Against The Forgotten

Natoshia Baer

My incredible husband hasn't stopped cheering me on since the first time I told him I wanted to publish a book. He puts up with me babbling over scenes, characters, and the problems that I create within my own story. The late nights, the long days when I lose track of time, my screen turned up too bright when I write in bed and everything in between. You never doubted me.

You will forever be my always.

I also couldn't have done this without our entire family. And my incredible BETA readers, thank you for reading the hot mess I dropped in your laps and being such amazing friends for me to lean on.

The amount of support I have received is so much more than I could have asked for.

Thank you to everyone, especially you, for reading my ramblings.

Enjoy the adventure ahead.

Contents

Content Warning

This book contains themes not suitable for readers under 18 years of age.
Content includes choking, morally grey MC, stalking, possesiveness, explicit scenes, fighting gore and death of a loved one.

Chapter 1 - Larissa

Sweat drips off my chin and I swipe at it with my shirtsleeve. I take a moment to breathe as the wind kicks up around us and rustles the trees as the birds chirp overhead. Eric is breathing hard and sweat drips from his chin as he slowly shakes his head at me while I plan my next move. I flash a grin at him before snatching my wooden staff up from the ground and charging at him. Eric grunts and raises his own staff to block my swing, exactly as I predicted, since he has done this same move every time I advance on him. Using my momentum as I step around him, I twist and sweep the staff behind Eric's knees in a quick arch. His knees buckle, pitching him forward. Eric goes down for only a second, rolling to jump back to his feet.

"Damn, Larissa, I hate when you do that. It stings." He grumbles, rubbing the tender skin behind his knees. I lean on my staff and shrug at him.

"You blocked my swing the last two rounds. I had to get creative." I walk past him and grab my water bottle from the grass, dropping my staff next to his. Eric sits on the ground, grabbing his own drink as he tries to hide his smirk.

"All these fighting lessons have paid off." Eric gives me an approving nod. I sit on the ground, kicking off my sneakers and socks to stretch my toes out in the cool grass.

"You are getting better, but you still have a long way to go." Adrian says, strolling up to us with his hands in his pockets. I squint up at him and let a yawn slip out.

"I can take you." I finish drinking my water with a smug grin.

"A snowy day in Hell, little sister." He scoffs. Eric rolls his eyes, being accustomed to our bickering.

"We need to get to the Elder Council meeting because you can't be late again. Mark and Dad need us there to introduce the new leaders." He holds his hand out for me and I groan. My body was aching from spending my day training at a brutal pace, and these meetings are a different kind of agony.

#

Adrian and I walk up to the large doors at the Town Hall and I notice our father waiting for us. I stand taller, pushing my shoulders back with my chin held high under his scrutiny. He nods to Adrian, holding the door open as we step inside.

"You found her and made it on time. I'm impressed." He gives me a pointed look.

"I was late one time, and nobody can let it go." I groan, following him into the building. My steps echo off the empty walls and I frown while looking at the now familiar building. Some of our mother's paintings hang on the walls, each of them depicting Nephilim and angels, locked in battle with demons. The pain of loss will always be in my heart, but small reminders like these awaken it over again.

"I still can't believe this world was all around me, yet I never saw it." I mumble as we cross the floor to the meeting room.

"Because you weren't looking for it." Adrian says.

Levi opens the door and I flinch when it emits a shrill squeak as it swings open. Everyone seated around the long rectangular table looks up at us, but I don't pay attention to them. I can feel the pull before I see him, like a gentle caress leading me home. My stomach still flips after all this time when Blaine winks at me and pulls the chair out next to him, nearest the head of the table.

I quickly take the offered seat and scan the faces of those around us. Levi sits at the head of the table, with Adrian at his side. Marley gives me a tiny wave from beside Adrian that

I return with a smile. Mark and Elaine are sitting awfully close to each other beside Blaine, whispering with their heads bent together. A man and woman who look to be in their late forties are to the right of Marley, staring at me with uncomfortable intensity.

"Jane and Emery, would you care to introduce yourselves?" Levi nods to them, sitting back with his arms crossed. We all turn our attention to the man that stands first.

"My name is Emery Saint. I have been a proud member of this Nephilim community since I was just a boy. I appreciate the honor you have given by asking me to serve on the Elder Council, Levi. Thank you." He nods, his bright blonde hair falling slightly into his face. The man has a tall frame, with piercing blue eyes that lock onto mine as he sits back down. Something inside me fidgets in discomfort at his scrutiny as Blaine shifts forward in his seat to whisper in my ear.

"That would be Jake's father," he says. Realization dawns on me as I remember the tall man with the blonde braided hair from Marcy's team. The small woman next to Emery stands up next, nervously brushing her short brown hair back from her eyes.

"Hello. I am Emery's wife, Jane. It is a pleasure to stand on the council to help rebuild our community." She sits down quickly. I sit in confused silence for a moment, but Marley interrupts.

"While it is so lovely to have you both here, I wonder what will happen now." She absentmindedly brushes her hand along her braids.

"What do you mean, Marley?" Mark asks. She simply shrugs and leans around Adrian to look at me.

"We have already dealt with one traitorous family that nearly got us all killed just so their child could get ahead." I speak up, and Marley nods once. Elaine sighs softly and Mark pats her hand.

"Are you questioning my loyalty?" Emery grumbles, looking between Marley and Levi.

"That is not what she meant, Emery. For a member of the Elders Council to betray their community, it has shaken all of us. The lingering distrust isn't easily brushed away. We will work together to rebuild our homes and trust." Levi says. The other Elders nod, showing him nothing less than the respect he commands.

"I mean no disrespect, but why do children sit in on Elder Council proceedings?" Emery asks, his eyes flicking between Blaine and I.

"There are no children here, Emery." Jane whispers.

"Blaine and Larissa are a vital part of the Nephilim as a whole, and Adrian has more than earned his place at this table. Each person you see has a seat because the majority cast its vote in their favor." Levi says, and I can hear the annoyance slip in his tone for being questioned. I sit taller, trying to focus on the conversation, but Marley keeps locking eyes with me and raising her brows.

Before I can figure out what she's trying to tell me, Mark catches my attention.

"You three should head home, we will be here for a while and you won't miss anything." Mark pats Blaine on the shoulder and I see Emery scowl at the gesture, just for a moment. By the time I blink, his face is impassive, and I question if I'm seeing things. Blaine stands up and holds his hand out for me to take and Adrian nods to our father before walking out ahead of us. I pull my phone out and check the screen.

"How is it already after seven? I'm starving." I groan. Blaine laughs and wraps his arm around me.

"Then let's get you home. See what Elaine left us for dinner." He kisses the top of my head and I smile to myself.

Chapter 2 - Blaine

I kick my shoes off with a yawn and step into the kitchen as Larissa trails behind me. Grabbing the oven mitts, Larissa follows the smell of pot roast to the oven and pops the door open. Elaine turned the oven off but left the food inside to keep it warm, just as we expected.

"Oh yeah, my mouth is watering." Larissa says excitedly.

"We have been living here for barely a month and Elaine has moved the silverware three times?" I grunt, still rummaging within the wooden drawers. Larissa giggles, kicking at the one right below the open drawer I'm looking through.

"Elaine really liked the kitchen at the old house. This one is a lot different, so I think she has a hard time finding a permanent place for everything." She waves her hand to gesture at the pale-yellow walls, black appliances, and small window above the sink.

"It is a lot smaller than the one Mammon blew apart." I admit as I scoop the meat and vegetables onto our plates, making a third for Adrian. We walk to the round dining table in silence as I vividly remember the day they attacked Nephal. Suddenly, Larissa's face becomes slack as she slumps into her chair. I know exactly what's happening, as if I was reliving the same memories that she's been sucked into.

A woman wearing a shining golden dress is standing near the house with her mouth hanging open, as if she is still screaming silently. Confusion sets in until I see the giant red stain spreading across her dress. I grab Larissa and we run back through the crowd, away from the house.

A demon emerges from the broken remains of the house. Her jaw falls open at his overwhelming size. His body seems to be made of black sludge, resembling a man in shape. I can't make out any defining features except where his eyes should be are just empty black pits that strike fear straight through me.

"Larissa, come back to me." I snap my fingers in front of her face, and she sucks in a deep breath. Her eyes slowly focus on mine, and the redness in their depths makes my heart ache.

"Another episode. That's the second one this week." My voice is low as I brush her static filled hair back down.

"I'm managing them, Blaine. It's just stress. I can't take sitting here much longer while Lilith could be out there somewhere, rebuilding her army just as we did. She isn't dead, and something is happening. I can feel it." She shivers, clutching onto my hand.

"Listen to me, Angel. You fried her, demon or not. There's no coming back from that." I stop talking when Adrian walks into the room, still towel drying his hair.

"Pot roast? Great, I'm starving." He drapes the towel over his chair and starts eating. I sit back in my seat but give her a pointed look. She shakes her head, pleading with me to keep it to myself.

"What is going on now?" Adrian asks.

"You tell him, or I will." I threaten. She picks at a carrot for a moment, avoiding looking at either of us until Adrian clears his throat.

"I had another episode. Not that important." She talks so quietly I almost can't hear her. Adrian sets his fork down with a clang and blows out a breath.

"They are getting more frequent. Dad said this is more than trauma and I think he's right." Adrian says, looking at me as I share the same concern. Larissa pushes her seat back and stands up quickly in irritation.

"I'm already full, so if you'll excuse me, I'm going to bed. I'm tired." Her words come out harsh. Adrian sighs as she stomps out of the dining room. I jump from my seat, catching her by the elbow and duck into the alcove beside the stairs leading to the bedrooms. I grip her jaw, forcing her to look at me.

"We are just worried about you, Angel." I whisper, desperately looking into her eyes as she tries to pull away.

"You're treating me like I have the word fragile written on my face. When Lilith came for me, I watched dozens of people die. You died, Blaine," her voice catches and she stops, taking a shuddering breath. "So yes, I am a little on edge, but I just want to move on." She swipes at her eyes in aggravation.

"I understand, but we can't just move forward like nothing happened. You need to process everything. Stop shutting me out." My thumb brushes her lip, tugging it out from between her teeth.

"I am processing, in my own way." She gives me a reassuring smile, taking my hand and dragging me up the stairs without looking back. I can't stop the groan as she pulls me towards her bedroom.

"Sex doesn't count as coping, Angel. Remember how your dad reacted the last time he caught me in your room?" I lean forward to whisper in her ear. She snorts a laugh as I shut the door behind us. My eyes devour every inch of her and a knowing smirk curls her lips. I'm obsessed with this woman and she knows it.

"He was pretty pissed off. If you want to go back to your room, be my guest." She shrugs, dropping my hand to pull her shirt off over her head while sauntering towards the attached bathroom. I prowl after her, not making a sound until she peers back at me and sucks in a startled breath. Pressing my body against hers, I pin Larissa to the door. Running my hand across her jaw and down her throat, I make her shiver against my touch as I stop to gently grip her throat.

"If you want me to go, then I will." I say, enjoying the feeling of her pulse fluttering against my thumb.

"I need a shower." She whispers. I smile, pressing a soft kiss to the top of her head, using my grip on her throat to pull her out of the way and open the door for her.

"Don't take too long." I slap her ass, making her stumble with a heated look thrown my way as she shuts the door.

I drop into her bed, taking a deep breath as I inhale her scent. It reminds me of comfort, of a home I never knew I would have.

#

The bathroom door shuts with a soft click as she finds me laying in her bed, with the lights off and my arm thrown over my eyes. I stay still, letting her think I'm asleep as she lets out a content sigh. I peer under my arm to see her looking up at the bright moonlight streaming through the sheer curtains. Larissa turns to me and I let my eyes slip shut as she comes to the bed.

"You are a bed hog." She whispers, crawling into bed next to me. She wiggles close and I roll over, pulling her against my chest and rubbing my nose across her neck.

"You smell so fucking good, Angel." My voice is husky from dozing off and it makes her melt in my arms. Realization makes me stiffen and lift my head, eyes suddenly wide open as my hand palms her bare ass. A groan rumbles from my throat as my hand trails up her side, moving to cup her breast and squeeze gently. A soft whimper escapes her lips and she twists her fingers into the hair at the nape of my neck, crushing her lips to mine.

I roll onto my back, dragging Larissa with me until she's straddling my lap. In one swift motion, I sit up and grab the hem of my shirt, pulling it over my head. Without giving her a chance to look me over, I dip my head into the curve of her neck. At a painfully slow pace, I trail kisses down her chest until she's squirming.

"Blaine. *Please*." Larissa begs. I grip her thighs tightly and rock her across my erection.

"Maybe I should teach you to be patient." I taunt her, catching her nipple between my teeth. She sucks in a breath as I pull free, my tongue darting out to flick across the swollen skin. She pulls my hands away from her hips and climbs off the bed, holding her finger up to stop me from dragging her back to me.

I arch an eyebrow but don't dare to say a word with the sultry look she's giving me. Her lips curl a sly smile as she grabs the waistband of my jeans and pops the button loose, tugging them down my thighs. Just when she crawls back into my lap, my entire body jerks when my senses all go on full alert. I grab her by the hips, pushing her away.

With no time to explain, I jump out of the bed and pull my shirt over her head, quickly guiding her back into the bed. She opens her mouth to question what I'm doing, but I push her into bed and silence her words with a long, passionate kiss. A chill abruptly creeps over the room as I melt into the shadows. Larissa sits up and looks around the room, still trying to wrap her head around my actions. I stand in the dark bathroom, rolling my eyes when I realize I'm standing here, buck ass naked.

"Come in?" Larissa says cautiously. I hear Levi step into the room, he flicks the light on and it casts a glow beneath the door.

"Just wanted to make sure you were doing okay. Adrian said you had another spell." He mutters, then clears his throat uncomfortably.

"It was a short one this time, no reason to make a big deal of it." She mumbles. I can hear the floor creaking as Levi sighs and steps towards the door.

"Okay, I will let you get some sleep. Tell Blaine that I said goodnight." I can hear the mild touch of disappointment and frown, wondering if he knows I'm lurking in the shadows. *Shit. My jeans and boxers were still on the floor.*

"I am an adult, dad." Larissa groans, the blankets ruffling as she tries to hide her shame.

"I know that. Did your mother talk to you about being, *ahem*, safe?" He coughs. I have to bite my hand to stifle the laughter, knowing she must be in there dying of mortification.

"Dad, stop. I promise you we are being *safe*." Larissa whines, and part of me hopes he tries to drop a birds and bees conversation on her. The light flicks off and her door slams shut with more force than necessary. Larissa blows out an aggravated breath when I poke my head out of the bathroom door with a grin.

"Not as sneaky as I had hoped." My shoulders drop in a half assed shrug as I give her a mocking smirk. She shamelessly watches my still hard cock bounce with every step. But I stop at her dresser, grabbing her a pair of pajama shorts. She pouts, sticking her lip out as I pull the blanket back, slipping the shorts up her legs, peppering them with kisses. Unable to stop myself, I press my face between her thighs and drag my tongue across her wet skin. Her back arches and I draw a gasp from her lips, making me chuckle as I pull her shorts the rest of the way up.

"That's not fair. You can't just tease me."

"Trust me, Angel. Tomorrow you are all mine. But for tonight, consider us successfully cock blocked." I chuckle, brushing my nose along her jawline and sending goosebumps across her soft skin.

"You could have warned me he was out there. It's not fair you can shadow jump while I get stuck with the sex talk." She hisses at me. I just shrug without remorse, burying my face in her boobs and clamping my teeth onto one.

"Life isn't fair." I mutter as she yanks my head away. "Now lay still, feeling you squirm makes me so hard that it hurts. We are running dangerously low on condoms. Maybe Levi can grab some for us on the next supply run, since he's concerned about us being safe." Larissa smacks the back of my head and I laugh.

"You need to get some sleep, Angel. Tomorrow, we get to meet with the Trackers. Hopefully, we will finally get some information on Lilith and Mammon." I affectionately kiss the top of her head. The two of us lay in comfortable silence, and I snake my hand under her shirt to press it over the beat of her heart. Mine matches it exactly, and with Larissa wrapped in my embrace, I can finally rest.

Chapter 3 - Larissa

I have to fight to pry my eyes open. My head feels as if it is spinning on an axis. I sit up slowly, struggling to see around the room. The overwhelming smell of sulfur makes my eyes water in the dim light. Sweat makes Blaine's shirt stick to me as I stand from the gravel and brush myself off. The room is so dimly lit I have to hold my hands out to feel around until I bump into a wall. The stone feels cold against my skin and I rest my head for a moment as another wave of dizziness strikes me. I don't know where I am, but my gut is screaming at me. I have to get out of here.

My eyes fly open at the sound of shuffling feet. Ducking low and using my hand to feel along the wall, I scuttle backwards when a flame dances into sight. From a hallway, a tall figure emerges with a lantern in his hand that swings with every step, casting misshapen shadows across the walls. The light fills the space and instead of gaining clarity, I only become more confused when I see the rest of the room. A throne sits to my left, where the man is walking towards. As he steps up, he snaps his fingers, and the room erupts with flames inside sconces that hang around the area. The heat stings my skin for a breath until it dies down, the room bright with the glow of flames. I get a good look at him now, his black hair is short and swept back with too much gel and his beard is short and messy.

I shift my feet, my toes curling against the gravel while I hold my breath. I flinch against the sharp points that dig into my skin but I don't dare to move from my hidden position. From where I'm crouched, I can see almost the entire area, but still have no idea where I could be. Dark gray and white carved stone makes up the walls and high ceiling. Across from the throne are rows of seats, and in between the two is a stone platform.

Where the Hell am I? I glance up at the tall man as he sits on the throne and stretches his neck from side to side. He looks familiar, but I can't place where I know him from. Before I can decide what to do, a man in a crisp black suit walks in from the same hallways the other appeared from, except he is dragging something behind him.

Wait, not something, but someone. A girl kicks ferociously even with her hands bound above her head. The man in the tux throws her onto the platform and she lets out a pained gasp. Someone tied a black fabric bag over her head, and her tattered clothes are covered in blood. I can't tell who she is even as I strain to see when the man kneels and gestures to her.

"Lord Mammon, the girl still refuses to tell us anything. She has been uncooperative and even broke Raymond's nose." He snarls. My heart thunders in my chest as I realize who the man on the throne is.

"He knows that if he is going to play with our guests, then he should ensure they have been restrained. Remove the bitch's hood." Mammon's deep voice sends fear through my being.

The young man yanks her hood free, and I have to clench my eyes shut for a moment. The poor girl's face is a swollen mess. I can see broken and missing teeth as she gasps for air. Her left eye is swollen shut and lacerations cover her face. The woman's short blonde hair is covered in dirt and dried blood that has dripped down her cheek. A small pink scar shines on her neck, a freshly healed wound.

"Nephilim don't heal quickly down here, do they?" Mammon cackles. Bile rises as I look back at her. She's a Nephilim.

"I have been very forgiving. But you have stepped upon my last nerve, girl. Where is she?" Mammon stands menacingly. The girl opens her mouth weakly as she struggles to clear her throat, and her demeanor suddenly changes. She holds her head up with pride and looks him in the eyes.

"Up your ass, Mammon." She snaps. Part of me celebrates her bravery until Mammon raises his hand and flicks his wrist. Without thinking, I run forward, screaming for them to stop. Nobody looks at me. They act as if they can't even hear or see me.

The man behind her pulls a dagger from its sheath. I'm too

late as he swings it down, right into the girl's heart. Her mouth opens in a silent scream and rage fills me as static crawls across my skin, building.

"Get away from her!" I scream. Mammon's brows draw in confusion and his head snaps towards me.

Suddenly I'm falling through the ground. Everything vanishes into a black cloud above me as I flail in terror.

#

"Hey! Wake up, I'm here Angel! Snap out of it!" Somebody screams in my face. I fight even harder, struggling to get away. Strong hands grip my arms and shake me.

"Larissa, it's me!" Blaine yells. My eyes finally focus on Blaine's terrified expression above me. My entire body is trembling as I swing my head, looking around the room. I'm in my bedroom, safe, and Mammon is nowhere to be seen.

"What just happened?" Adrian's worried voice comes from beside me, but I can't look at him. Nausea hits me like a wave, and I slap a hand over my mouth as I leap out of bed. Blaine catches on and runs to the bathroom behind me. I kick the door, trying to shut him out, but it bounces off his outstretched palm.

"You aren't leaving my sight, Angel. Puke doesn't scare me." He grumbles. As I empty the contents of my stomach into the toilet, he grabs a washcloth and runs it under the faucet.

I look up at him weakly, tears burning trails down my cheeks. Blaine hands me the washcloth and helps me stand, wrapping an arm around my waist as I wipe my face. After brushing my teeth, I let him lead me back to sit in my bed. Levi is pacing by the door and Adrian is sitting on the edge of my round lounge chair.

"Talk to me, please." Blaine pleads with me, clutching my hand in his. Taking in a shaky breath, the dream flashes through my mind, crystal clear as if I was watching a movie.

"I saw him. I saw Mammon." My voice is a broken whisper. Levi stops pacing and stares down at me. Adrian sits forward and leans his elbows on his knees.

"This wasn't like your other flashbacks." Blaine says. I shake my head from side to side as I pick at the skin around my nails.

"It was so different. I don't know where I was, but I saw him kill a girl. He said she was a Nephilim. I tried to save her, but I was too late and it was like I wasn't actually there. Until he saw me. Mammon looked right at me." My voice cracks and the lump in my throat becomes painful. Blaine rubs the pad of his thumb over a single tear that has escaped the corner of my eye.

"Okay, take a deep breath and start from the beginning." My dad says, nodding for me to continue.

When I finish retelling everything, my entire body is trembling from exhaustion.

"Do you think she could have been soul searching?" Adrian asks our dad. He frowns and shakes his head.

"She hasn't been there before, so she wouldn't have been able to project her soul. Soul searching is only possible when the person has physically been to a location prior." My dad explains to me and begins pacing again.

"Pretty self-explanatory." I snort. A yawn hits me and the room spins, forcing me to clutch my head in my hands as an involuntary groan escapes.

"Whatever she did, wherever she went, it exhausted her. We can figure this out in the morning. You need to get some sleep, Larissa." Adrian stops to squeeze my shoulder reassuringly and nods to Blaine when he leaves. My dad looks at the doorway, then back to me.

"I could sit in the chair. To make you feel safe." He offers, but I shake my head.

"No, I feel safe here." My words are a lie and I have to force a tight smile. Blaine tenses next to me and gives me a sidelong glare. My dad nods to himself before walking out. He closes the door behind him and I slump back on the pillows.

"You are a liar." Blaine says quietly, laying beside me.

"How do you know that?"

"Well, you just admitted it." He leans over me, caging my head between his arms as his weight pushes me into the bed.

"Your eyes keep darting around the room. Every noise makes your body tighten and don't forget that sometimes I can *feel* your emotions." He groans when the tears slip from my eyes. I reach up to caress his cheek, wanting to reassure him.

"Mammon saw me. I could feel how badly he wanted to kill me at that moment. I had to watch them murder that woman, she was so young Blaine." He wraps me tight in his arms as sobs break free.

"I won't let him touch you, Angel." His chest rumbles against my cheek as I fight to slow my crying. Even if I am safe, how many more will end up with the same fate as she did, because of me?

Chapter 4 - Larissa

Stretching my arms above my head, I twist my body as I try to wake up. Blaine's arm is wrapped around me, and he pulls me back to his chest. Smiling to myself, I try to sit up, but he pulls me down with a low growl.

"Where do you think you're going?" He grumbles into my ear. A shiver snakes up my spine. *There is nothing sexier than his sleepy voice and he knows it.*

"We need to get ready for the meeting, so don't try anything funny." I scold him. Blaine tightens his arm around my chest and slides his hand down my stomach, flattening his palm against me. He presses his hand against me harder while slowly grinding against my ass.

"I'm not trying, I'm *doing.*" He kisses just beneath my ear before nipping at the sensitive skin. My phone alarm beeps from the nightstand, and I lunge for it. Blaine dives over me to silence it, flipping me onto my stomach and pinning me with his weight as he does.

"You are going to get us in so much trouble." I laugh.

"Well, I am part demon." He pushes his knee between my legs, forcing them apart.

"But you're so sweet and innocent." I tease, hiding my smile in the pillow. Blaine kneels behind me, lifting his chest off my back. When I try to sit up, he puts his hand between my shoulders and shoves my face back down into the pillows. I curse him, my words muffled by the puffy fabric, only succeeding in making him laugh.

Keeping enough pressure to hold me down, he drags his knuckles up my thigh before pushing my shorts aside. I suck in a sharp breath when the cool air hits between my legs. Blaine drags his fingers around my clit, rubbing small circles. Painfully slow, he pushes his finger inside of me then drags it back out. I let out a breathy moan, waiting for more, but he moves his hand off my back. I turn my head and lock eyes with him as he sucks his glistening finger that was inside me.

"The only thing sweet here is how you taste. And I promise you, I plan to savor every inch of your body." He flashes me a grin and my body trembles. *That was so fucking hot.* Blaine grasps my hips and lifts me up onto my knees before grabbing the waistband.

"Don't you dare move." He says right before yanking my shorts off. I turn to face him, but his palm strikes my ass, making me yelp at the suddenness of it. Before I have a chance to smart off, he pulls my back to his chest and slowly smooths the sting away with his hand.

"I've told you already, Angel. Don't move." He kisses my neck gently. The contrast between his rough grip on my hips and tender lips is making my head spin.

His fingers skim up across my ribs, pushing my shirt until he can grip my breast in one hand while pulling my shirt up over my head. I lean my head back against his shoulder and whisper in his ear, "What if I don't listen?" His sigh causes wet heat to slick between my thighs.

"I was really hoping you wouldn't." Before I can ask, he grabs my throat and flips me onto my back on the mattress. I giggle at him and he shakes his head with a ravenous smile.

"My delicate Angel, laying here with nothing on except my hand around her throat and a pretty smile on her lips." He says. I bite my lip as he keeps his grip on my throat with one hand while trailing the other down my body slowly. He stops just before touching where I need him most and I let out a frustrated huff.

"Blaine please," I say. He tilts his head at me, pursing his lips as if he's thinking. I squeeze my legs together, desperate to ease the ache between them.

Blaine grips my thigh and yanks hard, "Spread your legs,

and grab behind your knees." He demands. I do as he says and try to bite down on my insecurity as I lay fully bare to him. Blaine lets go of my throat and kneels between my feet, grinning as he slowly rubs his hand across the slick that has dripped down my ass.

He dips his face down and drags his hot tongue across my sensitive flesh, pulling his name from my lips on a whimper. This only spurs him on, and he digs his fingers into each of my thighs as he starts flicking his tongue over my clit. Just as I'm panting, right on the edge, he stops. Blaine sits up and licks his lips clean with a crooked grin that flashes his fangs.

"Don't forget, those pretty little sounds are only for me. Do you think you can keep it down?" He reminds me. I nod quickly in anticipation, at this point I'd probably agree to chewing off my own arm for relief.

"Good girl," He whispers, and I close my eyes as a shiver passes over me. He pulls his shorts off and kicks them out of the way. Blaine slowly presses himself against my entrance, gathering my slick.

"Look at me, Angel." The gruff tone in his voice makes me lock eyes with him. "Take a deep breath," he commands and I do exactly that. He presses into me, slowly at first while watching me intently.

I bite my lip, holding back as he drags his hips back away from me. Blaine presses his palm over my mouth and I scrunch my brows at him in question. He answers by slamming himself into me at such a sudden pace I lose hold of my legs. I wrap one of my hands around his wrist, smothering my panted cries of pleasure.

Shadows darken the room and their chill crawls across my skin, adding to the overwhelming sensations. He sets the pace I need and the quiet room is filled with the sound of our bodies colliding, my smothered cries and his breathy moans. Blaine reaches between us, using his fingers to press my overly sensitive nerves in small circles. That's all it takes to send me over the edge, clenching around him as I cry out against his hand. His thrusts become erratic as he chases his own orgasm and Blaine's fingers bite into my soft skin above my hips as his movements stutter with a deep groan. His forehead drops to mine as he hovers above me on his elbows.

I smile up at him in bliss, hooking my leg over his hip as he kisses my forehead. His hands start gently massaging my hips and thighs as he brushes his nose over my jaw.

"That was incredible," I whisper. He pulls back to wiggle his eyebrows and press his lips to mine.

"It always is," he says. I snort and pat his shoulder affectionately. "Good to see your ego is still thriving."

"My ego thrives because I never have to ask if you've *finished*." He says in a smug tone, grinning at me as he stands. "Let's get dressed before I bend you over this bed." He slides his eyes over me as I stand. I'd much rather stay in bed with him all day, but I force myself to get dressed and follow him downstairs.

We walk into the kitchen and Adrian is already leaning against the counter, drinking his coffee. He holds a cup out for me, and I happily let the heat sink into my palms. His eyes stay locked onto me without saying a word.

"You can stop staring at me like that." I mumble, grabbing the creamer from the fridge. I fill my cup the rest of the way while I wait for him to speak up, but he just keeps staring at me.

"Seriously Adrian? Knock it off." I snap. Blaine raises an eyebrow and steps around us, heading outside with his coffee as he feels another sibling war coming on.

"What happened last night wasn't normal, and I'm worried that something is changing." He says.

"I'm fine. Maybe it was a fluke." I say, even though my gut tells me otherwise. Adrian sets his mug down and opens his mouth, but Elaine walks in, interrupting him.

"There you are child. Come here. I heard about last night." Elaine walks in and grabs me in a tight embrace.

"It was just a bad dream, Elaine. I promise that I'm okay." I hold on to her tightly for a moment before letting go. She gives me a sad smile and brushes my cheek with her hand. I grin when I realize she is wearing a flowy pastel blue dress with long sleeves that flutter around her as she walks.

"You look really nice!" I say. I glance down at my leggings and tank top, wondering if maybe I should have dressed a little better. She laughs softly, and I catch a glimpse of her blushing.

"Well, thank you, it was a gift." She winks at me before ushering us out the front door, only stopping long enough for me to throw back my mug and finish off my coffee. Blaine is sitting on the porch swing with his feet propped up and a serene look on his face as he holds my jacket up for me.

"You ready for this, Angel?" He asks when he gets up to walk beside me. I haven't stopped to think about the trackers lately, about what they have found while hunting down Lilith and Mammon.

"What if they didn't find anything?" I ask him, squinting at the sun that tries to shine through the dark clouds. I pull my zipper up, shivering against the cool wind. Blaine shrugs his shoulders and lets out a leisurely yawn.

"Whatever they've found, we will deal with it together." He says, his fingers lacing with mine as he gives my hand a squeeze.

Chapter 5 - Blaine

When we walk into the town hall meeting room, I stride in behind Elaine. She walks right to Mark, and he gives her an appreciative once over.

"You take my breath away, Elaine. I'm glad you like my gift," He kisses her cheek and she giggles. Adrian chuckles behind me.

"I don't know why they try to hide it. Everyone can see what's happening." Larissa says under her breath to Adrian. He snorts and walks past us towards his dad.

"Some of us actually like keeping things to ourselves." He calls over his shoulder. Larissa rolls her eyes at him and turns to find a seat across from the trackers. As soon as we sit down, I can see her trying to recognize the faces of the team while Levi calls for everyone's attention.

"Our trackers have some exciting news. First thing tomorrow morning they will follow a lead they recieved from a Cambion of Mammon's whereabouts. We will send a squad in behind them after they can confirm his location, but until then, what we say is not to leave this room," His voice fades out as the feeling of my panic begins rushing through our bond.

Larissa's eyes are locked onto the woman across from us, and I frown as they stare at each other. The woman brushes a hand over the fresh scar along her jaw, glaring at Larissa who is openly staring at it.

"What is it, Angel?" I reach over and shake her arm softly. Levi notices the rising tension and calls her name more than once. Larissa jerks backwards as she realizes the entire room is staring at her.

She grabs my sleeve and stands up abruptly, "I'm sorry for

interrupting. I need a minute." A blush heats her cheeks as she rushes from the room with me on her heels.

I stop in the hallway, giving her room to pace as she shakes her head and bites her lip. After a few tense moments of me patiently waiting while she composes her thoughts, Larissa stops moving and faces me.

"That girl in there. Did you see her?" Her voice is low, as if she's afraid somebody could be listening nearby.

"You have to be more specific than that. I was watching you from the moment we sat down." I brush a strand of hair from her face, but she shakes her head and it falls back into place.

"Blaine, it was *her*. The girl with the short blonde hair, and the scar on her jaw. I'm positive that she's the girl from my nightmare." Larissa hisses. My brows scrunch as I stand up straight, remembering the woman she described.

"Are you absolutely sure?" I lean forward, gripping her chin as I peer into her eyes. She knows I don't doubt her, and I can see how startled she is.

"Okay, give me one second." I turn and step back through the doors to the meeting room. All heads turn to look at me, most filled with irritation and distrust. I nod to Elaine and Adrian before turning to leave again. The two of them follow me out without any hesitation, just as I knew they would.

"What is it?" Elaine rubs Larissa's arm supportively. I lean against the wall across from them and nod for her to go ahead.

"The girl in there with the short blonde hair, do either of you know her?" Larissa wraps her arms around herself, hugging her elbows. Adrian furrows his brow for a moment before answering. "She was in my class at the Academy. Her name is Celia, I believe. Why?" He asks.

She looks around us, making sure nobody else has crept up before speaking. "She's the girl I had that dream about last night. I saw Mammon tell that man to *kill her*." The words rush from her, as if she can't contain them any longer.

Elaine's facial expression stays passive as the moments

drag by and I hold my breath, wondering if they heard her at all.

"Well, she is alive, so it might not have been another episode. What if you have seen her somewhere before, after the attack? Maybe you were right about this one and you were just having a nightmare." Adrian dismisses it with a shrug.

"I think he may have a point. You've been pushing yourself so hard lately, my sweet girl. You need to take it easy once in a while, or the stress will begin to pull you under." Elaine says, brushing Larissa's hair back from her cheek maternally. Larissa's shoulders sag as self doubt sinks its claws into her and I refuse to sit back any longer.

"What she went through was not just a bad dream," I step forward, pressing my chest to her back as I stand supportively behind her, "I have chased away more of her nightmares than you can count. I've held her while she relived that day repeatedly. And I am telling you, this was different." My voice is flat, refusing to leave room for argument. Larissa holds her head high and my heart fills with pride.

"She dream walks, Blaine. I'm sure reality and imaginary lines are getting blurry for her, but you shouldn't feed into her anxiety." Adrian waves his hand dismissively. She glances back at me, her cheeks pinking from embarrassment of being written off again.

"I know what I saw, what I *felt*. She has the exact scar as the girl from my dream and," Larissa begins, but I interrupt her, grabbing her shoulders and twisting her until she is facing me.

"What if you had a vision?" I ask. Her mouth opens and closes as she struggles to understand what I'm suggesting.

"You know better than that. She has never had visions before and that gift is nearly unheard of." Elaine says, but she doesn't seem sure.

"*Nearly unheard of*, Aunt Elaine. Not impossible." I remind her.

"She doesn't have the blood of a witch. Did you even pay attention during lessons at the Academy? Only Nephilim born from the blood of a witch can have visions. Even then, her visions would have started young." Adrian snaps, just as Levi walks out of the meeting with Mark close on his heels.

"You missed the entire meeting. They are close to finally finding Mammon and possibly Lilith, so this better be good," He mutters, rubbing a frustrated hand over his eyes. Mark chuckles at Levi, amused by his friend's exhaustion.

"Larissa is having visions." My words come out nonchalantly. Larissa's eyes widen when Levi and Mark both snap their attention to us.

"Damn it, Blaine! No, she is not." Adrian throws his hands up. Levi looks between us, waiting for one of us to explain. Elaine takes Mark's arm and asks him to walk with her, leaving us drowning in tension.

"That girl in there, Celia. She was the woman I saw last night." Larissa whispers. His brow wrinkles as he takes in what we are saying.

"Visions aren't a gift that many Nephilim possess," He offers, squeezing her shoulder affectionately "What if you accidentally fell into her nightmare?" He asks. She looks up at him in confusion.

"She lives a few houses down from us. What if you dream walked into her nightmare? They are tracking Mammon, so I'm sure she has had her share of vivid bad dreams. Have you taken that into consideration?" He asks.

"No, I haven't. That would explain how it felt so real. But I still want to warn her," Her voice is quiet once again, and I blow out an irritated breath. Before anyone else can speak, the rest of the Elders council walks through the doors with the team behind them.

"I'll talk to them. We can catch up at home." Levi says, turning away from us. Adrian hangs back with their father, his eyes shooting daggers at me.

Larissa takes my hand and rushes ahead of everyone to step outside, needing the fresh air. The two of us walk towards home without saying a word the entire way. My thoughts are racing, something in my gut is screaming at me that this is something more. I know my woman, and if nobody else will believe in her, I sure as Hell will.

Chapter 6 - Larissa

"I think we just need to accept that it was a dream walk. Maybe I should apologize to her." My words come out with a groan. Blaine makes a disgruntled noise beside me.

"It doesn't sit right with me, Angel. When you dream walk, your body is limp. You don't show any emotion or make a sound. You were thrashing, screaming, and you shocked me." He grumbles.

"Maybe you should start sleeping with rubber on." I poke his chest with a raised brow. He looks up at me finally, just to wiggle his eyebrows. I roll my eyes and elbow him, motioning to the backyard.

"Let's go train for a while. I need to burn this tension." I hop from foot to foot, accentuating my words. When we step into the back yard, Blaine is already stretching his arms above his head. His shirt rides up just far enough for me to get a peek at the hard lines between his hips. My mind immediately remembers what it's like to drag my tongue over the taut skin on his body, all the way down to his-

"You look pretty thirsty, kitten." He taunts me in a low voice.

"It's a shame there's nothing out here to fix that." I do my best attempt at a sultry voice and it works. Blaine opens and closes his mouth before stalking around me like a predator hunting its prey. I watch closely as he prowls around me, a mischievous grin on his lips.

"I will not hold back, so fight me off." He grins at me as I watch him, waiting for any slight movement. I take a slow, deep breath and pull the tingling from my chest. It spreads slowly, but I have been working hard and have better control of my abilities.

I envision stretching it down my arms and into my palms, smiling when I see the familiar sparks dance across my hands. The electricity crackles in the air, but it doesn't deter Blaine.

He suddenly plants one of his feet and launches himself towards me. I throw my hands up, prepared to take him down. Except he stops a foot away and winks at me as a chill dances across my skin. Blaine drops into the shadows at his feet and I curse under my breath. Spinning in circles, I search the trees' shadows for any sign of him. After a few minutes, I let out a frustrated breath, dropping my static protection.

Goosebumps crawl across my body and I don't react before he shoots up through my shadow behind me. I reach for my dagger at my hip, but he is clutching it in his hand as he pins my arms to my chest with his, crossing them and pointing the blade at me.

"You should never drop your guard. I thought I had taught you better." His deep voice rumbles through my back. I swallow hard, suddenly distracted by how he feels pressed so tight against me. All the heat in my body has settled in between my thighs and creates a longing ache. Blaine leans forward and places a soft kiss on the side of my neck. His familiar scent of smoke makes my heart race.

"What now, Angel?" He whispers.

"What?" I croak out. His laughter shakes both of us, and I melt a little more into his grip.

"If I was a demon, you would be dead. How can you get away?" He bites my shoulder, pressing his fangs into my skin just enough to sting. I shamelessly give him more access to my sensitive neck when I tilt my head.

"Well, I wouldn't be having trouble concentrating if it was anyone but you." I huff out, arching my back against him. He sucks a breath in through his teeth as my ass grinds against him.

"Maybe you need a different opponent." A booming voice startles us and Blaine swings towards him with a growl. Jake stands at the corner of the house, with his arms crossed and a bored expression on his face.

"Hmph. I'm just here to help." Jake says to Blaine. I nod and step forward, trying to put distance between us so I can think straight. But Blaine still has an arm wrapped around me. I roll my eyes and offer him a smile.

"That would be great, Jake. Did you cut your hair?" I ask in shock. Jake is nearly six foot eight and the last time I had seen him, the sides of his head were shaved with a long blonde braid down the middle.

He ruffles his now shaggy shoulder length hair and shrugs, "It was a pain to take care of." Blaine slowly drops his arm from around me as a small blur of orange fiery hair streaks towards me. I stumble backwards, laughing as Ella grabs me in a tight hug.

"We are totally here to help you. Blaine texted me about the dream vision thing and I have a feeling that things might get weird soon." She beams at me. I bite my lip as I think about the nightmare.

"You need more people that trust your instincts, Angel." Blaine says to me before turning to Ella and Jake.

"Do either of you know Celia? She got placed as a tracker after she graduated from Academy. Short blonde hair, wicked scar right here," Blaine points to his neck. Jake nods, but Ella looks confused.

"I don't know many of the trackers. They spend most of their time away from home." She and Jake both patiently listen as I tell them the full extent of my nightmare, dropping the bomb that Celia was the girl I saw. I pace, waiting for them to say something.

"You may have seen her before. Could just be coincidence." Jake says. Ella rolls her eyes. "Or that girl is about to get held captive in Hell. By Mammon and a stabby guy." She shivers and zips her fuzzy pink jacket up to her chin.

"I fully believe she had a vision. This was so different from anything else I have seen her go through." Blaine says in a tight voice.

"She isn't a witch." Jake crosses his arms and stares up at

the darkening sky. His tone isn't hostile, just flat.

"What if she is the first? There is that whole prophecy thing, so she's obviously not normal." Ella says excitedly, and from anyone else the comment might sting. Blaine looks at me and nods his head slowly.

"Whatever it is, my dad is dealing with it." I wave my hand, just wanting to drop the subject for now. Blaine squints at me before sighing and waving to Jake.

"If you hurt her, I'll break every bone in your body. *Slowly.*" He snarls at Jake. I swallow audibly and Ella mouths "*Hot*" to me, wagging her eyebrows. A wall of muscle is towering over me, and for a minute I have second thoughts.

"Eric said you were getting good. Let's see how good." He cracks his knuckles and I bounce on the balls of my feet. The moment I nod, Jake charges right towards me, throwing a right hook at my ribs. His punch makes contact as I dive back. My breath hisses between my teeth and I try to block the pain out.

Kicking my foot outwards, I manage to land a blow to his hip. Without thinking, I react with anger and almost immediately regret it. With no time to get my bearings, Jake grabs my ankle and throws me to the ground. The impact causes all the air to leave my lungs in a *whoosh.*

He drops his weight on top of me, trying to pin my arms, and I can hear Blaine shouting in the background. Gasping in a breath, I try to pull my power forward and the familiar tingle ripples across my skin. I buck against Jake, throwing him off balance before pushing my static out around me with a pained grunt. Jake shouts and lets go of me, rolling off.

Oh no you don't, get your ass back here, big guy. I push up onto the balls of my feet and leap onto Jake's back as he tries to stand.

"Shit, that stings!" He howls, trying to toss me off. I wrap my arm around his throat and clutch my wrist.

"Concede!" I pant. He nods and taps my arm. I drop off him and stagger backwards, clutching my side where he hit me. I'm smiling from my victory while Jake shakes his head at me.

That smile falters when the air chills and I see Blaine storming towards us. *Shit.* Jake puts his hands up in surrender.

"Demons won't go easy on her." His voice sounds annoyed. Blaine storms past him and gets in my face.

"Are you hurt?" His eyes are black and I can see him trembling with rage as he looks me over. I cup his cheek and brush my thumb across his dark stubble.

"You should see the other guy. I totally kicked his ass." I smile at him. His lip curls and he groans.

"From now on, you train with me and only me." He leans close to my ear, his breath tickling my neck.

"I'll be in your room tonight, so I can check every inch of you for any *injuries.*" His low voice causes my thighs to clench. When he pulls back, he looks more controlled and his eyes are back to the perfect shade of brown.

I bite my lip to hide my smile as we walk towards Ella and Jake. *I wish things could stay like this, with everyone I care about in this bubble.*

Chapter 7 - Larissa

Nearly two weeks had passed since my nightmare and every day I became more convinced it was just a dream. We were training late into the night on hand to hand combat and my entire body was sore when I dragged myself out of bed in the morning. It was just after nine a.m. but I wanted to crawl back under the warm blankets.

I stagger into the kitchen, drawn by the warming scent of fresh coffee. Blaine smiles at me, offering me a slice of his toast. I stuff a piece in my mouth while Elaine sets a cup of coffee down and motions for me to have a seat. Blaine and I look at each other in confusion. Elaine's hands are trembling, and she hasn't sat down with us.

"You both need to eat up and waste not a minute." She turns and goes back into the kitchen, scrubbing at a stack of plates in the sink.

"Elaine, what is going on?" I ask. She shakes her head and dries her hand on a towel.

"Hurry and go make yourselves presentable. I swore to Levi I wouldn't spill a word to you, either of you." She points at Blaine. He slowly stands up and stalks over to Elaine.

"Aunt Elaine, you promised we would never have secrets after my mom died." He crosses his arms and stares down at her. I gulp down my coffee, waiting to see if she gives anything away.

Elaine whips around to face him, and the anger on her face startles me. It looks so out of place.

"You don't dare to pull that card with me, boy. You aren't too big for me to still put you on your backside." She wags a finger in his face and I choke back a laugh when he actually looks a little scared.

Elaine sighs, drying her hands on her apron.

"Larissa, the trackers are back. What they found, it's not good. Please, for the sake of my old heart, tidy yourselves up. They are all meeting here soon. I must run a few errands, so I will be out for a bit." Her eyes shine and I realize she is fighting off tears. Blaine and I both quickly clean up our dishes and go to our rooms to get changed.

I pull out a white button up with short loose sleeves that flare out and a pair of black jeans. I'm standing in my bra and panties when my door clicks behind me and I swing around, grabbing my dagger off the dresser and pointing it level with Blaine's throat. He gives me a sly grin and steps up to the blade.

"You know, if this is a new kink, then I am definitely into it." He laughs when a blush heats my cheeks. I set the dagger on the dresser and he frowns at it.

"You should get a thigh holster. And a bigger blade." He says.

"Leave my little dagger alone. It was a gift from Adrian." I grab my blouse and begin buttoning it, but Blaine pulls the fabric from my hands and does it for me.

"It's kind of funny," He stops just over my chest "I can sense you." He breathes. I wait for him to continue, but he just finishes buttoning my shirt and hands my jeans to me.

"Blaine, what do you mean?" I ask, finishing dressing.

"Do you feel it? That pull that demands we obey, demands we touch." He trails a finger down my cheek. His touch sends a shiver over my skin. I nod slowly, understanding exactly what he means. All this time, I thought it was just me being obsessed with him.

"I can feel your emotions, but only in glimpses when you're overwhelmed by them. Wherever you are, my heart leads me right to you. It's been stronger lately. When I finally get my arms around you, the bond nearly purrs." He pulls me against him. My eyebrows shoot up as I feel the bond buzz, punctuating his words.

"Do you think this is because of the prophecy? Because it

fated us to have this bond?" I ask, my throat feeling thick. Blaine shrugs and turns away, pulling me after him.

"Don't know, and if I'm being honest, don't care. My heart and soul are yours, with or without the damn bond." He kisses my hand, but his reassurance doesn't quiet the little voice that questions our true feelings. When we reach the living room, my father looks at me with eyes that show every bit of exhaustion.

"What's going on?" I ask. He shakes his head once before turning to look over his shoulder. Mark is arguing with a man I recognize from the trackers' meeting. He is almost the same height as Mark, with bright blonde hair shaved to the scalp. His beard is shaggier and his entire demeanor is on edge. He has scars crossing his right arm and fresh marks on his cheek.

"Larissa, listen to me. That man in there is the leader of the trackers. He was also Celia's fiancé-" I cut Levi off, looking over at the men arguing in hushed tones.

"Wait, you just said *was* her fiancé?" When Celia's fiancé turns to look at me, I can feel the blood drain from my face. He doesn't even try to hide his look of disdain for me.

"So, you're the one working with demons?" He snaps at me. His voice is low and cracks, giving way to the heartbreak in his words. I just shake my head no, fighting back the bile that is rising as my unease grows.

"You are no hero," He spits the words.

"I never claimed to be." My voice is soft, but I hold my head high.

"Celia is missing. But I'm guessing you already knew that? And get this, Mammon has her in Hell. You knew, you knew and did *nothing* to save her!" He points at me, his arm shaking. But tears have broken free and cut sharp lines down his cheeks, showing the broken man beneath the anger. I bite my lip hard, trying to hold back my own tears.

"That is enough, Lane. I know you are hurting, but you won't speak to her like this. She did nothing wrong to deserve your wrath." Levi's voice booms through the room, startling even me.

I sense the chilling touch of the bond, and some of my emotions slip away between flashes of anger. I look over my shoulder to see Blaine struggling to control himself. Even warring with his own feelings, he still tries to ease some of my burden. But I don't know how much longer he can remain calm, his eyes are black and the tick in his jaw is picking up speed.

"You are covering for her because she is your daughter, but that bitch isn't one of us-" *crack*. The sound registers before I even see Blaine move. In the blink of an eye, he appeared in front of Lane and landed a hard punch to his jaw. Lane staggers sideways, holding his jaw with a look of shock on his face. Blaine grabs the front of his shirt and straightens him up.

"Apologize to her." His voice is so low I can barely hear him. Levi moves to intervene but stops as Mark walks over and grabs him by his upper arm.

"If that were Mary, the boy would already be dead by your hands. Let Blaine deal with this, Levi." He whispers. That seems to shake him, and he gives one sharp nod. Lane looks between the two of us before mumbling, "I'm sorry." He looks back up at Blaine.

"If that was *her* missing, you'd blame the person who predicted it too." His entire demeanor has changed. It's as if his mask of rage has melted away to show how much he's struggling. Blaine lets go of him and steps back.

"If looks could kill, you would have to bring Blaine back to life a second time." Mark laughs beside me as I continue to stare at Blaine with irritation at his reaction.

"Lane, I truly am sorry. I warned your fiance about what Larissa had seen in her nightmare. Celia and you both brushed it off as if it was nothing but a dream. I tried to intervene on Larissa's behalf." Levi gestures to the couch and Lane drops back into it. We all sit around the living room and I make sure to put myself between him and Blaine.

"What is the chance that this is actually happening? Your nightmare, coming true I mean." Lane stammers, dragging his hand across the pale stubble covering his cheeks.

"I honestly don't know. I wish I knew more, or could make sense of what I had seen, I'm so sorry." My throat feels thick as I struggle to swallow, guilt constricting me. Blaine grips my thigh, his fingers digging in just enough to ground me and help me draw in a breath.

"What happened when she went missing?" Mark asks, sitting forward with his elbows resting on his knees and fingers entwined.

"We were at one of Hell's gates. A secret contact had left it open for us. Celia was one of the two to scout ahead. But out of nowhere, they attacked us from behind. Next thing I knew, her partner was dead on the ground, Celia was nowhere to be found and the gate had been locked." He buries his face in his hands when he finishes. I rub his shoulder, offering comfort for a moment. From the corner of my eye, I see Blaine's expression full of sympathy as he looks at me, no doubt imagining himself in Lane's shoes.

"Do you have any idea who the contact was?" I ask. Lane scoffs at that.

"What part of 'secret contact' makes you think I know who it is?" He snaps.

"Hey, I'm just trying to help, so maybe take it down a notch." I bite at him, rubbing my temple as a headache throbs. Blaine's laughter vibrates through my chest and I roll my eyes at him. Now that I focus on it, I can feel his anger feeding my own through the bond.

"Can everyone just take a moment here? We know where she was last, and I know you will disagree here Levi," Mark gives him a pointed look before continuing, "Larissa saw the room Celia was taken into. What if we manage to figure out who it was that opened the gate and she can describe it to them?" Mark sits back as my dad shakes his head no.

"How many people can open the gates?" I ask.

"Only greater Demons, so including Mammon, there are seven. We can talk more about them later," Blaine says, shifting uncomfortably beside me.

"I have always wondered if the rumors were true about you," Lane says quietly, his words meant for Blaine. I look at him with my brow furrowed.

"Be careful what you say next, or it will be the last words you ever speak," Blaine says. I feel the temperature drop around us and put my hand to his chest, ready to stop him from picking a fight.

"Stop it, Blaine. Lane, quit antagonizing somebody you won't win against." Mark rolls his eyes and sits back. Lane grumbles and Blaine puts his hand over mine, holding it over his heart.

"What if it was Mammon? Maybe he just set you all up?" I offer. Lane shakes his head and rubs a hand over his tired eyes.

"No, because didn't you say Mammon was asking Celia for the whereabouts of another 'she'?" Levi asks me. I nod. "Yeah, he did. If it was Mammon, he would have ensured the girl he's looking for was the one at the gate." I look down at my socks, trying to process what we are talking over.

"My guess, he wants you." Lane says. My whole body feels as if it's pulled under ice water.

"You're right. It has to be. The way he looked at me, in that dream. He was shocked, but there was something else in his eyes. Excitement." I hide my face in my hands. Not only did I see Celia's death before it happened, but I am the reason she is going to die.

"This evening we will work on finding out who opened the gate. I'll start with whoever was in contact with the middleman. Eventually we will track them down. We don't know she's dead yet. Just try to hang in there." Mark says, standing and walking over to Lane. "Let's get you home, kid." Lane nods and stands up.

"We have to find her," He says to me before getting up and walking out with Mark. I flop backwards on the couch and groan.

"It's going to be a late night. I wonder if Elaine made more coffee." Levi says.

Chapter 8 - Larissa

If Blaine doesn't stop pacing, I'm going to throw apple slices at his damn head. Just as the thought crosses my mind, he walks back across the living room. I groan and throw a slice at his head, which hits its target.There is suddenly a very annoyed Blaine towering over me with his arms caging me against the back of the couch.

"Grown-ups use their words, Angel." He leans down and bites a piece of apple from my bowl, using his tongue to pull it into his mouth without breaking eye contact.

"You are driving me crazy. If teaching me is really this stressful, then somebody else can do it. Grown-ups also get their own food and don't have to make it so sexual." I pull my bowl away, but he just plucks it from my hands.

"You are mine, which means your snacks are my snacks." He leans over me, holding a piece to my lips until I open my mouth. Blaine pushes it between my lips and when I bite the tip of his finger, he groans.

"Such a tease," He grumbles. I take the bowl back, but I catch him smiling out of the corner of my eye. He drops beside me and stretches his long legs out in front of him to prop them on the coffee table.

"Teaching you isn't what has me concerned for once, it was what Lane said." He admits as I turn sideways and drape my legs over his lap.

"Blaine, you can't just punch somebody because they talked shit to me, or about me."

"I will defend you with my last breath, Angel. That pissed me off and I won't stand by while somebody disrespects you. But that isn't what I was referring to."

"Lane said that he had wondered if the rumors were true. You heard him?" He asks. I nod, so he continues.

"The Seven Kings consist of Lucifer. His sin is pride. Mammon, you know him, and his sin is greed. Asmodeus is Lust, but he doesn't associate with his brothers. He was also the leader of the Seven Kings, but when Lilith killed his mate, he left Hell. That's where she stepped in and took over. None of the others stood against her. Leviathan's sin is envy, and Belphegor is sloth, but we haven't heard from them in over two millennia. Satan is the most known in the mortal world, his sin is wrath. Lastly is Beelzebub, and he is associated with gluttony."

"What Lane said about rumors, he meant the ones about who my father is. He is one of the Kings. My mother did everything she could when I was young to protect me, keep others from finding the truth. But I trusted Marcy. I told her, she let it slip to her mother and you can imagine how well that went. Bertha spread some bullshit rumors. She said that my mother was a traitor before her passing, and I was a half-breed spy." He snorts, but I can see the pain in his eyes. I take his hand in mine, trying to soften some of his discomfort.

"Whoever gave her the time of day just looks like a bunch of idiots, don't they? Bertha turned out to be the traitor, throwing stones in her glass house. You didn't deserve any of it and I am so sorry you had to go through that." I cup his cheek and he leans into my palm.

"I'd go through it all over, just to kiss you for the first time again." He leans forward, placing a searing kiss on my lips. My heart rate speeds up at the intensity between us, leaving me flushed as he pulls away.

"You are so cheesy," I smile at him.

"I try my best," Blaine's face becomes serious again, "But you deserve to know. Lucifer is who fathered me."

"And his sin is pride? That makes sense."

"Yes, it is, Angel. He's a bastard, and I hope never to see him again. He came to take me away once when I was little. My mother stabbed him." His smile contradicts the dark story and I bite back a laugh.

"We don't know for sure who they are working with, but if he is the one helping the Nephilim track down Mammon, then we just need to be prepared. I sent a message to an old friend after our meeting with Lane. He should be here this evening. I can't imagine he has anything better to do," Blaine shrugs.

"Is this one of those situations where you don't tell me who it is for *'suspense'*?" I use a mocking tone and he laughs.

"I just like watching you squirm when you don't know everything." He shrugs and I elbow him in the ribs, but he doesn't even flinch. Adrian walks into the room and sits across from us in a chair, rubbing his eyes.

"They had the meeting without us." His annoyance is obvious. I sit up quickly.

"Are you kidding me? I should be there. This is about me!" I snap. Adrian just shrugs.

"Dad said that he would tell us what he could, but that we should sit tight. Apparently, something else came up. Mark looked pretty shaken." Adrian blows out a deep breath and lays his head back.

"Lane must have told him something else on their way home. I haven't seen him since then." Blaine says.

"Maybe somebody else on the team offered more information or something?" I offer, still annoyed at being left out. Like we are a bunch of children that are told to stay out of adult conversation, they're assholes.

"Not really anything we can do now," Adrian sighs. Blaine stands up and kisses the top of my head "I'm going to make a quick call, see if that friend of mine could meet us sooner." With that, he walks out while I glare at the back of his head. Adrian sits up and looks at the doorway, then back at me.

"What was that about?"

"More of the whole *'You'll know when you need to know'* bullshit. Apparently everyone around here is pulling it today." I pick up my coffee and groan when I realize it's gone cold, but drink it anyway.

"I couldn't find Elaine after I got home. Where is she?" He changes the subject.

"She left to run errands." I frown at the heavy feeling that has settled into my stomach, that I keep pushing aside.

"Where were you last night?" I ask. He looks away and checks the time on his phone.

"Dad said you all met around ten this morning. It's nearly five now. She should have been back." He says. I furrow my brow and just shrug. Elaine likes the peace of running errands, and this isn't the first time she has been gone all day.

"She will be home any minute. We can cook dinner for her tonight." The words roll off my tongue, even though I don't believe them. I tip my cup up and sigh when I realize it's empty Just like the feeling in the pit of my stomach.

#

Just over an hour later, Adrian and I are following Blaine out through the woods behind the town. I'm grateful I'm wearing sneakers and jeans as we stumble through the overgrown area.

"So, am I correct in assuming that we are leaving the wards because the person we are meeting up with is a demon?" Adrian asks. Blaine smiles over his shoulder at him and gives a nod. Stepping through the wards is something I haven't adjusted to, feeling as if you're walking through a heavy and invisible curtain. Blaine stops and looks around for a moment before walking off in another direction.

"You know where you are going, right?" I ask. He laughs and takes my hand in his.

"Just a little further, there's a clearing I used to come to a lot when I needed a break. Your impatience in and out of the bedroom can be astonishing, Angel." He grins as a blush heats my cheeks and Adrian groans.

As we reach a slight break in the trees, Blaine holds up a hand for us all to stop. I look around, but after a few moments, I still see nothing. Just as I'm about to ask Blaine what we are doing, black smoke rises from the ground. It snakes upwards into the open space, forming two figures holding hands. One is easily a foot taller and much broader than the smaller one.

As if sucked back by a vortex, the smoke slips back into the ground and my eyebrows raise in surprise. The man in front of us is a little more than just intimidating. He is wearing a white button-up shirt with the sleeves rolled up and the top buttons undone. The tight shirt strains against his muscular build, tucked into spotless black slacks. His hair is tied back at his neck, but a few black strands frame his sharp features. What catches me off guard is how gentle his eyes are. A stark contrast to his sharp cheekbones and cut jawline that is shadowed with stubble.

His eyes are locked on the woman beside him, caught in their own little world. She smiles up at him. Her sweet round face is flushed, and her chest is rising and falling fast under her simple black spaghetti strap dress. He brushes a blonde strand of hair away from her face and Blaine clears his throat, interrupting.

"Oh, I'm sorry! I still get a little disoriented traveling like that." The girl offers us a shy smile. "It's nice to meet you. My name is Piper." She holds her hand out to Blaine, and he shakes it.

"So, you are the one who tamed the big bad King of Kings? It is an honor to meet you, Piper." He turns and holds his hand out to the man.

"Uncle Asmodeus, you're looking as old as ever. What does she see in you?" He laughs and my eyebrows shoot up in surprise. The mysterious old friend that he called for help was a King of Hell? Asmodeus rolls his eyes and shakes Blaine's hand.

"I look younger than you. Stop calling me Uncle. It feels weird." he says with a deep, growling voice. Piper finishes introducing herself to Adrian, who is white as a ghost, before walking right past my outstretched hand and hugging me. I awkwardly pat her back and look at Blaine for help. He just smiles and keeps talking to Asmodeus.

"Asmodeus acts tough, but he told me all about you guys. So do not let that rough exterior fool you." She laughs, stepping back. "Sorry, I am just really excited to meet somebody who has the gift of visions as well. I kind of knew I would meet you," she winks at me, and I scrunch my brow.

"But they said I couldn't have visions without any witch's blood, so that makes no sense." I mumble. She shrugs. "You never know. I'm a witch and I would bet that you are as well," she says in an excited tone. Asmodeus walks over and takes my hand in his.

"I wish we were meeting under better circumstances, but I am honored to meet the one who took Lilith down with her own hands. I bet those same hands keep him in line." He points to Blaine, who rolls his eyes.

"Asmodeus is a dirty old man," Blaine stage whispers and Piper giggles, tucking herself into Asmodeus' side. My heart clenches when I see the obvious love they share. It's nice to see another couple unable to keep their hands to themselves.

"Our mother was just a normal human. We are only Nephilim." My brother says flatly. I nod beside him, "He's right, we would have known. Our father would have known." I say. Asmodeus shares a look with Piper before looking back at us.

"We need to sit down for this conversation," he says.

Chapter 9 - Larissa

Convincing our dad to temporarily drop the barrier was much easier than any of us expected. Mostly because Blaine lied and said it was an informal visit. We couldn't tell him what we were actually doing. Levi would never let us go digging around for something he had deemed dangerous. We were all sitting around the living room, and I was itching to ask Asmodeus a dozen questions.

"Asmodeus, you have shown the Nephilim nothing but loyalty. So, you are both welcome to stay as long as you wish. Congratulations on your engagement, as well. I need to have a small meeting with these three." Levi says while waving at Blaine, Adrian, and me. Asmodeus nods, taking Piper's hand in his. "We will wait here," he says, while she smiles sadly at me. *What is that about*?

We follow Levi into the dining room and sit when he motions to the chairs. He looks so tired, almost defeated.

"I know you are upset about being excluded, but we have our reasons. For starters, emotions are running high, and the rumors of your vision have become so misconstrued. Mark and I wanted to get hold of this before it ran away. When we find out anything of substance, I will tell you. Until then, please just try to relax and stay put. No more leaving the ward without telling a member of the Elder Council. Am I clear?" He asks. We all nod like scolded children.

"It's nearly seven and Elaine still isn't home." Adrian points out. Levi nods. "We know where she is, don't worry." Before just turning and walking out of the house.

"That was weird, right?" I ask them, but they both seem lost in their own thoughts.

"Maybe we should just throw pizza in the oven and call it a night." Blaine says, as Asmodeus and Piper walk in.

"Okay. Now that your scary dad is gone, tell me about your vision. Could you smell things, feel the dirt under your toes?" she asks me. I sit and think for a moment before answering her.

"Yeah, I could smell the damp air. It was like an old basement mixed with sulfur. I could feel everything around me, too." I tell her. She looks at me with a serious expression.

"You had a vision. When Blaine called Asmodeus and explained everything, I did a little digging. Mary was the daughter of a coven leader." I wait for her to finish. The confusion must be obvious on my face because she sighs and sits beside me.

"I'm talking about witches. Mary fled the coven when she was young. Just after the murder of your grandmother, who was one of the most powerful coven leaders. She died during a ritual spell that went wrong. The other leaders were so power hungry that they kept going, draining her life force. According to my aunt Willow, Mary saw everything. She was so scared that she turned and just ran. Poor girl had just turned 16," Piper nervously bites her lip as I shake my head, standing abruptly.

"You have got to be kidding me, right? My mother wasn't a witch." Even as I say the words, I don't know if I believe them. How well did I really know the woman that was capable of hiding the truth about me for eighteen years? Blaine grabs my hand and pulls me back to my seat.

"I know, Larissa. First, you find out you're Nephilim. Then you're told that your dad is alive and you have a brother. The prophecy and now this. I'm so sorry, I just thought you should know the truth." Her voice breaks as she covers my hands with hers. I see the threat of tears in her eyes. Asmodeus kneels beside her and cups her face in his hands.

"She knows you mean well, my love." He kisses her cheek.

"I'm sorry, Piper. I shouldn't even be surprised that my mother had another fucking secret." I laugh, but my voice has no humor in it. She shakes her head sadly.

"Once you leave the coven, your power weakens. While it will never fully go away, she probably wanted to forget the entire thing. Mary saw her mother die, sweetie. My aunt was in the same coven, and she left shortly after as well. Your mom was just a young girl and she was scared. She left to stay with her father, and I'm sure she met Levi shortly after. I think she may have just wanted a fresh start for her new family." She offers with a shrug. I nod to her, but I feel nothing. It's as if I'm empty. Adrian and I are witches now, on top of everything else that we're dealing with.

"So, what does that make me?" Adrian asks. Piper taps her chin with a bright pink fingernail.

"I can't say for sure, but there have only been a couple of witches to pass their gifts onto boys. It's rare that you even have a brother at all. Typically, we only have girls." She says. Adrian sighs and pats my shoulder as he walks to the kitchen.

"Yet again, the weight of the world is on your shoulders, and I am useless." He chuckles.

"Hey, don't say that." He turns to look at me and I smile at him. "You could make a pizza. I'm starving." He groans and rolls his eyes, but still turns the oven on as we all laugh and try to move on from the conversation. My mom is a witch, therefore I could have visions just as Blaine said. As if I didn't have enough on my plate.

#

Asmodeus shakes his head at Adrian, dismissing his idea entirely. "I know Mammon, there is not a chance he set this entire debacle up. It's too sloppy for him. If he could find you, he'd have killed you by now. I wonder if this ward has anything to do with his inability to track you." He speculates for a moment.

"The coven who set this magic was really powerful, according to our father. I'm sure he ensured they took extra precautions." Adrian squints at me, "And I'm sure Mammon hasn't stopped searching for you, even for a moment. So, when we went out of the ward," Adrian trails off. Blaine rubs a hand over his eyes and groans.

"You don't really think I'm that stupid? Piper here cast a cloaking spell. She is one of the most powerful magic users this world has ever seen," Blaine brags and Piper blushes. Asmodeus just beams at her with pride, rubbing circles on her cheek with his thumb as if he can dust away her embarrassment.

"I did my very best. I doubt anyone could do a tracking spell that is stronger than my cloak." She beams at me and I take a deep, reassuring breath.

"We could go to the gate," Piper muses aloud. "I can do a spell of sorts. Maybe I could see who opened the gate, if I could pick up on any energy?" She says. Asmodeus shifts beside her, looking agitated.

"I don't like it. What if Mammon is still watching the gate?" He asks. She nods and pats his hand. "Then we will have to be extra safe."

"I want to come with you." As soon as I say it, Blaine cuts me off. "Absolutely not, Angel. I'm not willing to risk your safety," he snaps.

"But it's fine if my mate puts herself in danger?" Asmodeus grumbles.

"I agree with both of you. It just isn't a good idea yet. We should give the Elders council more time to figure this out. Running head first into danger is just stupid." Adrian chastises. Piper rolls her eyes at me and I nod back at her. Just then, my phone vibrates, and I pull it from my pocket.

"Hey dad, everything okay?" I ask. Levi huffs out a breath before responding.

"Is everyone still there?" He asks.

"Yeah, why?"

"Nobody leaves tonight. I will be back late. Don't wait up." *Click.* I stare down at my phone for a minute.

"That was weird, like, really weird." I say, looking at Adrian.

"That was Dad. He asked if we were all still here then said, *'Nobody leaves tonight'*. He sounded more on edge than usual." I tell him.

Adrian barely reacts. "They probably figured out who opened the gate and are heading to meet with them now. This is good."

"Asmodeus, you and Piper are welcome to use my room. I barely sleep in there anyway." Blaine gives me a heated look that sends a shiver through my body.

"We will absolutely take you up on the offer, thank you. I'm happy to meet you all, but I'm exhausted. Portal jumping takes a lot out of me." Piper says as they excuse themselves. Blaine shows them to his room before coming back in and sitting beside me.

"I guess we should all get some sleep until the Elders decide to tell us more." Adrian waves goodnight as he walks away. Blaine takes my hand and pulls me behind him to my room. When we get inside and close the door behind us, Blaine pins me against the door frame.

"I knew you were having a vision, what Piper said about your mother just confirmed it. You will never cease to amaze me," He says, kissing my neck. I tip my head back to give him easier access.

"You didn't doubt me, not even once. You stood by me, Blaine. Thank you." My fingers curl into his shirt, dragging it over the taught muscles of his back.

"The only time I won't stand beside you is if I am in front of you when you are in danger, or behind you when you lead us. You are everything to me, Angel." He whispers, his admission sucking the air from me as I struggle to say anything at all. I hope he can feel my love for him flow through the bond when words fail me. What can I say, when a simple I love you pales in comparison?

"Come on, let's get you in the shower." A cocky smirk curls his lips a moment before he grabs me and throws me over his shoulder. I kick my feet, playfully fighting against him. This doesn't deter Blaine and he just swipes the shower curtain out of his way to turn the water on. He smacks my ass, making me yelp in surprise before pushing me under the water.

"Blaine! My clothes!" I squeal under the slowly warming spray of water. He grins at me, yanking his shirt and pants off before stepping in.

"That is unfortunate." He gives a dark laugh, dragging my wet shirt over my head. His lips are on mine before my shirt hits the ground. I cringe at the sound and shake my head at him.

"You're gonna have to mop that up." I grumble. He grins and brushes his nose against mine as he drags my pants down my legs.

"Worth it," he whispers. He presses my back to the frigid wall, gripping the back of my neck as his lips meet mine. I cling to his shoulders as he deepens the kiss, his tongue dragging across my lips. When we finally break apart, I swipe the water from my eyes and catch my breath. Blaine rubs his thumb over my kiss-swollen lips before grabbing my shampoo and waving his finger, telling me to turn around.

His fingers rake through my hair with just the right pressure while he massages the shampoo into my scalp. The intimacy of him rinsing my hair, then softly massaging the conditioner into each strand makes my knees weak. Blaine cups my throat as he pulls my back against his chest and drags a washcloth across my breast. The rough fabric over my sensitive nipples makes me squirm against him. My movement only pushes him on as he drags it between my legs. I let out a whimper at the sensation, pressing my thighs together.

Blaine chuckles and washes himself, watching me as he slowly strokes over his length. I reach between us, pushing his hand out of the way to tease him the way he did to me. He grips my hair, turning my head up to look at him while he thrusts against my hand.

"I need you," I whisper, pleading with him. Blaine guides me beneath the water, quickly scrubbing my body as his heated gaze stays locked on mine. He finally shuts the water off and grabs a towel to wrap around me. He wastes no time, grabbing me up and storming back to the bed while I wrap my legs around his waist. Water drips from us as he throws my towel onto the bed before laying me back on it and covering my body with his. Tonight wasn't about taking our time, this was about helping each other chase away the tension of our day.

"You're incredible, Angel. In every damn way." He says quietly before thrusting forward. My mouth drops open on a breathy moan as he moves his hips slowly. His eyes never stop skimming over my entire body with so much admiration, I nearly fall apart under him. Blaine pulls back to flip me over onto my knees. He grips my hips, lining himself up before slamming into me. I fall forward onto my elbows with a cry of pleasure as he picks up his staggering pace. My face buries into the bed in my half-hearted attempt to silence the screams as I clench around his cock.

Blaine grips my hair, yanking my head up as he rams into me one last time, his thrusts slowing as he follows my orgasm with his own. He wraps his arms around my waist and pulls me sideways with him while we catch our breath, still entwined.

"I love you, Angel." He whispers against my hair, kissing the back of my head.

"I love you," I murmur, a sleepy smile curling my lips.

Chapter 10 - Blaine

Larissa jolts awake, panting hard as she frantically scans the room. I sit up and gently wrap my arms around her, "It was just a dream. I'm right here, baby." Larissa relaxes and I yawn while reaching to pick my phone off the nightstand, Larissa flops against me and rubs her face across my chest.

"Pretty sure your dad just got home, or Elaine. I heard the front door, and it's barely five in the morning," I groan, pulling her tighter against me. After kissing me on the cheek, she pulls away to find a pair of pants.

"Just a little while longer. Come back to bed." I dive forward, grabbing her leggings as she tries pulling them on. Hopping on one foot to escape in a way that makes me smirk, she unfortunately finishes dressing.

"Come on, I need to see who it is. Just have a weird feeling." She whispers. Giving up I sigh and concede, grabbing my sweats off the floor as she pulls my shirt on over her head.

We step silently into the hallway, but I stop when I hear hushed voices coming from the dining room. Larissa waves for me to follow behind her, motioning for me to be quiet. I grin and wrap my arms around her, pressing my lips to her ear. "Try not to scream, Angel," I say before wrapping us in shadows, dropping through them to teleport to the bottom the stairs, then the laundry room.

The sensation of falling through the frosty air is familiar to me, but Larissa thrashes in my arms. I just clutch her tighter to my chest, hushing her as she opens her eyes. We are on the far side of the kitchen, pressed to the wall of the pitch-black laundry room. I lean towards the open door, straining to hear.

"They deserve to know, Levi." Mark snaps, his voice

sounds thick.

"I told you already, they will eventually. Now is not the time. You know as well as I do they would go rushing off, right into Mammon's lap." Levi hisses. Larissa steps closer, the both of us holding our breath to hear Mark's lowered voice.

"Larissa just began trusting you and you're going to throw all of that away when she finds out. What if they can help? If it was Mary out there, you'd do everything for her!" His voice rises and Levi hushes him. I stiffen behind Larissa and she glances up at my face. She can't make out much in the dark, but it's obvious something they said struck a nerve.

"My children putting themselves in danger wouldn't save Elaine, Mark. I care for her too. She is my family, and I will ensure we do everything. Mammon will keep her alive. We have some time." He says. It suddenly feels as if something has sucked all the air from the room, and I can smell faint traces of electricity. I grip Larissa's upper arms and whisper in her ear.

"Angel, pull it together." I plead. But she can't hear me. Not over her racing thoughts that I'm sure mirror my own. *Mammon kidnapped Elaine.* The light above us flickers on. *He is holding her hostage, most likely torturing her.* I curse under my breath, trying to shake her, but I yank back when static builds across her body. Larissa kicks the door the rest of the way open, letting it slam off the wall as she storms into the dining room. Levi holds his hand up to stop her as we get closer.

"Larissa, what are you doing down here?" He looks behind her to stare at me. But it's a mistake, because I'm just as enraged.

"How dare you? Elaine is in danger, and you were planning to lie to us!" She shouts. Her anger only grows, and I watch as spark dance down her arms and light up her fists. Levi shakes his head as her hair lifts, floating around her face.

"You can't do anything to help. I didn't feel it was necessary to tell you." He says in a calm tone. I can't help but to throw my head back with a cold laugh. The sound is devoid of humor and Levi snaps his attention to me.

"You just decide what is necessary information now? She

is the only family I have left!" I snap.

"He didn't want you to run after her. Mammon would love to get Larissa's soulmate. He'd break you, boy. That would kill Elaine faster than any demon could." Mark's voice is soft. I almost don't see him, slumped in a chair with his head in his hands.

"She was there when you weren't. How can you say it wasn't necessary for me to know?" She chokes back a sob, trying to pull her power back as a lightbulb above us bursts.

"Can either of you honestly tell me you wouldn't have run off, putting yourselves in danger the moment you knew?" Levi turns to his daughter, eyes bloodshot with unshed tears. "I can't lose you again, Larissa. There will never be a day that I don't regret every moment I was away from the two of you!" Levi shouts at her. She shakes her head at him.

"That doesn't mean you get to hide things like this from me, you are no different than my mother!" She cuts her hand through the air, turning to leave. Larissa stops short when we see Adrian standing at the bottom of the stairs.

"Adrian," She says, but he cuts her off.

"Elaine is probably being beaten and tortured for information *right now*. This isn't about you. It isn't about any of us, it's about her." His voice comes out in a hiss and some of my anger dissolves into shame as he walks closer to stand next to Larissa.

"What happened, Mark?" I ask. Larissa takes Adrian's hand in hers, grounding herself as we stand together.

"Elaine said she had a few errands to run. I tried to go with her, but that stubborn woman stopped me. Said what she was doing would be over quickly, and that they needed me here for the damned meeting." Mark says. The broken sound in his voice cuts through me. Larissa clears her throat, and I can see her fighting back tears. Adrian wraps an arm around her, awkwardly patting her arm. He doesn't know how to comfort his sister but is trying his best, even as he falls apart.

"She didn't say exactly where she was going?" I question,

pacing the room with my jaw clenched and eyes locked on the ground.

"She was picking up some things from town and meeting with somebody, an old friend. I didn't even ask who. I was so distracted by everything." Mark's voice was steady again. Adrian steps away to sit next to him, patting his shoulder as he slides the chair out.

"I won't stop until we get her back," Levi says to Mark before turning to Larissa, "We got Mammon's message, it isn't much to go on but from Larissa's vision we can assume he is in King's Castle." She frowns, and I know she's imagining her vision.

"What is King's Castle?" She gives me a questioning look. When I turn to say something to her, I stop and look over her shoulder.

"It's where the King of the Kings live." Asmodeus' deep voice startles her as he walks in, leaning against the wall and crossing his arms.

"Piper had trouble sleeping, so she will be in bed for a short while longer. Am I right to assume the disruption came from you?" Asmodeus asks Larissa. She nods slowly and he shakes his head at her.

"Your emotions are dangerous when they are the only thing in control of your power." He grumbles, walking over to the coffee pot.

"King's castle is in Hell. It was mine when I ruled, but after I fled, Lilith took over. Now it seems Mammon is trying to sit on my throne." He says.

"Since you are the King of Kings, why don't you just take it back?" She says, as if it's an obvious answer. I take her hand in mine, pulling her closer.

"It's not that easy, Angel." I brush my thumb across her cheek and she leans into my touch. Knowing that Elaine is being held down there makes me want to run straight to her and save her, the way she did when I was alone. We'll face Mammon the way we did with Lilith. Nothing will stop me. I look up from the floor to see Asmodeus watching me, his eyes mere slits as he slowly takes a drink of his coffee.

"Mammon would have to give the crown over or it would be a fight to the death." Levi says. He turns to Mark. "May I see the note once more?" He holds his hand out and Mark places a piece of paper in his outstretched hand.

"He grabbed her so that we would come running to save her and he'd be able to get to Larissa?" Adrian asks. Mark nods and offers Larissa a smile that doesn't reach his eyes.

"He is offering to trade her life for yours, I'm afraid. But Elaine would die before she allowed that." His voice is raspy. *Her life for Larissa's.*

"So, when do we go?" She asks. Every part of me becomes rigid, like I've been doused in freezing water. I shoot my hand forward and grip her chin, forcing Larissa to look up into my eyes.

"You are not going after her. We will take care of it, and you will keep your ass here where you're safe." My voice is lethal but she jerks away from me, a defiant gleam in her eye.

"Elaine will *die* if we don't do what he says!" She throws her hands into the air in frustration. Asmodeus sets a cup of coffee in front of Mark, then turns to tower over her.

"What if he kills her when you walk into *his* kingdom, then saulghters you where you stand and your death would be for nothing?" He asks. Larissa swallows hard before opening her mouth and closing it.

"Larissa, we need to do this carefully if we want everyone to live." Adrian sounds exhausted. Asmodeus perks up and turns with a smile on his face. Piper pads into the room with a yawn and gives an embarrassed smile to everyone.

"You let me sleep with all this excitement?" She asks him as he dips down and nuzzles her neck.

"Asmodeus, everyone is watching!" She giggles, pushing him away. He just smiles as she takes his cup and leans backwards against him.

"What's going on?" she asks, realizing the tension. I wrap

my arms around Larissa, needing to pull her close so that I can rest my chin on the top of her head. Mark looks like he would rather be anywhere but here.

"I wish we were still in bed," I groan and Levi clears his throat.

"Sleeping. I'm tired, old man." I snort as Larissa bumps me with her elbow.

"Larissa, would you mind showing me the garden? You can catch me up to speed." She gives her a pointed look and it makes me uneasy.

"Yeah, I guess I can do that." She says awkwardly. I begrudgingly let her walk away after placing a loud kiss on her cheek. Watching them leave with their heads bent together has suspicion clawing its way across my skin as I cross my arms and watch them through the window.

Larissa

We walk in silence through the dying garden, and I pull my sweater tight around my body as a frigid breeze picks up. Piper glances behind us, towards the house, and snorts at something.

"Asmodeus and Blaine are both staring at us through the window." I glance back and can see them clearly in the bright kitchen.

"It's still dark. How can they see us so clearly?" I wonder.

"Demons have great night vision, Blaine never told you?" She asks as we sit on a bench under the trees.

"He doesn't enjoy talking about that side of him, so I don't ask." I mumble.

"So, Elaine is missing and Mammon is just a cliché villain who wants your life for hers?" She asks, popping her lips as she waits for me to answer.

"I had a vision of you asking me to teleport you into King's Castle," she shrugs. I sit up straighter as an idea blooms.

"Piper, you could do that? You can drop me in with her, then pull us out before he ever realized I was there!" I say excitedly. Piper sighs and pats my leg.

"I wish it were that easy, but King's Castle has a powerful ward against magic. A spell like that would have to be powerful and untraceable. What if it drains me and I can't pull you out?" She sounds worried. I chew on my lip for a moment.

"If I could somehow get in, would you be able to pull me out?" Her brows draw together as she contemplates this.

"I can only teleport what I'm touching," she stops, getting lost in her thoughts. I bounce my leg as I wait, resisting the urge to shake her, "Unless I can get us in, then you teleport us out! If we can get to my aunt's coven, meet with them and see if any of your dormant powers could awaken." She stops suddenly and tilts her head. "Are we including the men in these plans?" She asks.

"No! Not yet." Guilt worms its way into my stomach immediately at the thought of hiding such a big secret from Blaine.

"They're coming now. We will meet up later and figure something out." She whispers, taking my hand in hers. I smile to myself, feeling a strong connection with her. Asmodeus and Blaine walk up, holding a steaming cup out for each of us.

"May we join you?" Asmodeus asks Piper, giving her a wink.

Chapter 11 - Larissa

Sweat has soaked the front of my gray shirt and I'm trying desperately to slow my breathing. I quickly drag my slick palms across my pants to get a better grip on my dagger. Leaning back against the tree for support, I concentrate on the feeling of rough bark and mossy smell to calm my racing heart.

Each deep breath pulls the scent of moss and the earth into my lungs. *Snap.* The air freezes in my throat, the twig breaking sounds like an explosion in the dead silence of the surrounding forest. He's close, too damn close. I look above me, gauging if I can make it up the tree without drawing his attention.

The sound of crunching leaves even closer has me closing my eyes as I plead with my thundering heart to slow down. *I'm out of time. He's only about thirty feet away.* Cursing under my breath, I squat down and prepare to launch myself up when the smell of freshly burnt firewood drifts past me.

"Trying to fly away, little birdie?" His voice is right behind my ear, taunting me. I drive my elbow back, putting as much force into it as I can. Blaine grunts, not expecting the blow to his ribs. I turn on my heel and sprint into the woods, my feet pouding across the uneven ground. Relying on directional instincts I *don't* have, I try to find a way out of the woods

I finally catch sight of Piper jumping up and down excitedly, cheering me on. My excitement crumbles as her eyes widen and she frantically waves me forward.

Too late. Blaine slams into me, sending the both of us tumbling to the ground. He turns his body to shield mine and take the brunt of our fall, but it still knocks the air from my lungs.

"*Sonofabitch,*" I wheeze as one word. Piper holds her hand out, helping me off Blaine, who is grinning wildly. I drag my eyes down his body, making it a point to lick my lips and he groans.

"Chasing you is so thrilling, Angel." He stands up and dusts the dirt from his pants before brushing his lips against my neck and whispering, "I think we just found a new game to play in the bedroom," Blush burns my cheeks as he winks at me.

"Why didn't you shock him?" Asmodeus asks. I look at Blaine then back to him and his expression is full of annoyance.

"Wait, are you serious? Because this is just *training,* I can seriously hurt people with my powers." I say. Asmodeus takes his jacket off and cracks his neck from side to side.

"Asmodeus, is this really necessary?" Piper's eyes are enormous as she looks between us. Blaine steps in front of me, crossing his arms and staring daggers at him.

"No." He says firmly.

"She loves you, so this is just a game. But what if a demon is chasing you? What will you do then? You won't be there to save her every time." Asmodeus rolls his shoulders. Blaine turns pleading eyes towards me, "I don't want you to get hurt, Angel."

"Then I won't. I'll kick his ass." I grin with confidence I don't even have. Asmodeus chuckles and Piper shakes her head with a smile.

"No secret king powers," she wags a finger at him then turns to me "Try not to fry him, I plan to get laid tonight!" She giggles. My phone chimes from the ground where it's resting on my jacket and I nod for Blaine to check it while I stretch my legs.

"Ella said she is bringing Jake and Eric over," He snorts when another message pops up "She is asking if Adrian will be here." Blaine says.

"Tell her he will be here," I turn to Piper. "She and Adrian have the hots for each other but neither one will do anything about it." I shrug. He tosses my phone back down and gives me a thumbs up. "I told her to 'come get that dick'," He winks and I roll my eyes at his antics.

Asmodeus walks up and immediately kicks my leg, not

giving me any warning. I dive to the side but still take the hit to my thigh. Letting out a groan, I flinch from the sharp pain and Asmodeus shakes his head.

"A demon doesn't warn you before they attack, and they will not take it easy on you." He swings a punch towards me, catching my ribs.

Hissing a breath between my teeth I try to resist curling in on myself. Asmodeus steps forward again, and this time I react. As hard as I can, I swing my fist out and aim for his throat. He is quicker than me and jumps back as I graze him. Huffing in frustration, I step backwards and make sure not to take my eyes off of him.

"If your moves are always this predictable, you will not stand a chance." He warns me before diving directly at me. Without thinking, I pull my powers forward and kick a foot out at him. Asmodeus takes the full force of my kick to the side of his knee and lets out a grunt of pain. Before I can celebrate, he slams me to the ground.

"Asmodeus," Blaine's voice is raised in warning. I desperately try to fight him off me, but the fall pinned one arm under me with the other between us. His weight and the impact are making it hard to breathe and black spots swim across my vision.

"Your tiny *sparks* won't always be enough. Some demons can disable powers. What will you do then?" He hisses before grabbing my throat in his hand. "Stop panicking and think." His words are calm even as he slowly cuts off my airway. I struggle to catch a breath, wheezing under his grip. *He's going to kill me. I'm about to die.* Panic takes hold, but suddenly the fear is pushed aside by blinding rage. The force of anger washes through me uncontrollably, and I gurgle, trying to scream.

"Asmodeus, enough!" Blaine's shouting pushes through the haze.

The tingling comfort of my power becomes a full-blown vibration across my entire body as I unleash it with everything I have. Asmodeus' weight suddenly vanishes and I suck in a breath, coughing and gagging at the ache. A cold flood circles me and causes a shiver to tremble down my body from the sweat that has soaked my clothes.

"Angel, I'm here. Look at me." Blaine's hands cup my cheeks and I peel my eyes open. His face blurs above me. "Blaine? Oh God, did I hurt him?" I rasp out, trying to sit up.

"No, but you were going nuclear," He whispers, kissing my forehead. When I glance around, I realize Blaine had used the shadows to pull me away from Asmodeus.

"I lost control. This rage came over me and it *consumed* me." I shake my head and try to make sense of what happened. Blaine nods and looks away from me.

"It was mine. Watching and just standing there while you fought to breathe, I couldn't take it. Even though I knew you weren't in any real danger, I think I may have forced my feelings through the bond." He sighs and I push his arms aside to bury my face in his neck.

"We will figure out this thing with our bond, together." I reassure him.

"Oh my gosh, are you alright, Larissa?" Piper runs up and helps me stand on shaking legs.

"I'm fine. Is Asmodeus okay?" I ask. He is sitting on the ground, staring up at the sky. He turns his head to look at us when we walk towards him.

"You have an incredible power, but you can't harness it well with your inability to control your emotions." He says. Piper blows out her breath as she sits beside him.

"What he means is, you will be a badass if you just keep practicing control." She corrects, patting his hand. Blaine smacks my ass and puts his face against my neck.

"She is a badass," He says with pride, "Here comes Ella, and she is on a warpath. You better lookout." Blaine whispers. Ella storms up to me and grabs me by the shoulders.

"How dare you," she states. I shake my head. "What do you mean?"

"Elaine was kidnapped, and you didn't think to call me? I

thought we were best friends." Sadness makes her words thick and I can see the tremble in her lip. Pulling her into a tight hug, I sigh.

"Ella, I'm sorry. I was just trying to process everything." In truth, I was struggling to accept the reality that Elaine wasn't coming home anytime soon. Ella gives me a knowing look as Eric, Adrian and Jake walk over to sit with us.

Blaine takes care of introductions and Piper excitedly shakes everyone's hand. Asmodeus looks like he'd rather have a black hole open under him.

"What the Hell happened to you?" Adrian asks, staring at my neck. Blaine explains our attempt at training and Adrian shakes his head.

"I appreciate you trying to help. But if you choke my sister ever again, I will kill you." Adrian says calmly, locking eyes with Asmodeus. I watch as Asmodeus lip twitches, as if he's fighting back a smile. Blaine grins beside me and I shake my head at him, desperately begging him to break the tension.

"Don't worry, Angel. He doesn't mean when you beg me to choke you." Blaine whispers loudly. I bury my face in my hands, hiding my mortification. Eric howls with laughter. Even Ella and Piper are giggling but Adrian looks disgusted.

"I only tolerate you because she loves you," He reminds Blaine.

"Then you'll always be stuck with me," Blaine grins, taking my hand in his.

"Okay, so no choking, got it. But how are we going to rescue Elaine?" Eric asks, playfulness gone. We sit in silence, everyone unsure of how to answer. Piper and I exchange a look and I shake my head at her once.

"Oh no, share with the class. You two have a secret." Ella pouts, calling us out. Blaine bumps me with his shoulder, but I can't look at him.

"Not really, just trying to train me. You know how I can't really control the static, it's either super tiny or explosive. I really struggle to find balance. So Piper and I were going to work on that. She was going to help teach me control." Piper clears her throat and I clamp my mouth shut to stop the rambling. Ella nods as if it makes sense, but Eric is staring daggers at me. Jake stands up and motions for me to do the same.

"Attack me." He tells me. I stand slowly, unsure of what to do.

"Charge up, however you need. Then hit me with it. Hurt me, without killing me." He explains, holding his hands up defensively. I nod in understanding and close my eyes for a moment.

"Do you have a death wish? Closing your eyes during a fight isn't just idiotic, it's dangerous. What have you morons been teaching her?" Eric calls out.

"I know that it's dangerous! But it isn't easy to pull the electricity forward without using emotion." I snap at him, throwing my hands in the air. Blaine walks up behind me and nods for me to look at Jake.

"Breathe in, slowly. Hold it for a moment while you search for that feeling." He reaches around and softly presses his hand below my breast. "Drag it outwards as you breathe out. You know how to do this, Angel." I do as he says and sweat breaks out across my brow. I imagine the tingling spreading until it vibrates across my skin.

Blaine takes a step back "*Good girl*, now you just need to amp it up a little. Add another layer over it, maybe two for good measure." He chuckles when Jake looks bored, dancing from foot to foot. My breath catches from him praising me and a low rumble sounds in his chest as he backs away again.

I step up to Jake and he takes a lazy swing at my ribs. As I throw my arm up to block him, a ball of electricity *shoots from my palm.* It slams Jake's shoulder and throws him backwards. I stagger from the force of it leaving my body, falling right into Blaine's outstretched arms. I stand up, looking down at my hands in shock as Jake stands slowly with a groan.

"Okay, that sucked." He grumbles, trying to roll his shoulder. My eyes go wide when I see the charring on his shirt and some of the fabric is burnt away.

"Jake, I am so sorry," I say. He just waves me off, thankfully not upset.

"I'm not volunteering anymore. You didn't tell me she could do *that*." He elbows Eric when he sticks his finger through the hole in his shirt. Guilt fills me as I see the red, irritated skin underneath.

"That's because we only focus on swords or hand to hand. I'm not dumb as a rock like some people, Jake." Eric jests back, but he is looking at me with curiosity.

"Okay, that was badass," Ella says.

"I wonder what other secrets you're hiding in there, Angel." Blaine whispers when I turn towards him. His eyes are full of pride as he looks me over before dropping a kiss to my forehead.

"To be honest with you, I am glad she figured that out on you and not when we sparred," Eric says to Jake, clapping him on the shoulder. Jake gives him a dirty look while Piper beams excitedly at me. Asmodeus has his head tilted, not speaking. I turn to Adrian, who looks startled more than anything.

"Can you try to do that again, but on purpose?" Adrian asks. I shrug my shoulders and look around nervously.

"What should I aim at?" I ask, still flexing my hand and staring at it as if it's an alien attached to me and not part of my body.

"Oh, could we have a bonfire? I'd kill for a s'more." Piper says. Asmodeus laughs and wraps his arms around her. We all began gathering wood so I could test out my new *trick* and so Piper could have s'mores.

Chapter 12 - Larissa

After nearly an hour of learning to summon and toss balls of electricity, we are all sitting around the bonfire together. While Piper happily eats so many s'mores, I question where she is putting them.

"You're going to get a cavity." I say as she spears another marshmallow. She sticks her tongue out at me and holds the stick over the flames. The smoky scent of burning wood brings me comfort, even as the guilt soaks my bones. Here I am, surrounded by loved ones while Elaine is suffering. And to save her, I have to do it behind Blaine's back.

"You'll have a bellyache, you're cut off." Asmodeus says, snatching the bag of treats from her and tossing it over to Blaine. Piper grumpily blows the fire off her extra crispy marshmallow and offers me one.

"No thanks, I'm actually about to go in and grab a drink." I start to stand, but Blaine stops me.

"You rest a bit. Using your power like that had to be pretty draining." He says, standing up. Piper nudges Asmodeus and he sighs, standing up to go with him without question. She waits until they're out of earshot and peeks around the fire to check on the rest of the group. Eric and Jake are arm wrestling. Poor Eric is struggling while Jake doesn't even look like he's trying. Ella and Adrian are sitting together, watching them while cheering.

"Those two look cozy, don't they?" Piper whispers. I smile and nod, picking up a stick to poke at the burning wood.

"I can't stop thinking that we are here, and Elaine isn't. It's all my fault," I say under my breath. Piper lays a hand on my shoulder and huffs.

"That's why we are making a plan. What if we went back

to my coven, and asked them for help? If you could harness your witch abilities, then we would have a real shot at a successful rescue mission." She says, sincerity in her eyes.

"If you're confident that they would be willing to help, then when do we leave?"

"I don't think we should do this without telling anyone." She looks me directly in the eyes, tilting her head.

"With that said, if it was my aunt in trouble, then I would move Heaven and Hell to bring her home safe." She squeezes my hand in hers. "But at least broach the subject with him, okay?"

"I'll try, but I know he is going to stop me." I say sadly.

"Well, bat your eyes and take your top off. Boobs work great when you want to get your way." She giggles and I shake my head with a smile.

"If he shuts it down, then we will do things our own way. We meet here at three am and walk to the outside of the barrier. From there I will do my best to mask and teleport us to the coven. But Larissa, he will come for you. Blaine loves you." She says.

"I know. I love him too. Which is why if this doesn't work, then I'm turning myself in. I can't put him in danger to save Elaine when it's my fault she's there and he would do everything to stop me." I look up and go silent when I lock eyes with Ella, who squints and purses her lips. *Shit, she definitely heard some of that.*

Blaine holds a bottle of water in front of my face as he sits down. While working up the nerve to talk to him, I take it and sip on the cool drink.

"I can feel it, you know?" His voice is soft.

"What do you mean?" I ask.

"Through the bond, you're flustered over something. I wish you would talk to me." Blaine brushes my hair back and I catch his hand in mine. I look back at Piper and she encourages me with a nod.

"What if there was a way to teleport in? Let's say a witch teleports herself and another into Elaine's cell. They grab her,

65

the second witch would then teleport them back out. So fast, Mammon wouldn't even know." I say excitedly. Blaine looks at me like I have grown a second head.

"Mammon will know the moment anyone opens one of the Gates, which is what you do to get into Hell to teleport anywhere inside. He isn't stupid. He has the entire palace spelled against magic, I'm sure. Why don't we just wait to see what the Elders have to say and maybe you don't run off and get yourself killed?" He snaps at me. Heat burns my cheeks as embarrassment hits me.

"It was just an idea we were going to pitch to the Elder's, Blaine." Piper tries to smooth it over, but he just snorts at her words.

"Larissa would hand herself over in a heartbeat if it meant saving Elaine. Usually I love how you put everyone else first, but I can't lose you. We will find another way." He says, his tone final with no room for argument.

"You aren't even giving me a chance to try." I say, defeated.

"I said no, drop it." He snaps. I huff out a frustrated breath and throw the stick into the fire. Sparks fly up around us and one lands on Asmodeus' pant leg. He gives me a glare as he sticks his thumb on it, smashing it down.

"When you react with emotion, that happens, Angel. People get burnt." Blaine says.

#

I look over at Blaine's slowly rising and falling back as he sleeps peacefully beside me. As gently as I can, I slip my legs over the side of the bed and tip toe to my dresser where I left a pair of jeans and t-shirt. Dressing silently, I keep checking to make sure he doesn't wake up and as I step to the door, I turn and blow him a silent kiss.

"I hope you'll forgive me," I whisper. The door shuts with a soft click behind me and I hold my breath, listening and waiting. The house stays silent as I pad down the stairs to grab my shoes and jacket from beside the door. Just as I open the door, I hear a small thud from upstairs. Without thinking twice,

I lunge through the door open and yank it shut behind me. I sprint around the side of the house as my heart races. Piper blinks at me with her brows drawn as I run towards her.

"What happened?" She hisses. I shake my head and motion for the woods.

"We gotta go, now." I huff. Piper lets out a sigh.

"Asmodeus is going to realize I'm gone. When he and Blaine come for us, they will not be happy. Are you sure you want to do this?" She asks me. I look back up at the house and for just a moment, I think I see a flash of somebody moving in the dark window.

"I can't ask you to do this and put a rift between you and Asmodeus," I say. Piper rolls her eyes and puts her hands on her hips as I jump in place, stuffing my feet into my shoes.

"Shut up, I offered to do this and I've done worse. Asmodeus will be fine." She waves a hand.

"Let's go," I say, turning to jog towards the woods. We do our best to keep our steps light but quick as we reach the fallen leaves. It's already hard to navigate under the moonlight but clouds rumble across the sky, blocking what brief vision we had.

I stumble forward, clutching my chest as panic cuts me deep and steals my breath. The bond vibrates and tears prick my eyes.

"Larissa, we need to go. Are you okay?" I turn my face towards her as I stagger forward.

"You're bonded, aren't you?" she asks, sadly rubbing at her chest as well. "I know, sweetie. Asmodeus is calling for me, too. Which means we are running out of time." She takes my hand in hers and we push forward, no longer trying to silence our steps.

The pain slowly burns into anger as we get close to the edge of the   border and a chill slips across my skin. *He's getting closer. We aren't going to make it.* Sweat covers my face as my lungs ache with the drop in temperature.

"*Larissa!*" Blaine's voice booms in the surrounding woods, full of rage and sadness. Sweat drips down my face, mixing with my tears as I shake my head. *Please understand, I'm so sorry.* I try to push it into the bond, forcing my feelings into the thread that connects us. He pushes back immediately with anger and betrayal. My heart feels as if he is pulling me to him. Piper dives through the barrier, suddenly yanking me right behind her.

"Asmodeus no, I'm sorry!" She cries out, grabbing my arms as he runs full force towards us. I glance back and nearly cry out in fear. Asmodeus looks like a God of death, one that only wears plaid pajama pants and black combat boots. Any other time, the sight would have been comical, except he was terrifying. With Blaine right on his heels as the shadows swarm and circle him in his rage.

Blaine locks eyes with me as Piper throws her hand wide, tearing a portal open beneath us and I drop down with her as he lunges towards us, a second too late.

Chapter 13 - Larissa

I mouth *"I love you"* to him, just as it feels like our bodies are being stretched and twisted. It isn't painful, but extremely uncomfortable. When Piper breaks away from me, I stagger and fall back to land on soft dirt. Turning to brace myself on my hands and knees, I wretch onto the ground. My eyes water and my throat burns as my fingers curl into the dirt, my nails burrowing into the wet soil.

"I didn't really have time to warn you how dizzying the first time can be. I'm sorry, but this is pretty normal." Piper says, holding my hair back for me as I swipe my mouth clean with the back of my hand. Shakily, I stand and look around us. I'm amazed at how the forest seems as if every plant, down to the moss along the trees, has a dark glow to it.

Piper leans against me, holding a hand to her forehead as she gives me a timid smile. Teleporting takes its toll on her, and she was doing it for me. Everyone just kept sacrificing for me, and I knew that I couldn't stop now. I couldn't let it all be for nothing.

"It's luminescent magic. They use it as natural light here to not disturb the earth as it sleeps." A woman's voice chimes behind us. I swing around, startled to see a woman in a dark robe. She reaches up and pushes back her hood, giving us a bright smile. Her hair is a soft blonde filled with gray, the same color as her eyes that reflect the moon.

"Auntie!" Piper yells, throwing her arms around the woman's neck. She holds her tight and smooths her hair back. The touch is so maternal, it causes a pang of grief to ripple through my chest as I think of my mother and Elaine.

"You are Mary's little girl, no doubt about that! My word,

you really are the spitting image of her." She says, smiling as she cups my face. I take a small step backwards and give an awkward laugh, unsure of what to say or do. Piper takes my hand and gives it a reassuring squeeze.

"I called my Aunt Willow to warn her we were coming. I caught her up on basically everything." Piper says with a sad smile, rubbing at her chest. I mirror her movement, trying to brush away the ache coming from the bond.

"They're already tracking us down, aren't they?" I ask her. She gives a light chuckle and nods.

"There isn't magic strong enough to hide the bond from them. Only one thing can sever the bond," Piper says, her voice dropping low.

"What is it?" I ask.

"Death is the only thing that will ever fully break a bond between soulmates." Willow says darkly before waving us to follow her into a *tree*. She walks right through it, before I can even digest what they've told me. *We will always feel connected unless one of us dies.* I'm reminded of the pain I felt on the day Lilith killed Blaine.

"Okay, just watch your step here." Willow says as we follow her. Everything goes dark and I throw my hands out, clutching onto Piper as she pulls me along behind her. I'm struck by a sense of familiarity as the energy crackles through the air around us and I take in the world we've stepped into. The houses that line the stone paths are built from logs, with ivy and flowers crawling up the sides. We follow the path through the town and I'm amazed by the glowing flora everywhere. I nearly lose my footing when my eyes travel up the massive trees that encircle the entire village, their limbs reaching into the dark, clouded sky above us.

Piper bounces excitedly next to me, her face nearly glowing under the different lights. Even though it is the middle of the night, the entire place is alive. People are out gardening in their yard, children are running excitedly through the streets and stop to stare as we pass by them. Merchants have stalls open as we get closer to the center of town, different food scents float around us and my mouth waters with each step.

Pulling us away from our gazing, Willow leads us into what looks to be an old style tavern. The inside is full of activity. People are laughing together over the sound of music that seems to come from the walls. A few of them stop to stare at us as we pass, giving us curious looks.

"I hate the smell of beer," Piper whispers to me as we stick close to Willow. She waves and smiles at the bartender. He nods respectfully to her before looking Piper over once until his eyes land on me. He is a tall man, showing off his very muscular figure with his white shirt unbuttoned and hanging around him. His hair is so black it looks like it has been stained with ink, and I'm startled when I notice two small horns peeking out from beneath his curly hair. His eyes drag slowly up my body, and he gives me a devilish grin, winking at me.

"I think he likes what he sees," Piper giggles as I roll my eyes at her.

"Not a chance," I say, glancing back at him one last time as we head upstairs.

The stairs head to a hallway with three doors and it opens to a large sitting area. Willow leads us all to the soft blue sectional that sits in the corner. Potted plants are all around us, on shelves between crystals, bones, and other trinkets. Willow smiles sadly at me as I sit back and try to relax.

"You have about three days at most before they get here, so we don't exactly have much time."

"I don't even have that long. I have to get to my Aunt Elaine before it's too late," I say sadly. Piper pats my leg and smiles at me.

"Finding your power will not be easy," she looks over at Willow, who nods and leans backwards.

"We will begin right away, but you need to know, you may have done this for nothing." Willow's voice is flat and void of emotion.

"What do you mean?" I ask.

"You may not even have the power you so desperately search for, but if you do, then we will help you unlock it. I'll send Cole up with a hot meal and some drinks, while I gather a few others for help." Willow says before walking away.

"I'm going to try something real quick." Piper softly bites her lip while concentrating on the wall across from us. For a long time, nothing happens. Suddenly, Piper tilts her head and I watch as her pupils blow wide. Her eyes glaze over as her body drops forward. I catch her before she topples off the couch.

"Piper?" My voice is raised as I shake her. Piper sits up, rubbing her face slowly.

"I'm sorry. Usually it's simple for me to peek in on Asmodeus. The wards here are really strong at blocking magic from coming, or going, I suppose." She looks sadly down at her clenched hands. Guilt pangs through me for getting her into this mess and she brushes a shimmering lock of hair from her face before putting a polite smile back on.

Chapter 14 - Larissa

The bartender from earlier walks down the hallway towards us, balancing a huge tray in his hands. He sets it down on the table between us and locks eyes with me, cracking a bright smile. His teeth are so white that they seem to almost glow against his dark skin. For a moment, I'm mesmerized by his one brown eye and one green.

"Welcome to Witches Willow, ladies." He gives a small bow. "My name is Cole."

Looking over at Piper I notice her brows are pinched as she watches him closely with a frown on her face. "Thanks, I'm Larissa and this is Piper." I motion to her. The frown only deepens, and he notices.

"Apologies, I work for your Aunt Willow. She told me of your plans, and I find it very brave that you would leave safety, and your mate, behind." He smiles softly at us before turning and walking away. I turn towards her and grab one plate from the tray. It has a bowl of what appears to be stew and slices of toasted bread next to it. She takes her own plate and looks back again, ensuring he isn't there.

"We don't trust him," she says before ripping a chunk of bread off with her teeth aggressively. Raising a brow at her, I take a glass of water to gulp down.

"Why? Because he is friendly?" I joke and she pins me with a serious stare, pointing her spoon at me.

"First, he looked right down your shirt. Second, he's part demon." She says, as if it's obvious.

"Asmodeus is literally the King of Hell and Blaine is part demon, too." I remind her. She rolls her eyes at me. "Yes, but they are the good guys. He isn't, and I can feel it. I don't trust him."

She says, obviously done with the conversation. We finish eating quietly and Cole comes back up to collect our dishes.

"Willow is waiting for you. I suggest you get a move on. She is not a patient woman," He whispers loudly to me before winking. I give an awkward laugh and follow him downstairs, while Piper glares daggers at his back. Willow waves us along behind her, out the door and down the pathway.

"When we get there, you step into the circle and wait while we say a blessing. Then we shall instruct you as we go." She explains to me quickly. We nearly have to jog to keep up with her as she weaves between people and heads for a small clearing. A million questions run through my head, but I'm too nervous to ask any of them. The clearing has unfamiliar symbols drawn in a circle on the ground, in a space about seven feet wide. Some resemble stick figures in different poses, while others are obscure letters.

There are two other women waiting there for us. One has all gray hair that is twisted into two buns atop her head. Freckles dot her soft brown cheeks that have begun to show signs of wrinkles. The other woman is young, close to our age. She has purple hair the color of a plum, and her expression is full of boredom. Willow holds her hand out to the older woman, and she steps forward.

"I am Anne," she smiles at us. Piper bows her head respectfully, and I follow her lead as the second woman steps forward.

"I'm Niko." She waves a hand at us, and we bow a little more awkwardly. Piper stands beside me as we face the other women, and step inside of the circle.

"We haven't the time to waste from what I've been told. Let's hurry along now." Anne waves her hand, motioning for me to follow Piper.

"Trust me?" She whispers. I hesitate for only a second before nodding. They all take hands and chant under their breath in an unrecognizable language while I fidget nervously. Piper bumps me softly with her hip and gives me a reassuring smile, but something has become restless within my chest. It feels as if my heart is a caged beast fighting to escape.

I try to push the feeling away and concentrate on Niko as she twists her purple hair into a bun. She steps to the edge of the circle and draws a blade from within her gray hoodie. Niko drags the dagger across her palm, wincing as red blood floods around the sharp object and spills onto the symbol at her feet. Then she kneels and presses her palm to the twisted image. As blood seeps in, the circle fills with a low blue glow and she steps away, nodding to Anne.

"What are you doing?" I ask, a little repulsed.

"Take out the dagger that your brother has the twin to," Anne's soft voice commands. *How the heck does she know that?* With my shaking hand, I pull the dagger from the pocket on my hip. Slowly, I hold the tip of my finger against the point and take a deep breath. The blade breaks skin when Piper reaches over and taps the hilt.

"Hey that hurt," I grumble, and she rolls her eyes.

"It barely stings, and you hesitated." Piper sticks her tongue out at me and I sigh. She was right, but I wasn't about to tell her that. My blood wells up and drips slowly down my finger and Anne nods to me.

"Repeat after me and clear your mind of all but our voices." She says and closes her eyes. I follow her actions and hold my hands outward, closing my eyes and trying to concentrate. But the urge to flee only increases in my chest, instinct warning me that *something* is coming. Something powerful. As I struggle to clear my thoughts, the bonds strumming picks up its pace. I can feel Blaine's agitation as he tries to reach me and it bleeds into desperation. His anger rips through me with so much force that it nearly brings to my knees and I cry out in pain. My body shudders and I stagger sideways, fighting against the pain as it courses through my head in agonizing waves.

"Larissa, you must push back. Listen to my words. Drive back against him or this won't work!" Anne shouts. I throw my head back and clench my jaw as tears drip into my hair. Struggling blindly, I dig into my power and imagine forcing it as a current through the bond. Using it to hold Blaine off, in the back of my mind, I'm desperately hoping I don't hurt him. The pain finally subsides and I fall to my knees in relief, unable to hold myself up any longer. Piper catches me as we both collapse and she holds me tight. Sweat covers my body, and she brushes my hair back while I stare at her through blurry eyes.

"I know it hurts, sweetie. But it's temporary," she reassures me.

"What happened?" I ask, struggling to stand with her help.

"You are opening the channel to your magic. When you do that, it can also change and even deepen your bond. I didn't think it would be so severe. I should have warned you." Piper says.

"I'm okay, it's not so bad," I lie, "But he's pissed." I chuckle and she frowns at me.

"Asmodeus is getting angrier by the minute, but I doubt Blaine meant to hurt you." She says sadly. Anne claps her hands and draws our attention back to the three women watching us warily. The wind kicks up, and I shiver against the chill of it. The smell of charred earth drifts past my nose and I look around us. Anne points at my feet and I glance down in shock. Where I was standing before is now charred earth in the shape of my shoes and I stare in shocked silence.

"Don't move from that spot. We must hurry now. Clear your mind once more and say, '*I open my soul to you, Selene, and accept the gifts you graciously blessed upon me*'." She says. I take a shaky breath and open my arms, tilting my head to the sky.

"I open my soul to you, Selene." Cool air brushes my hair back and light dims beyond my closed lids. "And accept the gifts you graciously blessed upon me." A chill creeps from my face and drapes over my body as I stand there. The sensation is similar to Blaine's shadows, but still so different that it's uncomfortable. In an instant, I feel like I'm sinking into the ground, unable to move my body. I can't scream or open my eyes as it consumes me.

Chapter 15 - Blaine

Feeling her pull away in the middle of the night didn't usually concern me. I have made jokes about buying her a giant hamster water bottle and hanging it next to the bed because of how much water this woman consumes. Brushing my hand over the empty place on the bed made me consider that idea more seriously as I picked my phone up to check the time.

That's when I noticed her full glass of water on the nightstand and the hair on my neck rose. The bathroom light was off as well, and I could feel her panic trembling in the bond.

"Larissa?" I call, rolling out of bed and pulling pants on as I rush around the room. Her phone is on the floor and most of her drawers are open as if she got dressed in a rush.

"Damn it, you stubborn fucking woman." I snarl, nearly ripping the door from its hinges as I thunder through the house. I knew she and Piper were hiding something, but I trusted her to come to me when she was ready. *I trusted her, damn it.*

"Asmodeus!" I roar, slamming my palm to his door once before shoving my feet into shoes and running through the front door. The giant demon is hot on my heels as he curses Piper.

"Why must she push me? Why must she test the limits of my patience and willingness to forgive her dangerous and selfish actions?" He stomps, nearly rattling the earth as we run through the woods. I can still smell her on the wind and I begin dropping in and out of shadows, moving quicker as we approach the border.

"Larissa!" I roar, seeing her and Piper running towards the rippling veil that is keeping her safe. She twists as Piper portals them, her eyes shimmering when I reach for her and *she pulls her hand away.*

"I love you" She mouths the words, and then she's gone. A cry of anguish rips from my lungs as the bond aches from the distance stretching between us and I slam my hands to the closest tree. My blackened fingertips and claws sink deep into the bark as I rip away chunks, throwing them in a blind rage.

Asmodeus grips my shoulder, and I swing to face him, swiping at his face. He slams a palm to my chest, landing me on my ass and knocking some of the fight from me as my vision clears.

"I am not your enemy, boy. Thank your stars for that." He points a finger at me, then holds his hand out to help me stand. My breathing is ragged as I take his hand and brush myself off, slowly calming myself. I rub a fist against my chest, frowning against the deep rooted ache that protests.

"It will not stop until she is close to you again." Asmodeus lays a palm over his heart as he looks to where they vanished.

"We have to bring them back. I have to get to her, Asmodeus."

"Let's gather some things, I can track Piper." He turns and leads us back to the house where Adrian stands outside, his arms crossed as he glares at us.

"Trying to wake the entire town?" he grumbles.

"Lariss and Piper took off and we're going to bring them back." I say, shoving past him. I'm not in the mood to explain anything and leave that to Asmodeus as I stand in Larissa's room. If I close my eyes, I can almost imagine she's here. Smell her sweet scent, hear her soft snores as she takes up the entire bed. Excitement trickles through the bond, so muted I almost miss it.

"Don't get too excited, my Angel. I'm hunting you, now." I grind my teeth as I dress, only stopping to press my face into her pillow. I take a deep breath through my nose, inhaling her as I grip the headboard.

"If you start thrusting into her pillow, I will leave without you." Asmodeus says from the doorway, and I reluctantly drop it while giving him a dry look.

"You know where they are, don't you?"

"Yes, but it will take us a day's travel and we must travel with peace. Once we get there, you cannot go about rampaging. The entire coven would kill you in the blink of an eye." He warns me, and I hold my hands up innocently before following him downstairs. Levi is waiting for us, pacing in front of the door with the look of a father whose child is late for curfew.

"Where is she?" he asks.

"Her and Piper ran off to join a cult," I roll my eyes, kneeling to tie my shoes as Asmodeus sighs.

"They went to Piper's aunt Willow, to her coven. They've got a plan to help rescue Elaine. Those two becoming friends was a grave mistake." He mutters, and I couldn't agree with him more at this point.

"So tell them to come back, *now*." He throws his hands up and Adrian walks out of the kitchen with a mug in his hand as he shakes his head.

"Yes, because Larissa always does exactly as she is told." Adrian says.

"Piper once eluded me for nearly three days in pursuit of a damn dragon. Nearly got herself burnt to a crisp." Asmodeus shakes his head and my anxiety only grows.

"Well, let's hope those two don't decide to go dragon hunting." Adrian snorts while walking past us, but I see the way his hand shakes and the fear in his eyes. He's worried about his sister, as he should be. Larissa was her own worst enemy and I wasn't going to let her off easy for this.

Levi puts his hand out, stopping me with a serious look. "Blaine, you bring her home." I nod and he gives my shoulder a squeeze before turning to walk away.

"Hurry along, I'm missing my stress reliever." Asmodeus says.

"Gross. Maybe you should dry hump her pillow before we leave?" I mutter as we walk back out into the night.

Chapter 16 - Larissa

"Blessed girl, one of her own kind and so alone. You have tainted your soul of an angel and blood of a Goddess by the one you call to from within. He carries a darkness that has bled into you. You will lose a beat of your heart when you face off against the Forgotten." A feminine voice chimes around me, the sound caresses my skin like a mother's hug.

"Who are you?" I ask, my voice trembling.

"It's me, Larissa. Open your eyes," Piper's voice is full of worry, and I realize she's shaking me. My eyes fly open, and I look around as exhaustion seeps into my body.

"Where did that voice come from? And what did she mean by 'I'd lose a beat of my heart against the Forgotten'?" I question. My legs shake and my joints all ache, "Oh, what the hell? Why does everything hurt?" I moan.

"Larissa, you have been standing here for hours, seven hours, to be exact. You were unreachable." Piper throws her arms up and I look around, realizing the sun was high above into the sky. My neck cramps and I twist it from side to side, not understanding how I could have stood in this spot for hours.

"We tried to reach you, but you were not within your own body. What did you see?" Anne steps close and takes my arm, guiding me to a bench surrounded by flowers. The smell of lavender brushes across me as we sit, and I rest my head in my hands.

"I may have been out here for hours, but it was just a moment to me. There was nothing. It felt like I was still here with my eyes closed, and there was a woman's voice. She said something like 'having the blood of a *Goddess* with an angel's soul', that I was one of my kind and there was darkness tainting me. There was something said about the Forgotten, but what does that mean?" I ask, my voice low.

"The Forgotten are something unheard of these days. I wouldn't put much thought into that," Anne says dismissively.

"Do you think it was her?" Niko asks excitedly. I look up and Willow's face is full of wonder as she reaches towards me.

"It could have been Selene. She heard your call," her voice was full of awe at the possibility. My mouth opens and closes as I try to form the words.

"Selene is the Goddess of our coven, and every coven prays to a different God. She is a powerful entity who gives us our power from the moon. We bless every baby witch born within our coven on the first full moon after their birth, and they're given abilities from our Goddess." Piper taps her chin as she thinks it over.

"Are you thinking that she was never blessed as an infant, that the Goddess waited for her to seek her out?" Anne says to her, and Piper nods.

"It is the best explanation I have, honestly." Piper says to me. As the pounding in my temples increases, I groan.

"I think I'm overloaded. My head feels like it's going to explode." My voice is a high pitched whine. Willow says something about herbal tea and Anne follows her as they head towards the tavern. Niko leans down to pluck a stem of lavender and pulls out green leaves from the satchel at her hip. I watch with mild interest as she crushes it in her palms before closing her eyes and mumbling something. The crumpled flowers in her hands melt into a purple liquid that drips between her fingers, and she frowns a moment before shrugging it off and reaching towards my face. I jerk away and she rolls her eyes.

"Hold still. It's mint and lavender. I'm just rubbing it on your temples to help ease the ache." She grumbles, reaching out again to smear the oily substance onto my temples.

"I'm still learning earth magic, so I overdid it a little." She gives me an apologetic smile as the mint burns my nose and makes my eyes water.

"Astral witch learning earth magic? That isn't something you hear every day," Piper says.

"My father was from another coven. I've got a little from both parents, and there aren't a ton of others like me. Male witches are a bit of an endangered species." She says with a shrug.

"Yeah, no kidding! Do you have a bunch of siblings?" Piper asks. Niko laughs and shakes her head. "Nope, just me."

"Do most witches only have one type of magic?" I ask in confusion, grateful that the headache is easing up a bit.

"How much do you know?" Niko asks. Piper holds her hand out, giving a thumbs down and blows a raspberry.

"Real mature," I say to her, and she laughs. Niko shakes her head with a small smile before turning to me.

"As you heard before, each coven prays to a different God or Goddess. Different magic comes from different sources. Earth, water, fire, air and spirit, or also known as astral magic. There are also many other types." She waits as I look at her in confusion. Niko sighs and motions to Piper, "Her magic is astral, though from a different coven originally, her mother and aunt joined this one. Their other one was also astral, but Piper is all around talented." She says. Piper beams, but I notice the blush in her cheeks from the praise.

"You already know that I can open portals, which I also use to travel between realms. I can see the future with my visions. But I'm still learning how to use most of these gifts myself, especially when new ones pop up. It's difficult to find elders willing to teach me." Piper clears her throat and her cheeks redden.

"Her soulmate is the King of Hell, and some witches don't agree with their bonding. That train left the station though, so they can stay pissed off, or move on." Niko says. Piper relaxes and looks at me.

"Asmodeus and my powers, which reside within our soul, blended into one. His gifts changed and affected mine. He saved my life and I love him, even if the coven refuses to accept it." She says it as if it doesn't matter, but I can tell she is carrying a heavy weight.

"You can't control who your soulmate is," I say and Niko snorts.

"Yes, you can. You cannot control who your soul calls to, but you sure as hell choose who to mate with. If you give consent to your body, then your souls *could* fuse. Hence the word *soul* and *mate*." Niko says and Piper blushes.

"Is the sex good?" Niko says and catches us off guard, both of us looking at her with wide eyes. She cracks up and shrugs.

"There's very few men here and I can't leave until I finish training. I'm on a dick hiatus, okay?" She says. Piper and I can't stop the laughter as we lean against each other, interrupted as Willow and Anne rejoin us.

"Well, you girls are having fun," Willow says.

"You already seem better, but drink this just to be safe." Anne says as she pushes a cup into my hands. After taking a hesitant sip, I make a face as the bitter flavor coats my tongue.

"It's a very bitter tea, but it should give you back some energy so we can test what power Selene has gifted you." Anne says, nodding to Willow before turning to leave.

"I am needed for a meeting, but you know where to find me. I will see you later, Larissa. Blessed be." She calls to me, and I give a small wave. Willow sighs and motions to the cup. "Drink up," she says as I rub at my chest, noticing the ache has gotten worse. The bond is nearly dragging my heart from my chest, forcing me back to Blaine.

"Once we start, our magic and your concentration will help that to ease." Niko motions to where Piper is also clutching the front of her shirt. I tip the cup up and gulp down the thick liquid, nearly heaving it all right back up. I swipe my mouth with the back of my hand as I gag and Piper giggles, amused with my suffering. We follow Willow back to the circle, and I give Piper a weak thumbs up.

Chapter 17 - Larissa

Stepping behind the charred marks on the ground, I frown at the burns and rub them with the toe of my shoe.

"Never mind that, the earth is forgiving. Now, this will be a little difficult. You have the gifts of Nephilim and witches. We won't know exactly what gifts are from which side, but we could start with-" Willow starts.

"Portals," I blurt out, and she gives me an admonishing look for interrupting her. Piper gives me an encouraging nod, and Niko fixes her hair into a messy bun to keep it off her face.

"That is tough. Before you interrupted, I was going to suggest you first try to search for somebody." Willow says.

"Elaine!" I say excitedly, but she shakes her head at me.

"No sweetheart, you can't reach past Hell's gate. It's essentially another realm, and it's far too dangerous." Willow says quietly.

"Why is that dangerous? Mammon can't hurt me if I'm not actually there," I say.

"Your soul could become trapped in Hell while your body withers away here. Your soul would eventually fade out of existence." Niko says darkly and Willow clears her throat.

"Why don't you try Blaine? It would be a little easier." Piper suggests, and I nod to Willow even as I become uneasy.

"Well, the magic won't dampen the bond much, since you'll be using it to find him. Try to remember to separate your feelings from his or else it may overwhelm you, and you won't be successful." Willow says.

"I got it," I bite my lip and run a hand through my knotted hair with a cringe as I feel some of Niko's herbal goo, "At least, I hope I do." Niko steps forward and hands me a hair tie, whispering, "Sorry!" as she steps back. I tie my hair up in a high pony and nod to Willow for her to instruct me. She kneels outside the circle, Piper and Niko do the same in a triangular formation around me.

"All right, close your eyes and breathe in and out. Concentrate on one specific sense, like what you smell." Willow says.

"Lavender and a lot of mint," I mumble. Somebody *shushes* me and I peek with one eye towards the sound.

"She said concentrate, not speak." Niko nags and I huff, closing my eyes to focus. I let the smell of lavender fill my mind, envisioning I'm standing in a field of flowers as the clouds darken the sky above me.

"Now, imagine that leading you to Blaine. Follow it." Willow says. Suddenly I am standing in the same flower grove, looking down at a path of purple flowers leading between the dark trees that surround me. I glance at my hands and rub my arms against the icy breeze that has kicked up. It feels as if the wind is pushing me to follow the trail, so I do. *I'm only mildly freaking out here.*

I step over broken tree limbs, keeping track of the flowers that are becoming more spread out the further I walk until they stop completely. Sunlight streams through the trees sporadically and a large opening in the branches shines down on a single broken flower. It looks to be trampled. The path ends here, and I kneel to brush it with my fingers as I look around.

"What the hell is happening?" I whisper to myself.

"The brave little Angel has peaked out from her hiding spot amongst the trees?" Blaine's voice echoes around me, low and full of rage. I shiver as I spin around, searching the trees desperately for him as I hear twigs snap and see shadows jump just beyond my line of sight.

"You weren't listening, Blaine. I had to, please understand." I call out to him. A cracking sound echoes through the trees and fear mixed with excitement fills me as I back away.

"You didn't have to do anything! This is dangerous and

stupid!" He shouts. I flinch back and a growl comes from across the opening. Shadows are bubbling from the earth, taking shape. I realize the smell of smoke is drowning out the lavender and Blaine's emotions are becoming suffocating.

"Don't run from me, Angel. You know I'll chase you, and when I catch you, you'll be on your knees begging for forgiveness." His voice is a threatening deep rumble. I take a deep breath, turn on the ball of my foot and run as fast as I can along the path of flowers. A chill has chased me, nipping at my heels as dark shadows consume everything behind me. The flowers wilt and collapse, the field dying as I push myself faster.

Blaine slams me to the ground, and I cry out as we roll, coming to a stop with me on my back. His hand covers my mouth as he climbs between my legs and pins my body with his. Blaine is shaking with his thinly veiled rage. I just lay there with my eyes closed, not daring to move a muscle.

"Look at me, Angel." His voice gives nothing away as tears roll down my cheeks and I finally open my eyes.

"Don't cry, baby. Those witches will wake you soon enough. Until they do, you are going to listen to what I have to say." His eyes are bloodshot and he looks like he hasn't slept yet. "You betrayed me, Larissa. Sneaking from our bed to run from me in the dead of night. I begged you to stay, you agreed to drop it and you *lied.* Do you feel the bond? The way it screams for you to come back to me?" He snarls, prying his hand off my mouth. The brown eyes I love so much are now the color of burning coals and his fangs on full show. I open my mouth to speak, but he shakes his head at me, holding a finger to my mouth.

"Don't fucking start. I already know why you did it. You were being selfish." He hisses. Shock hits me like a wave and I try to fight him off, but he just gives a humorless laugh.

"You ran off to learn how to become powerful enough to get to Elaine because you are impatient. Even though there are people more qualified than you for the rescue mission. And you did all of this for nothing, because I'm bringing you home. Asmodeus and I are close. Do you realize reaching out to me just opened our bond even more? I can feel you, sense you more clearly. Come back to me and your punishment will be something you can enjoy." He warns me. An excited chill crawls my spine at the way he grinds his hips against mine.

"Please, I need you to try and understand. I can do this, if you would just trust me." I say around his finger. He slams his hands into the ground beside my head, but I don't flinch. No matter how far down in the dark he is, he will never hurt me.

"I can't trust you right now, Larissa."

"Blaine, I love you." My voice is a choked whisper as I feel the world crumbling.

"I'm going to catch you, Angel." He promises as I fade out, my tears still falling as I go.

Chapter 18 - Larissa

Piper keeps tossing and turning in the bed across from me, unable to get comfortable enough to sleep. I can tell she craves Asmodeus, his peace and warmth, to feel safe. Because without Blaine I just feel so cold, alone, and exposed. She sits up and looks over at me and I rise up, wrapping my arms around my legs to rest my chin on them.

"Scoot over, I can't sleep." She grumbles, stomping over with her pillow dragging behind her. I laugh and give her room as she climbs into bed beside me and leans against the headboard.

"I thought about trying to reach out to Asmodeus, even with that magical barrier on crack that keeps blocking me. But I know I'd turn to putty if he begged me to come back to him." She huffs. After Niko threw a glass of water in my face and I came sputtering out of the circle, I was shaken. Blaine has never looked at me like that, with so much pain and anger in his eyes.

To make things worse, I absolutely suck at portal jumping. I ended up in a tree, on the roof and in a stream, all within a few hours. We called it quits for the day and Willow tried to comfort me. "You are just tired, so get some sleep and we will be here tomorrow morning." The look in her eyes was more than just concern, but I couldn't put my finger on it.

"I'm sorry, you can go back. Tell him I forced you to help me or something," I shrug and she leans over to lay her head on my shoulder.

"I would never lie on you like that, dummy. I'm not going anywhere. Asmodeus will forgive me, after a few good spankings. That part I *am* excited about." She wiggles her eyebrows and we both dissolve into a fit of giggles. Piper lays back, and I do the same, the two of us staring at the ceiling in silence. Having somebody next to me is more comforting than being alone and I find her hand under the covers. She squeezes back and we just stare upwards in peaceful silence.

#

Willow woke us up early and we rose as slow as the dead. The bed was comfortable, but Piper snores and I couldn't stop tossing and turning. She brought us each a change of clothes, thankfully. My joggers feel as if they are made from a soft cotton, but don't do much against the cold wind when it kicks up. That didn't deter me from admiring the hand sewn green fabric each time I brushed my damp palms across them. Piper walks alongside me, humming to herself with a bright smile in her own little world. Willow also gifted each of us a cloak, and I snuggle into it gratefully as we walk across the grounds towards the same place as yesterday.

A few children are there, surrounding an older woman who is instructing them. Suddenly, two small girls holding hands seem to warp and vanish before our eyes. I suck in a breath, swinging around to search for them, but they appear behind us. The girls are giggling and skipping excitedly past us back to the woman.

"They are practicing their abilities. The one with blonde pigtails just time skipped. The girl holding her hands is what we call a booster. Her power strengthens whomever she is touching." Willow explains as we pass them.

"That woman is a teacher and she has raised up two generations from this coven alone. She's going to help us today." Piper whispers to me before bowing in respect to her as we pass. "She doesn't look *that* old," I whisper.

"It's because I'm not," The woman croaks, laughing as embarrassment covers my face.

"My name is Grandmother Sienna. But you may call me Granny." She winks at me as I follow Piper, bowing to her in respect.

"Alright children, back to your parents for snack time. We are done for the morning." The kids all excitedly ran past us, not sparing a look back on their way home.

"Come and kneel down in front of me, sweetheart." Granny says, sitting on a stone that has been carved into a chair. I do as she tells me and fidget nervously in the damp grass. Granny smacks my forehead and I recoil from her, rubbing the sting away as she squints her brown eyes at me.

"I said kneel, not wiggle. Sit still and breathe slowly, Larissa." She says and Willow nods for me to obey while Piper hides her giggles with a cough. Granny brushes her gray curls back and tilts her head as I sigh and obey her.

"Good, now I want you to imagine the room you have been staying in. Focus on it. Imagine every single detail. Describe to me what you see," Granny says.

"The wooden floor, I'm kneeling on the bed and looking towards the door. The walls are a shade of tan, like dried mud," Willow snorts when I finish.

"That's good, now tell me what you feel. Use your hands and feel around you." Granny uses her wooden cane to push my hands toward the ground.

"I feel the fuzzy blanket beneath me, how the mattress bends under my weight. And I feel the cool air around me." My voice is a whisper as my memory of the room becomes clearer.

"Is there anything you smell?" She asks.

I take a deep breath through my nose and use my mind to focus in the room, "Coffee. And breakfast, somebody is cooking downstairs. I can hear people coming into the tavern, chairs scraping the floor and their laughter." I tilt my head, waiting for Granny to instruct me again. I'm starting to get dizzy with my eyes closed and my stomach has started fighting against my meager breakfast. After a few moments, I peek through my lashes and nearly fall off the *bed*. No longer just in my mind, I'm kneeling on the bed Piper and I slept in. With amazement, I watch the dust float in the sunlight that streams through the window and warms the chill on my body.

"Holy shit," I breathe out, standing on shaky legs. The floor creaks under my steps and I spin in a circle, laughing excitedly. "I did it! I did it, Aunt Elaine!" I shout, jumping up and down. Tears blur my vision as I fall backwards onto the bed and stare up at the ceiling. *I'm one step closer, so I won't be long now. Just hang in there Elaine, please.* After calming my emotions, I do my best to repeat Granny's instructions. This time I focus on where I was before, imagining myself laying in the cold, dew covered grass. My mind brings to life the smell of flowers on the breeze as it catches loose strands of my black hair. It only takes a moment before I feel as if I'm falling through the bed and open my eyes to see a bright blue sky. *Oh no, I feel so sick.*

Rolling over, I clutch my mouth as my body threatens to heave up the cup of coffee I chugged for breakfast. Comfortingly, a hand strokes my back while Piper cheers behind me.

"That was quite a show. You opened a portal around your body and slid through so seamlessly." Granny says, pulling my hair back as the nausea passes, slowly.

"Wonderfully done, darling. The sickness will lessen the more you practice. As soon as you are ready, we will push further. Piper has offered to travel with you to be safe." Willow claps her hands together. I slowly stand with a triumphant smile on my face.

"Thank you so much, Granny." I say, wiping my mouth with the back of my hand. Granny waves me off with her cane before standing slowly and walking down the gravel path towards a few houses.

"I've taught far less gifted toddlers and you weren't nearly as stubborn *or* crafty," She cackles while hobbling away and Piper shakes her head. "Good to see that Granny hasn't changed a bit," she sighs.

"Where do we portal to now?" I ask, walking to link my arm through Pipers while she bounces excitedly and Willow sighs, "You girls aren't going to stop until you're exhausted on the ground, so we might as well go at it now." She laughs and walks towards the tavern while throwing her hands into the air. "I need food and more coffee first."

Chapter 19 - Larissa

"That shower was incredible," I say, scrubbing my hair with a towel as I walk into our shared room. Piper laughs and scrunches her nose, "Did you use enough lavender?" I fix the black nightgown Willow loaned me, fidgeting with the long sleeves. It's plain and comfortable but I envy Pipers' pink cotton shorts and matching pink tank top.

"I didn't realize it would be so strong. I only added like two drops to my hair and body wash," I groan. "Your aunt makes some crazy, strong essential oils. Unless it's mixing with that headache paste that Niko made earlier." I say and she covers her mouth to stifle a laugh before speaking.

"We make them with magic. One drop is meant for an entire bottle of soap! No wonder you stink so good," she laughs, and I snort at her joke. Throwing my towel onto a hook on the door, I flip the light off and walk over to grab my pillow and flop onto Piper's bed. We squirm under the covers, and I yawn into the darkness.

"You know Cole needs to learn some boundaries. He would have walked right into the bathroom if you didn't lock the door." Piper says with a sneer.

"He was only trying to bring towels up. Your aunt told him to put them in the bathroom. He didn't know anyone was in there and even apologized, Piper. You really don't like him, do you?" I raise my brow as she shoots me a glare.

"I can't stand him, something is *off*, and he wants in your pants. But on a positive note, you did phenomenal today. Considering I only had to help you twice. Next time, you will listen when I tell you not to push too hard," Piper says in a sleepy voice. I wouldn't have passed out if I had just listened to her, but

I have to push even harder if I want to get to Elaine in time. As if she is reading my mind, Piper finds my hand and gives it a squeeze. "You're doing your best," she says before turning onto her side.

"I just hope my best will be enough," I whisper, closing my eyes.

#

Cold air feels as if it has an iron tight grip on my throat and my lungs have begun burning for oxygen. My eyes fly open as my body tries to thrash on the bed, but I can't move. Not with the weight pressing down on top of me.

"Fucking hell, Angel. Lavender smells *so good* on you." Blaine's voice crawls across my skin. It's such a soft caress compared to the grip he has on my throat. My body responds to him immediately, going limp as he drags a hand up my thigh. His fingers stop just as he pushes my nightgown up over my hip and Blaine realizes I'm not wearing any panties. Digging his fingers in, he shoves my legs apart with his and settles between them.

"I gave you one chance to come back to me willingly. But I'm done waiting." His voice deepens in the darkness of our room. Remembering where I am, I stretch my hand out to find Piper is missing. The moonlight cuts through the clouds just enough I can see a flash of his smile.

"Her mate took her home hours ago. But I wasn't ready to touch you. I was afraid I'd hurt you if I did." He confesses. Without speaking, I reach up and caress his cheek. Blaine tilts his head and relaxes for just a moment before jerking away and laughing darkly.

"You would never hurt me, Blaine."

"You don't know that. I haven't forgiven you," He hisses out and I nod slowly.

"I love you," I whisper, and he shakes his head. The chill in the room drops a few more degrees, making my breath come out in a small puff.

"You say that as if it means anything," he dips his face down, brushing my lips with his as I strain against his grip to close the distance between us, "You came here intending to sacrifice yourself to save another. Is that what lovers do? They run off to die and leave the other all alone?" He snarls against my mouth and tears fall from the corners of my eyes. I try to shake my head, but the motion is slow with his hand around my throat.

"I've been watching you and I can't take another day of seeing you do this. The way you ran yourself to the brink today tore me apart. Piper had to bring you back more than once. I'm not good at watching somebody else save you. Not to mention, that little busboy who wants what is mine." He nods towards the door, and I purse my lips.

"You've been here all day?" My voice gives away my shock. He just grins again and shrugs.

"And you're jealous of Cole?" I ask with a soft chuckle. His eyes turn to slits as he grinds his hips against me, drawing a gasp from my lips.

"You do not say another man's name when you aren't wearing any fucking panties," He rumbles. I watch as he slowly licks his hand before cupping my bare skin. I bite my lip as he rubs his palm against me, just teasing as I squirm under him. *Is it fucked up that his anger made me wet?* He tilts his head as if he is listening for something I can't quite hear. Suddenly his face splits into a mischievous grin as he grips the collar of my nightgown with both hands. Before I can stop him, he rips it down the middle and the cold air hits my bare body, making me squeal.

"Blaine, what the hell?" I whisper. My brain is caught between sex crazed and annoyed at his lack of boundaries. A chair scrapes in the tavern under us and I plead with my mind that Blaine at least tries to be quiet. He isn't focusing on anything except me as he pushes the fabric aside and stares at my body. I fidget under his gaze after a few moments and cross my arms, feeling shy. Blaine grabs my hands and pins them above my head, making my heart race as he grinds against me again.

"Don't you ever hide from me again," he says with a stern voice. I open my mouth to argue with him, but he stops me. His mouth crashes into mine with punishing kisses as he forces his tongue past my lips. My body feels as if it has come alive under his touch, heat racing under my skin everywhere he is pressed against me. Blaine releases my hands and pulls back just enough to whisper, "Try not to move these." Both of his hands clutch in a tight grip, his fingers digging in painfully as his mouth descends on mine again.

I cry out as he pinches my nipples before rubbing away the pain. He chuckles against my lips as his hands stop their torment and drag down my sides slowly. The sensation makes me wiggle, tickling the closer he gets to my hips. Excitement makes my breath catch as he drags one hand down my leg. His rough hand hooks my knee around his hip while the other reaches between our bodies. Blaine uses his thumb, putting gentle pressure on my clit as he kisses my throat. I bite my lip to stay quiet when he suddenly bites my neck, none too softly. His fangs sting, threatening to pierce the skin before he pulls back and drags his tongue over the sensitive mark.

He sits back and yanks his shirt off over his head and unbuttons his jeans as my heart races. Metal clanging together from downstairs grabs my attention, but Blaine cages me in with his arms, raising a brow.

"Is there a problem?" He asks. I nod towards the door.

"There are people here who could hear us, Blaine." He just grins before pressing two fingers against me. I spread my legs wider, part of me not caring if anyone else is around to hear us. His lips brush against mine as he hums, "Try not to scream my name too loud then, Angel." Before pushing both fingers inside of me. I gasp at the pressure that builds as he curls them, knowing exactly how to shatter me. With a wicked grin, he leans down to push his face between my thighs. His tongue slowly drags across my clit as my breath comes in shallow puffs. *He has me wrapped around his finger, literally.*

"Blaine please," I beg him and he groans before clamping

his mouth around my clit and increasing the pressure until I cover my face with a pillow. He drags me just to the edge before pulling out of me and taking his mouth away. He rips the pillow from my grasp and throws it to the floor.

"I'm going to fuck you until you remember who you belong to," he says. I reach between us and grip his throbbing dick in my hand, stroking him. He drops his head onto my shoulder, sucking breath between his teeth. Blaine pulls my wrist away before gently kissing my palm. He guides my legs up onto his shoulders, his fingers clutching my calves so tight the skin begins to ache. I moan loudly as he slams inside of me, neither slow nor gentle. My lips curl up in a smile as he claims my body with his. *My body and soul.*

Blaine puts both hands on the back of my thighs, pushing them to my sides as he pounds into me harder. I can't stop crying out from the overwhelming feeling of being joined together. Something thumps to the floor beneath us, and I hear a muffled voice. My pleasure doesn't slow, but my eyes fly open.

"Blaine!" I huff in a warning, but he just shifts and uses his thumb to stroke my clit. That, along with his punishing thrusts, drags my body back to the pleasure I was so desperate for a moment ago.

"Larissa? Piper?" Cole calls just outside the door and I shake my head as Blaine smiles at me, "You feel so fucking incredible, Angel." He gives me a devastating smile. Two massive wings burst from his back in a flurry as he snaps them open in the moonlight.

"Oh fuck, Blaine," I whimper, only spurring him on.

"That's right, come for me darling." He commands. I can't do a thing to stop the waves of pleasure as they rush through me, crying out his name as I unravel around him. The door frame splinters, giving way as the door swings open and Cole storms in. I'm still shaking and panting underneath Blaine as he lays over me to cover my body from Cole's eyes. His wings drape around us and I fight the urge to brush my fingers through the coarse feathers near my face. Light fills the room, and I scrunch my eyes against it. Blaine cups a hand over my face, kissing above each eye as he shields them.

"Who the fuck are you?" Cole shouts, standing in the doorway.

"You didn't hear her the first time? Well, get the fuck out and give me another minute, maybe two. You'll hear her scream my name again." Blaine says. Before I have a chance to protest, he gives me a warning by pushing his hips against me, making me slap a hand over my mouth.

"Larissa, are you okay?" Cole says, annoyed.

"You don't speak to her ever again, got that?" Blaine snaps. Cole just snorts and leans against the door frame.

"How about you 'get the fuck out', before I tell Willow you're here?" Cole threatens, before his voice turns smug. "Don't forget that she ran away from you, buddy." I brace my hands on Blaine, trying to keep him calm as he reaches down beside the bed. Blaine grabs his button-up shirt off the floor to pull over me before tucking himself back into his pants.

While standing up, he drags his fingers through the wet mess he made between my legs, making me whimper. But then he turns and licks them clean, making a show of it while staring Cole down. His wings flutter when he shivers as if he's tasted the most divine dessert.

"Blaine!" I pull up the blanket, mortification burning my face, and Cole looks at him in disgust.

"Did you force yourself on her? That's the only way she'd have you, huh?"

"I'm going to snap your fucking neck with my bare hands." Blaine's humor is gone as he stretches his shoulders.

"Wait, stop it!" I grab his arm and pull him back to the bed.

"Let him try. I'm not worried." Cole winks at me, and I scowl as Blaine's hand shakes in mine. The overload of testosterone in here is making the air so thin that neither one is thinking clearly, obviously.

"Come with me. or I'll do it." Blaine says, just quiet enough I barely hear him. But from the look on his face, he means every word. I stand up and he grabs me in his arms, baring his teeth in warning once more towards Cole. He doesn't take the hint as he steps closer to us.

"You have got to be kidding, Larissa!" Cole shouts. Blaine takes a step back into the shadows, laughing sadistically as darkness swarms around us.

#

"You can't be fucking serious!" I scream and thrash against his iron tight grip in the cold, damp leaves. Blaine shakes his head at me, standing up and pulling me along with him.

"I told you I was bringing you home," he says, taking my hand in his. I plant my feet and send a shock through his hand. Blaine jerks away, grumbling in frustration.

"What was with that shit you just pulled with Cole? Threatening to kill him unless I came back before I was even ready?" Throwing my hands in the air, I stomp closer to him. "I still had more to learn. I didn't even get to ask about my mother." My voice wavers, giving away my tears that hide in the darkness of the woods.

"Why do you care about Cole? He had no business barging into your room like that." He spits out, "Piper's aunt can come to us and tell you about your mother. And I've told you, they are putting a plan together to rescue Elaine. I swear to you, if they don't then I will go in there with you to bring her back." he promises, clutching my face in his hands and resting his forehead against mine. I can feel the tremble in his hand, our emotions bouncing off each other even as my soul hums happily at being reunited.

I swallow hard and nod, shaking against the cold.

"Shit," Blaine curses under his breath. He wraps his arms around me, scooping my bare legs up to carry me. I wrap my arms around his neck and bury my face against his. I can't tell him I could never let him go with me. Not when Elaine's life was already on the line. I can't risk him too. Sighing to myself, I almost laugh at the irony that I thought he was behaving irrationally, when I feel the same way about Blaine risking his life.

"We are almost home, Angel." He says softly, kissing the top of my head as we push through the barrier that protects Nephal. *It protects everyone, except the dozens who died in the attack and Elaine,* I think bitterly.

By the time we reach the house, a chill has soaked into my bones from the cold. Blaine's shirt and the thin sheet have done little to keep the dreary weather away from my skin. When we walk in the front door, Blaine doesn't stop, even as Piper storms up to us with a look of rage on her face. Her hair is a mess, and her cheeks are a bright shade of pink. Somebody needs to tell her she is about as intimidating as a puppy.

"How dare you!" She shrieks, shaking her finger at him. He doesn't even look down, just steps around her. I give her an apologetic look over his shoulder and notice Asmodeus standing over her with fire in his eyes.

"How dare *you?*" He growls before turning and storming back towards Blaine's room as she huffs after him. He looked exhausted and shaken to his core. Asmodeus was so worried about her.

"He's just as pissed as I am." Blaine says, kicking my bedroom door shut behind us.

"I never intended to worry either of you, we were perfectly safe." I whisper. He sighs and sits me down on the edge of the bed to walk into the bathroom. While he gets the shower started, I wrap myself tighter in the blankets, shivering from the cold. I bury my nose in Blaine's shirt, basking in the smoky scent and smiling to myself at the comfort it brings me.

The comfort is short lived when my door swings open with enough force it bounces off the wall and nearly slams shut again. Adrian's outstretched hand prevents it from closing. The look on his face is enough to make me want to shrink back into bed and disappear.

"Going to pull a little magic trick and vanish again, Larissa?" He snaps at me, and I flinch from the cruelty in his voice.

"That's enough, Adrian." Blaine says, standing beside the bed with his arms crossed. He just snorts and looks back at me, waving his hand in Blaine's direction.

"He was animalistic. You sent this man on a warpath. I don't even want to talk about Asmodeus and our father, who was ready to start a full attack against the witches. Because of you being so damned immature and impatient!" He yells.

"What do you mean by an attack?" I asked in confusion.

"He threatened them to give you back. He had no clue our mother was a witch, so he was afraid they were using you. But you didn't take the time to think of anyone else before skipping off, did you?" He asks.

"I said, *that is enough.*" Blaine's voice is a low warning and I hold my hand up.

"The Nephilim sat back while our mother was murdered. Nobody saved her. I won't make your mistake." I hiss at Adrian, and he stares down at me, his face a blank mask. For a moment, nobody moves or says a word. Then Adrian slams my door shut as his thundering steps recede. I slump back, biting my hand to fight back the sobs. Blaine rubs his face and walks toward the door. I will not cry in front of him. I stand by my decision.

"You better hurry before all the hot water is gone." He says before walking out. Dropping his shirt onto the bed, I walk silently into the bathroom and shut the door behind me. Without bothering to check the water, I step in and slide the curtain closed. Hiding behind the fogged plastic as the water hits my skin makes biting back my feelings even harder. I yank the handle further towards the heat and hiss in a breath when the scalding water splatters over my skin. It doesn't burn away the pain inside, at the mess I have made with Blaine and failing at rescuing Elaine.

I fall to my knees and cry out, clapping a hand over my mouth as I fall apart. It seems like here, behind a flimsy curtain with water dripping down my face, is where I come to unravel. *Mom, what did I do?* How do I fix this? I've made a mess of everything. The way he looked at me before walking out, it was as cold as the day we met. My hair dangles around my face as I lean forward, watching the dark strands curl on the shower floor through the blur of tears.

I hear the door open, as if from a distance, and feel cool air brushing my skin.

"Oh sweetheart," Piper whispers. Her small hands pull me up, moving my face from under the water before she lathers soap into my hair. I don't bother trying to hide my body, feeling a strange comfort in her presence.

"Asmodeus is speaking with Blaine. His emotions and yours are bouncing all over each other since neither of you can control the bond." She says kindly before pulling my head back under the stream of water.

"Were you trying to boil your skin off?" She snorts but doesn't change the water as I glance up at her. She is standing in a black t-shirt and spandex shorts. The shirt is soaked and clinging to her skin as she smiles down at me.

"You are getting all wet," I croak, and she giggles.

"I'll dry off," She combs conditioner through my hair with her fingers, picking at the knots methodically, "This isn't the end. It feels like it right now, but he loves you more than anything. I don't think he really knows how to deal with all the ways you make him feel. And with Adrian, siblings fight, it's totally normal." She reminds me.

After rinsing my hair in silence, she steps out and grabs a towel for me and herself. The bathroom door cracks open, and Piper gives whoever is on the other side a glare.

"Just try to hear her side for one fucking minute," she snaps before nodding to me and shoving her way out the door. A small smile tugs at my lips but drops when Blaine steps into the bathroom and blows out a breath, no doubt looking at my puffy face.

"I tried to come back in, but she kind of threatened to stab me *and* Adrian in the balls. I don't think she was bluffing," he mumbles, looking at the ground while rubbing the back of his neck. I breathe out a small laugh and try to step around him, but he grips my arms, pinning me in the doorway. I hesitantly look up into his eyes. The rage has melted away and his soft brown eyes are broken. The same way I feel inside. Reaching towards his face so slowly, as if I'm scared that he will run from my touch, I rub my palm against his stubble and his eyes slide closed.

"Larissa," My name is just a whisper on his lips before he looks back at me, "I can't lose you."

"I don't plan on dying. Never in all eternity will I forget that pain of seeing your lifeless body cast aside in the dirt. Begging you to open your eyes, or for the earth to open and swallow the both of us. You need to know that I would never want you to feel what I felt that day." My voice breaks, but I push past, refusing to look away.

Blaine grips the back of my neck and guides my head back, "Swear to me, from here on out that we do this together." He says gruffly, tilting his head and raising one eyebrow.

"I swear it." He crashes his lips to mine when I promise. Blaine grabs my thighs and lifts me up, wrapping my legs around his waist and my arms around his neck. We pull apart, breathless, as he walks us into the bedroom and sits me down on the bed.

"It's nearly morning and your dad is downstairs. The Elders have reached a decision, and he wanted to tell us himself what was decided." He turns towards the dresser as excitement fills me. *We are finally coming, Elaine-* The world is sucked into a spinning black vortex of smoke and suddenly vanishes.

Chapter 20 - Larissa

Elaine looks up at me, a sad smile on her lips. Blood drips down her chin as she gives a rattling cough. Her dress is filthy and torn. Bruises cover her body as she lies on the cold, hard stone beneath us. Chains wrap her hands and end in a bolt to the ground. The room shakes as if an earthquake is trying to tear the kingdom down. I try to run to her, but she shakes her head at me as Mammon towers just behind her.

"Oh my sweet girl, you need to save yourself." She calls to me, her voice raw and hoarse. Mammon laughs and tilts his head, flexing his claws as he stares at my throat.

"You son of a bitch! Leave her alone. It's me you want!" I scream, running for him. I don't stop, even as chaos erupts around us. I kick dust up as nephilim crash against cambions. Demons slither in the darkness and their hisses send a chill up my spine.

"Larissa, stop!" Blaine cries out behind me, desperation in his voice as I grip a sword in my hand, running right towards Mammon.

#

"Please wake up." Blaine whispers as he grips my shoulders. I blink up at him, furrowing my brow while sitting up slowly. Glancing down, I realize I'm still naked and Blaine hands me my clothes.

"I turned around to grab you some clothes, and you slumped back. Scared the shit out of me, Angel. You were screaming again." He looks away and starts pacing.

"It was another vision, Blaine. I saw Elaine and Mammon is going to kill her. There were so many nephilim there with us, down in his damn castle. People were dying all around us, again. Because of me." I whisper, shaking my head as I yank my shirt over my head. Blaine stops pacing and looks at me.

"It's me you want," He whispers. I pull my jeans on while waiting for him to finish.

"You screamed that while I was trying to wake you. Were you trying to go after Mammon again?" He asks, throwing his hands into the air. I walk up to him and take his hand in mine, feeling it tremble as his anger surfaces.

"You were there with me, Blaine." I say softly and he looks at me, dropping his forehead to mine. "You promise?" He whispers and I nod. A knock at the door makes me jump, but Blaine just sighs.

"If your brother lays into you again, I can't promise to be nice." He says, kissing my cheek.

"I can handle it. He was upset, just as you were." I remind him but he just rolls his eyes and leans over my ear, "Except you belong to me, and nobody gets to be angry with you but me. We get to have hot makeup sex for a month now." He growls before smacking my ass and walking to open the door.

Adrian crosses his arms, looking over Blaine's shoulder to me. He doesn't even speak to me, just looks back to Blaine.

"You better get your girlfriend downstairs before our dad drags her out himself." He says before turning to walk away. I snort at him.

"Dramatic much?" I say. Adrian turns back around and looks at me with his mouth open, but Blaine swings the door shut before he can say a word.

"Like I said. You. Are. All. Mine." He stresses every word with a purposeful step towards me before wrapping his arms around me.

"Take us downstairs," he says, and I scrunch my brows.

"Show me your power, little witch." He grins and I smile back at him. I grip his sweatshirt and close my eyes, taking a deep breath.

Between one moment to the next, we are standing in the middle of the living room. Blaine is beaming down at me with pride, "You are incredible," He whispers.

"Imagine what I could do with just a few more days of

training." I grin at him, but he shakes his head once.

"You ran off to a group of strangers, putting yourself and Piper's life in danger, just to learn a few parlor tricks?" Levi says behind me, his voice calm but startling. I turn and cross my arms, holding my chin up and looking him in the eyes.

"I learned more than *tricks,* and they weren't just some strangers. Mom was a witch. I have a right to know about her and where she came from." I say defiantly. Levi crosses the room, brushing past me to look out the large window into the morning light.

"You are still a child," He says coldly, and I grit my teeth as he continues, "Acting on impulse, not thinking anything through. They could have killed you. Running away from the protection while Mammon has men scouring the earth for you. There are nephilim specially trained for this. Your mother apparently left that part of her life behind for a damn reason!" His voice rises and I feel small and insignificant under his angry stare. Like hearing for the first time that he isn't mad, just *disappointed.*

"You don't think I am capable of anything, but I took Lilith down when no one else could."

"This is different," He shuts me down, "You had an entire town fighting beside you and it still nearly killed you." He just isn't willing to listen.

"She left you behind." I say, putting as much malice into my words as I can. Somebody sucks in a slow breath behind me, most likely Adrian, but I don't care right now. The rage inside me causes my vision to tinge, the edges becoming red.

"Excuse me?" My dad says, stepping closer to me.

"My mother left you behind. Maybe she had a fucking point." I spit the words out. Levi shakes his head before brushing past me to leave.

"She isn't to leave the house unaccompanied."

"I don't need a babysitter!" I shout at him, but he opens the door, calling back over his shoulder.

"Since she wants to behave like a child, lashing out when

her feelings are hurt, we will treat her as such." He says before stepping out. It's then I notice the two Nephilim standing beside the door. Eric gives me a small nod, but the man beside him doesn't even look at me. Both are wearing warrior clothing, black from head to toe with weapons strapped to them.

"Eric, what are you doing here?" I ask, unsure.

"Please forgive me, Larissa. I couldn't say no to the Elders Council." He frowns at me while the guy beside him looks down at me with disdain.

"Levi gave us orders to guard you and ensure you don't leave, unattended or otherwise." The guy beside him says. He has short blonde hair with flat brown eyes that are surrounded by long eyelashes.

"Kade," Eric warns beside him. But it's too late. The lights above us flicker for a moment while I fight to regain control of my emotions. Blaine sighs behind me and puts his hand on my shoulder, nodding towards the kitchen. I follow behind, *and so do dumb and dumber.* I snort at their new nicknames and fight the urge to scream at them.

"It's not their fault, and fighting back will only put you in a worse spot." Blaine whispers. Before I can say anything, Adrian stomps past us, nearly knocking me over as he makes his way to the coffee pot.

"You are being such a bitch." I snark. He laughs under his breath and turns towards me.

"Pot, nice to meet you. I'm kettle." He sneers at me, and I blow out a frustrated breath.

"Larissa," Asmodeus says behind me, and I bite my lip nervously. Even Adrian raises his brow at the hulking King of Hell. I turn to look up at him and he contemplates for a moment before speaking.

"I'm glad the two of you are safe. Piper informed me of how much you learned, and your ability to control your newly found power." He says calmly. I hold my breath, waiting for his anger, but it never comes. He stands patiently, waiting for me to say something.

"I thought you would be pissed."

"Piper has made me hunt her down through scarier situations than this one. I detest being away from my mate, so next time I will accompany you." He says, and I nod once. Blaine grunts and I raise my brow. I wonder what trouble Piper has gotten into in the past.

"What my uncle said," Blaine says and Asmodeus sighs, "Not your uncle." Before turning and nearly bumping into Kade, who doesn't look as if he remembers how to blink.

"Can the guard dogs stand by the door, or somewhere out of the way?" Asmodeus asks, stepping past him.

Kade scoffs, "As if a demon isn't in the way. In a nephilim town." Eric closes his eyes for a moment. A chill creeps over my spine and I look up to see Blaine's clenched jaw. Asmodeus' dark chuckle comes from down the hallway, where an angry Piper is standing. I raise an eyebrow and tilt my head at her rumpled appearance. Her hair is a blonde mess behind her face, which is full of rage.

"They are welcome here. You aren't, so maybe go somewhere else. Out of sight." I raise one shoulder in a shrug and he glares at me. Blaine's hand twitches and the shadows behind Kade follow the movement. He's ready to put him out, the very moment he crosses a line, and that realization makes me smile. No matter what, Blaine will always have my back.

"Kade, maybe you should stand guard outside the front door." Eric says. Kade looks at all of our faces, realizing we vastly outnumber him and he stomps off. I giggle, unable to stop myself. A clatter at the sink startles us and we all turn to see Adrian shaking his head.

"You did something incredibly reckless. Taking off like that without even telling me. I didn't know until Blaine was shouting and stomping around the house." He seethes, and a pang of guilt aches in my chest. He yanks another mug down from the cabinet and pours a cup, holding it out to me. I take it gratefully and grab the creamer from the fridge.

"You use so much creamer, it isn't even steaming

anymore." Eric whispers and I flip him off.

"You don't get it. I *was* terrified that I had failed again." His voice breaks and the look of pain in his green eyes is an exact reflection of mine when our mother died. I sit the cup down and grab him in a tight hug.

"Adrian, I am so sorry," I whisper against him as he stands stiff, "I never should have said that. I didn't mean it, you haven't failed anyone. Not our mother and not me." I say, my voice thick.

"You can't do this again, Larissa. Promise me?" He says, clearing his throat.

"Promise," I whisper. He takes in a shaking breath and hugs me with one arm awkwardly, patting my shoulder as I pull back and he squints down at me.

"Don't think for a moment that I'm not still angry." He says and Blaine snorts.

"Good luck. I said the same thing. Maybe it's one of her new witchy powers." Blaine says, as he wiggles his fingers at me and I roll my eyes. Wiping my face with the back of my hand, guilt creeps in about our father. *What I said to him was even worse.*

Chapter 21 - Larissa

"Ella?" Eric asks. Snapping out of my thoughts, I look over to see Ella standing wide eyed, her blush nearly as bright as her red hair. She is wearing a shirt that hangs off her frame, with sweats that are so big on her they cover her feet. She opens and closes her mouth before clearing her throat and I swing my wide eyes at Adrian. He rubs his neck before walking over to her.

"Oh, come on! That is so gross, Ella." I tease, and she covers her face with an awkward laugh.

"We have all dealt with the both of you every damn night. You aren't quiet. Don't start with me." He warns me before taking her hand and walking back to his room. The look of happiness on his face when he whispers to her brings me some comfort, even if it was gross. Blaine steps aside when the front door opens, but it isn't Kade. Levi walks in with Mark hot on his heels.

"Eric can stay, but that *kid* by the door isn't welcome here." I say to Levi. He just stares at me, crossing his arms and setting his lips into a deep scowl.

"I'm so glad you are safe," Mark rushes in and grabs me in a hug. I raise my brows at Blaine, who smiles, shrugging. Levi clears his throat and Mark steps back, giving me a small nod of respect.

"I'm incredibly disappointed that you rushed off and told no one of your plans. Putting your life in danger to save Elaine's was not the way to go about these things. We must think with our minds, not our hearts." Mark says, giving a stern expression. I lean against the counter, sipping my coffee while he goes on.

"Elaine would be crushed if anything happened to you. She would blame herself, and I fear that would kill her faster than any demon." He says and I swallow hard, hurting my throat as his words hit me.

"You're right. I couldn't stand just sitting here, though. Nobody will give me a chance to be what I am supposed to be. Stop hiding me behind these damn walls." I say to Levi, not looking him in the eyes. I can't stand to see his disappointment, now that my anger has become regret.

"This is the only place you are safe," Levi says. I set my mug aside and mimic his stance, crossing my arms while staring at him. Sadness replaces his anger in a flash before his hard mask is back.

"I'm sorry," I say, quietly. Asmodeus takes Piper's hand and they head towards the living room. Blaine walks past us, clapping Eric on the shoulder and leaning in to say something as they follow. Mark takes a seat at the dining room table, just outside of the kitchen.

"For what, exactly? Because you were dragged back here, put in your place and now you don't want anyone to be mad at you?" He asks. I bite my tongue, fighting the immediate urge to say something I would regret. *Or zapping him.*

"I'm sorry for what I said." My words come from between clenched teeth, "Mom didn't run from you, she loved you." Levi's expression fails once more, and he blows out a breath.

"You are so much like her." He says and I falter, surprised.

"Mary always dug her heels in when she acted out of emotion, just as you do. Whenever a consequence would catch up, she apologized with that same expression. She was sorry for whomever she hurt, but not for the actions she felt were justified." He says, his voice softens when he speaks of my mom. She was his entire world. I remember the pain I felt when Blaine had died, the agony that still burns to my soul when he sleeps too soundly. Some nights I wake him, just to see him open his eyes and know beyond a doubt he is still here with me.

"Do you feel as if your actions were justified?" He asks. I don't even stop to think, I just nod and he gives a half smile.

"She would be proud of you." He says before turning. I grab

him in a hug, hiding my face in his shirt.

"Somebody is really emotional today," Eric says in a loud whisper. Levi hugs me tight, patting my head that barely comes to his chest.

"I'm proud of you too, for being brave. Disappointed at your lack of self-preservation." He says, and I roll my eyes as we pull away.

"I do hate to ruin this moment, but Levi, I believe you should tell her." Mark says. I look at him, then back at my dad.

"The team is about to leave on a rescue mission. Could someone ask Asmodeus and Piper to come in here? I'll get Adrian." Levi says. *They're going after Elaine.* It's finally happening. Blaine comes back into the room with Asmodeus and Piper following him. She has brushed her hair and is wearing jeans with a giant hoodie that swallows her petite frame. It says *"Down With My Demons"* I cover my mouth to cover my laugh as she grins at me and wiggles her brows.

"Sex hair didn't exactly feel appropriate, but the hoodie is fitting." She whispers, and I nod at her. Levi comes back downstairs, rubbing his face with an embarrassed Adrian and Ella behind him.

"Everyone is getting laid," Blaine chuckles as Levi glares at him.

"Speak for yourself," Eric says, giving us a sideway glare. Blaine leans close to my ear, "I still haven't forgotten the way he looked at you when you danced together. And I am not finished with what we started earlier." He whispers. I close my eyes and take a deep breath, shaking off the excited chill that climbs my spine.

"If we can all keep our hands to ourselves for a moment," Levi gives Blaine and I a pointed glare before continuing, "The team we gathered is going to go in for the extraction. Our silent partner, the one who has opened the gates in the past, sent a message. According to him, Mammon has mobilized a good portion of his army. He thinks that he may have found our town. However, our contact told us where Mammon is targeting and it isn't near this home." he says, taking a deep breath before turning to Piper.

"I am asking the two of you for help. I do not expect you to fight, just simply to help portal out any of whom are seriously injured and to limit casualties in case of failure." He tells her. Piper squeezes Asmodeus' hand, and he nods.

"I can help, too." Blaine says, stepping forward. My mouth falls open as I look at him, but he just smiles over his shoulder.

"Don't give me that look, Angel. I have something precious to protect, and I owe it to my mother. Plus, I'm the other half of this famous prophecy. I should be down there." He says to me. I shake my head, turning to my dad.

"Then I go." I say, standing taller. Blaine steps in front of me, anger flashing in his eyes.

"You aren't ready yet, Angel." He says in a warning tone.

"Yes, she is." Eric says. Blaine's eyes slide closed slowly, as the surrounding shadows pulse before he opens them again. Levi turns his attention to Eric, and he bows his head in respect to my dad.

"With all due respect, sir. I've seen how she has excelled during training. She is ready." He urges him and Blaine turns towards him.

"Stay out of this," He warns Eric. I grab his arm and Eric's dark brown eyes turn to slits as he stares at him.

"Larissa can manipulate her portals nearly as well as my own. I vote she comes along." Piper winks at me, and I smile at her.

"She did the right thing, leaving to train with her mother's bloodline. You would have kept her in a bubble." Eric says in a quiet voice. I pull on Blaine's arm, forcing him to look at me.

"I can't lose you, Blaine. Not again," I say, my voice breaking and his lips thin into a hard line. He gives Eric one last glare before turning back to Levi.

"That is what I was getting to. If you can follow orders, we could use you out there. Both of you." Levi says. I nod excitedly and Blaine pulls his arm from my grip, storming off. I go after him, but Asmodeus holds his hand up.

"Stay here, let me talk to him. Piper speaks on my behalf while I'm gone." He says before following him out. I blow out a breath, frustrated to be back at square one with him.

"You must do exactly as you are told, Larissa. Everyone's life will be on the line. If you disobey, then it could be the death of any of us." Levi says, giving me a stony stare.

"Have some faith in me. I can do this. I'm ready." He nods to me as I bounce on the balls of my feet.

"Adrian, you will be with me. Ella, we could use you on the field as well. Mark will be the one to grab Elaine. Larissa, you will be there to pull them out. Just outside of the border will be where we gather. That is right where you jump to. Then immediately get back to the safety of town."

"We will have healers on standby, ready to bring back any injured. If you run out of stamina, stay here. Don't kill yourselves trying to portal everyone." He says, looking at me and I give a small smile.

"How many warriors are we planning to take?" Eric asks. Mark stands up to speak.

"That is where we have struggled. We cannot take an entire army down to Hell. If Mammon's men return, then we would be caught in their domain. But if we take too few, they would outnumber us in the chance they catch us. Mammon could just kill Elaine, and we would be lucky if we escaped with our lives." Mark says and I scrunch my brows.

"What are we doing about Mammon?" I ask. Levi and Mark exchange a look before Mark answers me.

"This is strictly to save Elaine, but if it comes down to a fight, we will do whatever we can." Mark says. He looks nervously at Piper, who tips her head up, understanding flashing in her eyes.

"They expect Asmodeus to take back the throne." She says, her voice flat. She doesn't show any emotion, but that's how I know she's agitated by the idea.

"If it comes to that, which I hope it doesn't, you are

correct." Mark says.

"Those of you here, we need you to gear up. Larissa, most of us will wear these," Levi hands me a black hooded mask that only leaves my eyes exposed, "He won't know if you are there, so you won't be targeted directly. Same with Blaine." He says.

"But doesn't he have somebody trying to track me?" I ask. Levi looks at Piper, who smiles at me and winks.

"I'll do my best cloaking spell, trust me. Plus, it's hard to track somebody when your evil lair is being run down." She grins and I chuckle to myself. Just then, Blaine walks back in and holds his hand out to me while Asmodeus nods to me over his shoulder.

Everyone separates, each of us gathering our own equipment. I take Blaine's hand and follow him back to my room. When I walk in, there is something laying on my bed.

"Go on," Blaine says, nudging me forward. Slowly stepping forward I reach down, lifting the sword in my hands. Shimmering emeralds catch my eye where they are set into the leather grip.

"I had that crafted for you as a gift. Right now seems like the perfect time to give it to you." He shrugs. I hold the blade flat in one palm while staring in wonder at the reflective blade.

"It's so beautiful, Blaine." I say in awe. He steps up and hands me a sheath with a strap to place on my back.

"It's a short sword, which means you will have to get up close to use it. Try to avoid anyone who wants to kill you. But if they get too close before I can stop them, use this." He cups my face in his hands. I look up to his eyes and he gives me a kiss with so much fire I feel as if my lips are melting to his. Blaine pulls away and I blow out a breath I didn't realize I was holding. He lays his forehead against mine and I close my eyes.

"You are my entire soul. When we are down there, getting you back out alive is the only thing I will be able to focus on, Angel." He says and I lean back, looking up at him with scrunched brows.

"Blaine, you can't just protect me. You have to think about

the greater good," my voice is sarcastic, even as his words make my heart flutter.

"You are the only good left in my life, Angel. I will pull you from the flames while the world burns." He whispers. His words shouldn't make my heart soar the way they do, but I can't stop the tear that trails down my cheek. Blaine rubs it away with the pad of his thumb, "I won't apologize for putting you first. I'm not the actual hero in this prophecy, you are." He says. A small laugh escapes when I shake my head.

"I'm no hero, Blaine. But you are mine." My voice is just a whisper as I raise onto my tiptoes to brush my lips across his. "I love you."

Chapter 22 - Blaine

"I didn't realize there would be this many people." Adrian says, adjusting the blades he has strapped across his body. He gives a cocky grin as he nods to Larissa's new blade that is securely in its sheath on her back.

"I see you took my advice on the short sword," he says.

"You knew about it before I did?" Larissa says. I just chuckle and take her hand in mine.

"Just to be sure it was something you would like, I had to get outside opinions." I kiss the back of her hand and she blushes, her free hand reaching back to brush over the hilt.

"I love it." She says softly. I notice Adrian frowning while surveying the faces around us, and we all notice a few members from the Elder Council are missing.

"Where are Jake and his parents?" Larissa asks Adrian. He shrugs while pushing his long black hair out of his face until Larissa hands him a hair tie and he accepts it without argument.

"No idea. They're the ones who have been communicating with our inside source, so they should be here." Adrian absentmindedly walks up to Ella, who smiles at him while Eric stares up at the sky. Larissa catches Lane's eye, and nods to him. He just turns away from her and starts talking to Kade, who gives me a glare over his shoulder. *Of course they're friends.* Levi stands with Mark and someone who has already placed their hooded mask on. The woman turns around and winks at Larissa, coming up close to take her hands.

"Marley. Where have you been?" She says excitedly as they pull each other in for a hug.

"Back in my day, I was a tracker, believe it or not! I dove back into field work so that I could help locate Elaine and bring her home." She smiles at me, and I tilt my head in respect. She looks around us and sighs.

"What is it?" Larissa asks.

"I think your father did a good job of picking who should be here, so don't mistake my words as judgment. That group of four over there are my team, along with Lane. Then there is your team, and of course Levi and Mark. Plus the infamous Asmodeus and his lovely mate. I fear we may not have enough for what we are about to face." She says, sadness in her voice. I look around us, realizing she may have a point. There are less than twenty of us standing here, and Levi looks frustrated as we walk up to him.

"Are there more people coming?" I ask. He glances around us, then takes Larissa by the arm and pulls her aside.

"The Saint family stayed behind, and they convinced some others to do the same." He says.

"My parents may be afraid, but I am not." Jake's deep voice startles Larissa as he walks up to us, with a short man that has bright blue hair.

"Micah!" She shouts, hugging him in excitement. He laughs and hugs her back.

"Didn't think I would miss all the fun, did you?" He grins, winking before turning to find me staring down at him.

"Hey buddy!" He says, smacking my ass when he walks past. Jake snorts when my jaw drops open and I look at Larissa in shock.

"He's eccentric?" she says, shrugging as I glare at them.

"I'll break every bone in your body if you touch me like that again without buying me a drink first," I huff, breaking the tension as soft laughter fills the silence.

"So, do you think we can handle this?" Larissa asks Levi and he scrunches his brows while looking at her.

"We need to have faith." Is all he says before squeezing her shoulder and motioning for everyone to gather. He waits while we all quiet down and give him our attention.

"Getting to the gate will be easy. Piper has offered to open a portal to save us time on traveling. Just beyond our ward, people have already set up medical stations. The time has come for us to go in. Marley, your team will split up to help locate Elaine and scout ahead. Adrian, your team will oversee holding off any obstacles that get in the way. Larissa and Piper will portal out anyone if they are too injured to fight. Once we get Elaine out, we will call for a retreat. Everyone is to disengage and run, no exceptions." He directs us all with a firm tone. Voices murmur across the grass until Kade steps forward.

"Why should we run if we get the upper hand? Shouldn't we kill as many as we can?" He says, giving a cocky smirk.

"This is a rescue mission, maybe save the blood lust for another day." Larissa snaps. A few people around us chuckle, and Kade looks at me with disgust when I blow him a kiss.

"Larissa is correct. Our only mission is to save Elaine and get everyone home alive." Levi says, nodding to Piper. She takes Larissa's hand in hers and they step ahead of the group.

"Are you ready?" She asks. Larissa nods and holds up one of her hands while she does the same, giving eachother strength.

Chapter 23 - Larissa

I bend over and brace my hands on my knees, groaning as the nausea hits me. Portal jumping by myself is one thing, but Piper's kick me right in the gut every time. This time I am not alone. It seems a few of Marley's team aren't accustomed to portal jumping. Blaine rubs my back while chuckling at a young guy who yanked his mask off just in time to puke into a nearby bush.

Jabbing him with my elbow, I stand and look around us at the incredible scene. I can hear waves crashing just beyond a cliff that looks as if it drops off the edge of the world. Dark, thundering clouds have crept through the sky above us. We are standing just beyond what looks like an ancient, crumbling castle. The overgrown bush and sparse trees give us just enough cover to prepare for what we are rushing into. Levi walks up beside us and pulls his mask over his head, pointing to mine that dangles in my hand. I yank it over my face and Blaine helps me tuck my unruly black hair under the cap and into the collar of my jacket.

"The green eyes are enough to identify you, but that raven hair is a dead giveaway, Angel." He whispers, kissing my forehead before pulling his own mask down and winking.

"Remember your positions. Watch each other's backs. Asmodeus, let's go." Levi nods to him and we all begin our silent walk towards the crumbling gray stone walls. An eerie silence surrounds us as I struggle to slow my breathing. I'm on edge and unsure of what to expect. The only sound is the wind blowing as it carries the salty smell of the surrounding ocean with it. As we get closer, the pungent smell of sulfur taints the air and I cover my mask.

"It's not pleasant, but you'll adjust pretty quickly," Piper says beside me, squeezing my arm once before stepping ahead. The front of the broken and abandoned castle still has a door, though the wood looks decayed and it's overgrown with vines.

Asmodeus walks up to the door and holds his hands up before chanting under his breath. With a sudden puff of smoke that is quickly whisked away by the growing wind, the ancient hinges creak as the door swings open. It reveals a sinister entryway that makes me want to turn and run in the opposite direction. The inside is far too dark and looks as if we are stepping into an entirely different castle. It's too dark to see much of anything, but I can tell it's in much better condition than the illusion outside has given us.

I stop and turn in a slow circle, realizing the darkness has a heavy weight that slows our movements. It blocks out everything from the outside world, even the wind has stopped. We are standing in the foyer of a grand castle that doesn't show any signs of aging. Sconces come alive along the walls in a ripple, leading to a series of doors. Each one is made from what looks to be marble, and has intricate designs carved into them. Unfamiliar shapes and symbols attached to vines catch my attention.

Asmodeus walks straight to the first one and kneels, taking out his blade and piercing his finger. A few people whisper, but they fall silent when Levi raises his hand. We all watch as he uses his bleeding finger to drag it along a few of the symbols, making his way to the top. Blood fills in the carvings and they glow until he steps back. The outline of the door flickers and shifts as if a flame is dancing behind it before swinging inward. Everyone is holding their breath, waiting for something to happen, but nothing does.

Asmodeus nods to us and takes Piper's hand in his, leading the way.

"Why isn't he wearing a mask?" Ella whispers to me and I startle. I didn't notice that she had fallen in step beside me.

"Dude is a fucking tank. I doubt anything could help him

blend in." Lane says next to her, eyes going wide when Levi snaps his stare to us. Our steps are silent as we each cross the threshold, two at a time. The hallway we step into is wide enough for us to walk beside one another, but the dust covered stone walls feel as if they are closing in on me. I grip my dagger and pull it from my waistband, rubbing the hilt with my thumb for reassurance. Goosebumps race down my neck and back as a frigid chill grips me, making me glance back.

Even in the dim lighting, I can feel the comfort within those familiar brown eyes. Blaine winks and I smile, turning forward with more confidence. We come across another door, but this one opens with the turn of a knob. *Well, that was a little anticlimactic.* The room we walk into is dark and difficult to see, but we stick with our teams and stay on guard.

"We are within the castle. Keep your wits and blades sharp." Asmodeus says, his voice seeming loud in such an empty space. But nothing happens, even as the flames on the wall dance higher. *Something feels familiar about this entire place.*

Nothing happens until I nearly drop my dagger from the shock as it rips through me. *They killed her right there.* I stare at the throne to my left, where Mammon sat as he ordered Celia to be murdered. Realization sucks the air from my lungs before I can even look down. My feet scuff the ground as I stagger away from the massive stain right where I was standing. I press the back of my hand to my lips, fighting the bile as it rushes up to my stuffy mask. A hand grips my elbow and pulls me towards the rows of benches

"Shit, shit, shit." He mutters repeatedly, realizing exactly what's going on. "Angel, try to keep it together. Look at me." he demands, gripping my face in his hands as I turn to look up into his eyes.

"I didn't know this is where we were going to enter. I am so sorry." His voice is sincere, and I shake my head, trying to smother the guilt as it eats at me.

"I failed her and I can't let Elaine down too. Let's just keep moving." My voice breaks as I brush past him, but he doesn't stop me. Blaine knows if I stop to dwell now, every negative thought will consume me. Marley waves her group on, and they split into two teams. Each group takes a different hall. Micah and Jake go with them to lend a hand just in case they run into trouble. Aside from the two hallways they exited through, there are only two others. The way we all came through and another directly behind the throne.

"There isn't anyone here. Wouldn't they know we came through somehow?" I ask, not letting my guard down as we stand around.

"Not necessarily. Piper is casting an intense cloaking spell, but I don't know how much longer she can keep it up or how far the reach is." Adrian's muffled voice says before walking away. I glance over at Piper and her face is pinched in concentration as she grips Asmodeus' arm for support. *We have to find Elaine, fast.*

"He has changed everything, there never used to be a throne or a podium here. I had them removed long ago. I don't know where to look for a prisoner cell, but every hall connects back around. Be careful." Asmodeus warns as I walk away.

Chapter 24 - Larissa

"I'm going to check out that hallway," I say, motioning behind the throne. Blaine snorts and holds his hand out.

"After you." He says. Eric walks up and Kade pulls his mask off, just to show how annoyed he is by following me. *Fine by me, you can be demon bait.* I feel guilty for my thoughts, but only for a moment. Kade shoves past Blaine and gives him a disgusted glare. *Nope, fuck that guy.* Blaine just rolls his eyes and keeps walking, catching me off guard with his calm response.

The end of this dim hall takes a sharp right, opening into a larger path. There are doors scattered along the walls, but they don't look like prison doors. The first one opens with no resistance, and inside stands a stunning four poster bed with purple mesh fabric draped around it like a curtain. The room has a large rug in the middle and shelves built into the wall beside a smaller door that resembles a closet.

"Guess we found the guest rooms," Eric says quietly. I have to bite back my frustration as every door after is the same. This is obviously not the right place, and I can't stand the idea that she isn't here. An off feeling settles within my stomach, and I keep glancing over my shoulder.

"Something isn't right." Blaine says, looking around as we step into an open room with stairs leading up and another hall to the right. I nod to him and Kade chuckles as he turns down the hall.

"What, your demon side isn't happy to be home?" He says in a mocking tone.

"You're barking up the wrong tree, Kade. Knock it off." Eric warns him, casting a glance in my direction as I walk past. I charge after him, grabbing his shirt and spinning him to face me. Kade's eyes widen in surprise as I slam him against the rough stone wall, gripping the front of his shirt as my hands flicker with sparks. He tries to pull his face away from the small arcs, but I just apply more pressure.

"I'll fry your brain and leave you laying here for Mammon to find if you keep this shit up." My voice is just a hiss before I shove him away. When I turn around, I see Blaine staring at me with one brow raised. I brush my arms off, as if just touching Kade has dirtied me, and walk ahead of the men. Eric chuckles and sighs. "I tried to warn you, watch who you cross." I hear a scuffle as Kade hurries to catch up to the three of us.

"I thought you meant her boyfriend. Not her." He whines, trying to be quiet but failing in the silence of the underground walls. Blaine's eyes lock on me, but I don't turn to meet his stare. I'm not proud of what I just did, especially as the anger slowly fades. It'll be a wintry day in Hell when I apologize to him, and with how much I'm sweating, that won't be today. Blaine grabs my arm, yanking me back as he presses a finger to the front of his mask. I reach behind me, silently pulling my sword from its sheath.

Holding my breath for a moment, I hear what Blaine caught before the rest of us. The nearly silent echo of laughter comes from the path ahead of us. This laughter isn't from anyone I recognize, and it's followed by the clanging of metal.

"I smell intruders." A voice cackles, feminine and high pitched. The sound is getting louder, and we have nowhere to hide if we stay here.

"Back up, pick a room. Go now." Blaine whispers. I nod to him and grip Kade's arm. He tries to jerk away, but I just roll my eyes and teleport us back to the first room we had come across. Kade wrenches away from me, kneeling on the stone with his hand firmly placed over his mouth.

"Blaine and Eric must have hit another room," I whisper, "You need to get up. We have to hide." He nods and stands, turning towards the door. Enough light is coming in around the cracks that I put out the torch on the wall, smothering the flames with a decorative bowl from the dresser. I grab his arm and tug him back towards the smaller door on the side wall and yank it open. Grinding my teeth in irritation, I realize it's a closet with just enough room to shove him into.

I hear a scuff just outside our door, cursing to myself when I realize they're so close to finding us. Without a second to spare, I duck beside the dresser, pressing the flat side of my blade to my forehead. Distant sounds of a fight reach my ears, and I fight the urge to run out into the chaos. Blaine you better be okay, I swear to- *crack*. The door bursts inward, splintering everywhere in a cloud of dust. I bite my lips, stifling the shout of surprise that almost slipped out and gave away my position.

"I can smell you, sweetheart. Hiding is really such a coward's thing to do." A woman purrs. I leap up, swinging my blade toward the voice. I clip the arm of a tall woman with bright white hair braided down to the back of her knees. The light streaming through the doorway illuminates her olive skin, but her eyes are what makes me pause. They emulate a deep yellow glow that cuts through me, and strikes fear into my being. I screwed up by getting distracted, and she swings a wooden staff at my head. I jump back, narrowly missing the blow as it whizzes past my face.

Kade leaps from the closet, charging past me towards her.

"Kade!" I call his name and try to grab him, but I'm too late. She swats him aside as if he were just a pest. He hits the wall and slides down, groaning while clutching his arm.

"So, the rumors are true. They sent a team in to rescue the useless old woman." She coos, grinning as I point my sword at her.

"Where is she?" I ask, rage burning inside of me. Suddenly I hear a scuffle not far off. A man screams before the sound of metal hitting stone ends in silence. The cambion before me stops smiling, her bright yellow eyes flashing as she shakes her head.

"Zan," she whispers, her voice broken. I hesitate, unsure of her next move, and caught off by the sudden change in demeanor.

"Don't fucking touch her," Blaine says, stepping up behind her. His eyes are the color of ink, and the shadows in the room pull towards him. Blood drips from his right hand when he flexes his blackened fingers that are tipped with claws. She squints at me, her sadness vanishes as it's replaced by something sinister.

"The blood of my lover is on his hands. Yours will be on mine." She pulls the staff apart, revealing a long and narrow sword. I swing my own up to block hers as she aims right at my throat. Her emotions are clouding her judgment, making her sloppy. Blaine tries to leap at her, roaring as he does. Somebody else catches him off guard, running full speed into him. I swing at her, sparks dancing down my hands and she gasps, blocking my blow.

"It's you, the one Mammon is after." She says, her voice bordering on excitement. I grunt, pulling back and kicking her legs. The cambion woman dances backwards, giving me room to see Blaine pick up a man and throw him out the doorway. His face mask is gone, and his shirt is torn over his ribs. A deep wound is exposed and bleeding. But he doesn't show any sign that he is in pain when he pulls a small knife and throws it. It pierces into the man's eye with a loud squelch, the force of the blow knocking him back. He doesn't make a sound as he falls, his body crumpling to the floor.

"The blade, Larissa! It conducts." Blaine shouts as the woman runs at me. I grip the handle and push my power into my arms. As she swings at me, I duck and stab into her abdomen. The smell of burning flesh fills the air as she screams when I leap back. But I'm not fast enough. As she falls, her blade swings down. It clips my face as life leaves her eyes.

I suck in a sharp breath as I slap a hand over my cheek. Warm blood trickles between my fingers. Blaine runs up and grabs me, looking me over in concern. I breathe a sigh of relief, seeing that his side has already stopped bleeding. Tilting my head, I motion to where Kade is slumped against the wall.

"She hit him pretty hard. You need to take him back to Piper." I say and Blaine shakes his head, walking over to help him up.

"No, you can take him back yourself and stay there. You held your own, but barely." He grumbles. I roll my eyes and stomp past him, nearly running into Eric, who is leaning against the wall. His eyes widen as he takes in the blood smeared across my cheek, but I wave a hand and act like it isn't burning like a motherfucker. Eric shakes his head at me, then glances down at the body of a man laying face down in the dirt. This guy was tall with short brown hair and an intimidating muscle build.

"He almost got the best of us until Blaine went ape shit." Eric chuckles, clutching his arm oddly to his body. I step around him and give a small frown.

"I just killed his partner. She said her lovers' blood is on his hands." I say, glancing up at Blaine. He looks down at his stained hand that uses to help Kade stand and I can see the remorse he tries to hide.

"I ripped his throat out with my hands." He says, Kade's eyes widen as he glances sideways at Blaine. "Boo" Blaine whispers, making Kade jump. Eric chuckles, walking up to me.

"Do you mind trading him? I need Blaine to get this back in place." Eric says, grimacing as he walks towards Blaine. I nod, but Kade steps past me to lean against the wall. I noticed blood covering his neck, and I cast a worried glance back to Blaine. He nods to me in understanding before turning to grip Eric's arm.

"This is going to suck." He says. Eric sighs.

"I'm aware. Can you just do it please?" He asks. Blaine doesn't even flinch, just yanks his arm down into place with a sick grinding sound. Kade throws up on the floor and I'm tempted to do the same. Eric groans loudly, nearly falling over, but Blaine catches him. Eric straightens up and limps towards Kade, leaving a small blood trail as he goes.

"The dude with his eye poked out stabbed me in the thigh, got me pretty good." He chuckles, walking to Kade. I sigh, realizing Blaine is right and we need to take them back. I grab onto both their arms and focus on the throne room, and Blaine presses his chest to my back. He places his hands over mine and drops a soft kiss to my neck, and I welcome the cold shadows that caress my sweat covered skin.

Chapter 25 - Larissa

We drop into what I can only describe as chaos. Most of our Nephilim who came here are locked in combat with demons. They are distinctly different from their cambion offspring. Each of them has skin the color of ashes, paired with emotionless eyes. They're incredibly strong, and a few feet taller than most of us. Their features are startling human, but obviously demented. I watch in horror as Adrian dives onto one, driving his dagger into the creature's throat, only to be thrown off.

I leap forward, my blade already heavy in my palm. Blaine is trying to pull me away, but all I can see are the claws stretching towards my brother. He pulls a long sword from his back and swings it at the demon. It smacks into the creature's outstretched palm, burrowing into his flesh. Black blood oozes out, and he yanks his hand back with a hiss as smoke comes from the wound.

"They're forged in holy water!" Adrian shouts at me. I look at the sword in my hand and focus, pushing my power beyond just my hands. Imagining my weapon as an extension of myself, sparks crackle across the blade, arching in vast waves. Lunging forward, I plunge the blade into the demon's shoulder. It lets out a piercing wail so sharp that I'm forced to cover my ears.

"Larissa, duck!" Piper screams. I don't think, just act. Dropping to the ground, I look over my shoulder in time to watch her open a small portal with one of her hands. Asmodeus flings his sword into it, and she waves her hand. Her second portal opens just above me and the blade launches through it, sinking into the demon's head. He falls sideways, screeching as his body begins to burn and crumble to ash.

Asmodeus runs over and plucks his sword up, wiping it off

on his pants.

"Marley found her, but then we were ambushed. Demons swarmed her team and those of us here. Levi ran to help them, along with Ella. We need to go." He grunts, swinging and slicing the head off a demon that ran towards him. I turn around, realizing the amount of black sticky blood and ash that covers the ground. Blaine shouts across the field and I look up just to see him drag his long black claws down the face of a demon. The creature cries out and shoots his hand forward to grip his throat.

"Blaine, no!" I scream, running towards him. Blaine doesn't struggle, he pulls out another throwing knife and stabs it into the creature's throat. Over and over, he grips its wrist with one hand while mutilating its neck. The demon tries to drop him, but Blaine doesn't give him the chance. He stabs it into his neck and yanks sideways, spilling black ooze all over the ground and into his arms. My feet are frozen in place, not only at the brutality Blaine showed, but at what we walked into. We might all die down here.

Piper opens a portal quickly before helping Eric and Kade through. She calls for me, exhaustion making her stagger. Asmodeus runs to catch her, and I give him a thumbs up. Winking at Piper, I back away from them.

Her eyes widen as she screams for me, shoving at Asmodeus. I can hear shouting coming from the first hallway, the path Marley had taken the last time I saw her. Elaine is still down there, along with everyone else.

"Grab her! Fucking stop her!" Piper calls, her voice nearly swallowed in the fighting. I can't leave, not when Elaine is so close. Nobody else can get them out except for us. I won't leave that burden to Piper. She's already exhausted.

I have to do this, and I know I can. Without looking, I can feel Blaine and Adrian already gaining on me. Blaine is still in a rage from the fight, and it brings me an odd comfort. We will need his strength, considering the sounds of war that is waiting for us.

Screams bounce off the walls and I put my head down,

running as fast as I can. *Ella.* Fear makes my feet become numb, ice climbing my limbs.

"We have to get them out of there!" I shout over my shoulder.

"Larissa," Adrian starts.

"I know!" I cut him off. It took us mere seconds to get here, but it felt like minutes ticking past. My feet slip over the ground, something slick makes each step difficult. Adrian pushes me forward when I try to look down.

"Don't," He snarls. I swing and scan the battle in front of us. Cambions and demons are tearing into whatever they touch. Some have even begun fighting each other. Their blood lust is stronger than their sanity, as it slips away. I see Marley, her mask torn off and blood covering half her face. She cries out, stabbing two swords into the back of a cambion. The man under her screams and convulses as his wounds bubble. I stare in horror, and she looks up, waving me to her.

"They were waiting, down in the cells. As soon as we pulled Elaine out, they swarmed us. We never had a chance," she says, panting. I look around in horror, pleading for just a glimpse of *her.*

My breath stills, everything around us slows. Elaine is unrecognizable. She looks like a shaking pile of dirty fabric. Levi is clutching her to his side as he fends off a demon by shoving his hand into its chest and bursting flames from within. *Okay, that was badass, but ew.* I run towards them, brandishing my sword as a cambion female rushes them from behind.

"Get down!" I shout. Levi drops to the ground and covers Elaine's body with his own. I leap over them, spearing into the heart of a girl with soft blonde curls as I land. Her mouth drops open in shock and I try to yank my blade free. A sudden pain erupts from my leg and I look down, realizing she sunk a curved blade into my thigh. Pulling my sword from her now limp body, I trip sideways, leaning on the wall for support. The heat has become nearly unbearable as the smell of blood and sulfur boils in the air.

"Larissa, take Elaine and go." Levi shouts, pushing Elaine into my arms. For a moment, I forget the pain as I clutch to her frail frame. Tears bloom in my eyes as I look into her eyes. Her cheeks are sunken in, and the once shiny hair that framed her face is now dull and knotted. Even in this condition, she cups my cheek and smiles at me. Rage rears its head as tears trail down her dirty cheeks.

"You came for me, my sweet girl. I wish you didn't always throw yourself into danger." She rasps. I shake my head and hug her tightly. I'm afraid that she will disappear if I let go for even a moment. A hand presses to my thigh. "This is going to hurt." Levi says before ripping the cambion's blade out. I throw my head back, bouncing it off the hard stone wall as stars dance behind my closed eyes. My breath comes out in ragged pants as I swallow down my pain and Elaine rubs my arms.

"It's okay, I'm here." She says, comforting me even in her condition. Around us, the fight has died down. I glimpse Adrian backing a demon into a corner and the look on his face is crazed. Ella is sitting on the ground, clutching her arm to her chest as she watches.

Blaine comes up behind the demon, blocking his exit as Marley stands, holding a steaming knife in her hand.

"Marley can channel heat into anything she touches." Levi explains and I nod, wide eyed.

"We have to help get everyone out of here," I say as Adrian swings his sword, embedding it into the demon's head. She screams and falls over, black blood pouring down her face and into the dirt. Blaine runs to us, grabbing Elaine in a tight hug and looking us both over.

"Let's get you home," He says, "Both of you." But before we can move, Asmodeus roars from the entryway.

"Unhand her, Mammon!" The walls tremble, dirt falling as the world around us shakes. Marley is gathering all her wounded and nods at me.

"Go help him. Blaine can get more of us out than you can." She says. I can see the hesitation on his face.

"Go on, take Elaine too. I'll be right behind you. I have to help Piper." My voice breaks. Blaine closes his eyes, nostrils flaring as he nods. Before he walks away, Blaine rips his shirt off and ties it around my leg to slow the bleeding. I smile at him, and he kisses me hard before reaching for Elaine. She pulls away and shakes her head, taking my hand in hers.

"I'm staying with her. Go on and be quick." She tells him, her voice strong and unwavering. He must realize there's no point in fighting and jogs off, picking up Ella and nodding at Adrian.

"You should have gone with him," I say to her. "This entire mission was to save you, Elaine." I say, my voice thick. She gives a dry laugh and Levi walks ahead of us, Adrian trailing behind as we rush back to Asmodeus.

"If I did that, you would have no reason to stay back from what awaits us. You and I will stay out of sight. Let the men distract Mammon. Then we get out as soon as Blaine comes back." She says and Levi gives a thumbs up over his shoulder. He knew I'd stay back to protect Elaine. *Sneaky.* We stop just before the hall opens and I help Elaine sit to rest. Meanwhile, Levi and Adrian slink out. Mammon's back is to us as he faces Asmodeus.

He is truly terrifying, his ripped shirt exposes the sickly gray tone of his skin and I can't look away from the hollow black pits he has for eyes. Mammon's brown hair is slicked back, half of it is tied in a low ponytail and he bears a sharp toothed smile at the warriors facing him. Asmodeus is panting, his fists shaking as he holds two blades that appear to be made from pulsing black smoke. I watch as Adrian swings in, aiming for the back of his knee, but Mammon jumps into the air and lands a few feet away. With Piper dangling in his arm. Even with his back towards us, I can still see her blonde head as he turns his body. He has her arms pinned to her sides, but that isn't what startles me. Her head is limp and laying on her shoulder. *Not Piper, please no.* My heart feels as if it has slowed down while I wait for any sign she's still alive.

Mammon adjusts his grip and her eyes flutter for a

moment before she becomes limp again.

"Who is she?" Elaine asks, taking my hand in her fragile ones. I've never seen her as frail before. The thought catches me off guard and I look at her.

"Her name is Piper, she is Asmodeus' mate. She's my friend." My voice is low, trying to keep an ear out in case Mammon has anyone waiting to ambush us. Elaine grips my hand tighter, watching intently while covering her heart with her free hand. *She is praying for Piper.* After the hell she has endured, she is praying for a girl she's never met.

"I'll tear her heart from her chest if you do that again, boy." Mammon's voice booms in the room, making my skin crawl. Levi shakes his head, holding up both hands in surrender.

"We don't have to do this, Mammon. Just put her down." He tries a placating tone. Mammon just laughs, his hair falling forward. He has discarded his tie, and his shirt is unbuttoned at the neck with the black sleeves rolled back.

"You sent your hero home to hide behind her little bubble? And here I thought these two were buddies. What a shame that she doesn't give a shit about a dirty witch." Mammon says. I shake my head, wanting so badly to run out and kick his ass. Elaine tightens her hand on mine, squinting at me. I pat her hands, trying to convince both of us that I'm not going anywhere.

"Take me. Let the girl go and take me." Levi says. The longer we sit here, the faster my heart races. Mammon throws his head back with a demented laugh.

"Give her back to me or I'll rip your limbs from your body while you still live, Mammon!" Asmodeus shouts. But if he's afraid, Mammon doesn't show it. He shrugs and tilts his face towards her.

"This little blonde of yours smells delicious. Maybe I understand why you have betrayed your own kind to keep her bed warm. But she still doesn't hold a candle to the woman you threw away." Mammon says.

"Lilith finally got what she deserved." Adrian says.

Mammon swings to look at him.

"You will be the first to die, painfully slow while your father watches. As we speak, my army is gathering. You'll stand no chance. None of you." Mammon becomes animalistic at the mention of Lilith. He turns and yanks on Piper's hair, wrenching her head back onto his elbow. Light glints off something metallic in his hand as he raises it. Everything suddenly movies in slow motion. Asmodeus throws one of his weapons, aiming for Mammon's head with a shout of fury. But it misses its mark and sails past him. Mammon easily side steps it and ducks as Levi sends a ball of fire at him.

I yank my hand free from Elaine, locking my eyes onto the black knife he holds in his hand. It's nearly touching her skin, poised above her heart. Mammon could pierce through her bone in an instant, and she would be gone.

I run forward, ripping my mask away with a cry that bursts from my chest as power erupts from inside me.

I leap right through my portal and land on top of Mammon, catching him off guard and knocking him sideways. Piper tumbles from his arms to lie motionless on the ground. Asmodeus runs forward, grabbing her up and nodding to me as I stand up and back away. My leg feels as if it's on fire, and the pain makes my head spin. Mammon turns towards me, baring his teeth in a feral smile.

"Larissa, no!" Levi shouts. Mammon throws his hand back, catching him by his shoulder and throwing Levi aside. I don't dare look away, backing up as he advances. *I'm so tired.* The spots that dance in my vision won't clear, no matter how much I blink.

"I'm shocked you wouldn't just watch your little friend die. But you genuinely surprised me. I didn't expect you to be brave." He shakes his head, throwing the dagger out and sinking it into Adrian's arm as he runs towards us.

In the blink of an eye, Mammon is thrown sideways. Blaine is holding a block of concrete, panting as shadows swarm the room. He looks like an angel of death. I smile up at him, nearly falling as he runs to catch me.

Chapter 26 - Larissa

Nephilim began swarming down the hallway we entered from, and I look at Blaine in confusion. He grips my shoulders as he looks me over before kissing my forehead softly.

"Somebody is helping us. They sent word that you were all in trouble. I grabbed who I could and gave instructions to anyone else to follow behind. That same person opened the gate for us, but he was gone before I could see his face. Willow showed up and said Piper sent a message to her. We are all getting out of here, alive." he says, smiling. I look over his shoulder and push past, staggering to my brother, who is kneeling beside our dad. Adrian is clutching the wound on his shoulder tightly, but blood slips past his hand to drip down his sleeve. Our father is struggling to stand, already looking to help lead his people.

"I've got this one, Levi. You need to get the kids and Elaine out of here." Mark steps up. He is wearing full gear, while holding Elaine so gingerly. She is glaring daggers at me, and even in this state, I am a little intimidated.

"Stop running to face death, child. My old heart can't take much more." She scolds me and I nod, relieved. But it's short-lived. I swing around as the sound of fighting breaks out. Cambions and demons are pouring in faster than we can handle. There is no feasible way the thirty warriors Blaine led here can stand against all of them. I reach for my sword and Blaine stops me. He blinks and his eyes turn black, the firelight reflecting on them.

"You are going home, Angel. Right now." He demands. Looking back over my shoulder, I watch as the two sides collide. Each one a fight to the death. Mark kisses Elaine and softly pushes her to Adrian.

"As soon as we are home, I am going to marry you, my sweet Elaine." He promises before pulling his sword and swinging it into the nearest cambion. Elaine blushes, and the color of her cheeks warms my heart. Until Blaine is ripped away from me.

I look up as he turns, slashing at the hand dragging him back by his shirt. Black blood oozes, but Blaine's attempts yield nothing. The hand pulses, bubbling as it grows larger. Mammon is snarling as he throws Blaine against the ground with an inhuman roar. I try to run forward, but I'm stopped by a familiar cloaked woman.

"Piper is safe, Asmodeus demanded I bring him back so he could ensure you all safely make it home." Willow smiles down at me. I look behind me and wave to my family.

"Take them, now. I can't leave without him." I plead with her. Levi has fallen in and out of consciousness, and Adrian is too distracted to hear me. She sighs and nods, turning towards them. Throwing my sword up, I block a demon as she swats at Willow.

She slams her arm down onto my blade, screaming as electricity sparks into her before she yanks away.

"Willow, you need to hurry!" I shout. Asmodeus and Blaine are taking on Mammon together. Somehow, he still has the upper hand. I mentally plead with them to move faster. While I'm watching their backs, I stop paying attention to my surroundings. A female demon bats me across the face, catching me off guard. I stumble sideways, falling near the feet of a nephilim who is encasing their hands in ice and stabbing them into enemies. He hooks my arm with his freezing one and helps me stand.

I don't have time to thank him though, the demon leaps onto me. I swing my sword up and pierce under her ribs. We fall sideways, and I quickly get back onto my feet. She hisses up at me and the sound cuts off before I can make a move. A tall nephilim warrior brings her ax down, separating the demon's head from her neck. I nearly puke from the sight, but Blaine pulls my attention across the room once more.

He is slouching forward, wheezing. His shadows are sluggishly moving now, having used up all his energy. Asmodeus is hardly faring any better. His chest shows healing gashes from Mammon's clawed hands. But it appears Mammon is also wearing down. *We might have a real shot at this.* Those thoughts feel wrong with so many bodies cast aside, the smell of blood and sulfur saturating the air. Dust is being kicked up around us with every scuffle, and it's getting difficult to see who is a friend or foe.

I trip over a body, landing hard on my knees. Risking a look to see who I stepped over is an awful choice, and I scramble to my feet. There is no mistaking the cherry red pixie cut. Or the face of betrayal. *Bertha.* A former member of the Elders Council that had deceived all of us. She broke the protective barrier of Nephal after casting a deal with Lilith. Bertha became a traitor so that her daughter Marcy could be the hero. *Lilith didn't hold up her end of the deal.* The sound of her snapping Marcy's neck is ingrained in my mind. *Bertha and her husband, Dominic, grabbing Marcy's body and running off.* No one ever found them because they joined Mammon's army.

The castle walls shake, straining as Mammon grows taller. I'm pulled from my thoughts when I realize the walls and ceiling above us have serious damage from the battle that rages on. This whole place could come down on us.

Asmodeus waves his hands and a huge spear appears in his palm. It looks as if it's made of smoke, twisting, and moving in his hand. He throws it just as Mammon lunges for Blaine and hits him in the chest. Mammon falls forward, missing Blaine as he collapses to the ground. His impact causes chunks to fall from the ceiling, crumbling into the ground and crushing a demon.

Around us, Cambions have completely given up fighting and are running for the closest exit. There are no longer any demons left alive to flee. *We did it.* The witches have pulled nearly everyone out by the time I run to Blaine's side. He smiles at me, panting from exhaustion.

"You sure are stubborn. Why didn't you go home?" he mumbles. Tears blur my vision and I shrug.

"I won't leave you." I whisper. Asmodeus walks up to us, nodding to Blaine and clapping him on the shoulder. More stones crumble to the ground as the building shudders.

"We need to go before this place comes down on our heads." Asmodeus calls out. I look over to see a frustrated Willow. Adrian, our father, and Elaine are still here. Elaine has her no-nonsense face on, apparently refusing to leave without us. I glance over at Mammon's unmoving body as we walk past and bile crawls up my throat.

Something doesn't feel right.

"I told her I can only take a few at a time, but she won't budge without the three of you as well." Willow says, waving to Elaine. Guilt seeps in as I'm looking around the scene before us. Some nephilim weren't so lucky, and a few people stayed to help gather the bodies. I limp over to a body, recognizing the dusty hair.

"Lane, I'm sorry." My voice cracks as I whisper. *Mammon fell and I wish you could have seen it. I hope you can rest now, reunited with Celia again.* I kneel and use my sleeve to clean the dirt from his face, smoothing his hair down. "I'm so sorry," my voice trembles as I pluck bits of gravel from his clothes and hold his cooling body.

Someone near me lets out a shriek, pulling me from my thoughts. My head swings up, staring right into the enraged eyes of a beast born from evil. Mammon is rising, his body twitching as it stretches and *grows.*

The roof collapses by the main exit, kicking up a cloud of dust.

"Larissa, let's go!" Blaine shouts. I jump up towards him, but Mammon is too fast and grabs my leg, yanking it out from under me. *I can't portal, I would just take Mammon with me.* He drags me to him as I kick and thrash, desperately reaching towards Blaine. My nails break on the ground as I try to frantically claw into the dirt. Blood smears as my fingers scream in protest, but I can't give up.

Mammon swings his arm and rolls me into a pile of rubble. My back hits the sharp rocks and I fall face first into the ground with a cry. Using my shaking hands, I slowly push myself up onto my knees. I struggle to see as dirt and smoke fill the room. Coughing into my arm, I try to stand and swipe the cloud away. Blaine is there in a moment, bearing my sword. "Why is my shirt all wet?" I wheeze. *Oh, that is blood, a lot of blood.*

He drops into the shadows and appears behind Mammon. Blaine uses the blade to slash the back of his ankles, making him fall to his knees. The overgrown demon is shrinking down, losing more of his energy by the moment. But he doesn't stop. Mammon swings his arm and crashes it into the wall to rip off chunks of stone. He throws it at Blaine, knocking him over as he leaps up from the shadows. I use the last of my energy, forcing myself to run.

Not towards Blaine.

Not away from Mammon.

I snatch a discarded piece of a broken sword from the ground, the blade cutting into my palms when I do. It only forces me on. Pushing me beyond any limits. A primal cry rips from me as I push every bit of my power into the blade, swinging it at him. He holds his arm up to block, exactly as I had hoped. The blade sinks into his flesh, the smug smile he had drops as electricity courses through his body. I brace my feet on him and launch myself away. He convulses, falling over to spasm on the floor for a few moments before stilling. His mouth foams and his dark pitted eyes slide shut as black blood puddles under him.

Chapter 27 - Larissa

The smell of burning flesh makes my lip curl in disgust. More smoke has thickened the air, pushing down on us as flames crackle beside the throne. Mammon's lantern from my vision has shattered and broken atop the burning ornate rug. *Burn in Hell, Mammon.*

Hobbling over to Blaine, I choke up as he struggles just to stand. Blood covers his chin and neck, but I don't care as I throw my arms around him. We fall over and he laughs, looking at me as I prop myself up.

"Eric was right. You were ready, Angel. I never should have doubted you." He smiles and my heart soars as I cup his face. He pulls his hand off my back and stares at it in horror, realizing how badly I'm bleeding.

A commotion stirs up, and I turn to see smoke billowing towards us. Blaine and I stand, finally ready to leave with the others. But we are closed in by a thick cloud. I have no idea which way to walk, and my eyes are burning.

"Hold on!" Willow says and the sound of wind whistling filters through the chaos.

The air clears in time to see a spear sailing right towards my heart. But my feet don't move, not in time. Blaine is standing directly behind me, and I won't take another step. *I'd die for him a thousand times over.*

Someone knocks us sideways, just before the weapon can hit its target.

"You are infuriating, old crone!" Mammon shouts, storming over to yank his spear from Elaine's chest. He turns as a witch floats above the rubble, sucking the air from his lungs with her power. Another runs full force into him, sending him sprawling onto his back.

I crawl to Elaine, crying and shaking my head as I pull her onto my lap.

"No, Aunt Elaine. Not you. I can't lose you. I need you. Please." I whimper, rocking us back and forth. She weakly raises her hand to pat my cheek. Blood drips from her mouth and down her chin as she tries to speak. Blaine roars as he charges at Mammon while I desperately wipe the red droplets from her skin. If I can just stop the bleeding, she will be okay. Adrian and Asmodeus are rushing in from the other side, but I can't look up. All I can do is stare into her eyes as I watch her light dimming.

"She moved before I could blink," Willow whispers, kneeling beside us.

"We have to go, take us back. She needs a healer." I cry, not taking my eyes off her. Elaine shakes her head once, her hand dropping.

"It's my time, child." She rasps. I grip her tighter as if I can keep her alive if I just hold on.

"I am so proud, and your mother-" She stops, rasping in a breath.

"Tell me after we get back and you heal." I beg her.

"Your Mama is proud too. We love you, sweet girl." Her eyes blink slowly. Elaine's breathing has become shallow as more blood fills my lap.

"You can't leave me!" My cries are muffled as I bury my face in her hair.

"I love you." I whisper. *This can't be happening.*

"Don't go." She doesn't hear me though, her last breath leaving her lungs in a sigh. Elaine's face relaxes, as if she has found peace.

Her breath stops brushing the hair from my neck.

My hands tremble on her chest that no longer rises and falls.

The heartbeat beneath my palm has stopped.

She's gone. It's all my fault she's gone. Willow tries to comfort me, but I swat her hand.

"You should have taken her back when you had the chance!" I scream at her. She gives me a pitying look, only making me feel worse.

"Elaine?" Mark's voice is a broken whisper. My sobs slow when I look into his eyes, his pain open for the world to see. Piper is there, leaning against Niko. Her purple hair falls over her face as she tilts her head, taking in my shattered appearance.

"Oh no," Piper whispers, covering her mouth with a shaking hand. Mark falls to his knees beside me and softly brushes her dirty hair from her face. Agony burrows deeper in my chest as I slide her gently into his arms.

"She saved me. She did it to save me." I whisper, shaking my head as more tears fall. Blaine staggers up beside us, gripping his ribs as he looks down at Elaine. Mammon is struggling to even hold his head up halfway across the room. Asmodeus is swinging wildly at his face and chest while Mammon fights back against him weakly.

"Aunt Elaine," Blaine whispers, his voice breaking.

"Get her out of here, Willow." I whisper, standing and shoving Adrian's hand away as he tries to comfort me.

"Larissa, it won't bring her back." Adrian says. The sound that I let out isn't a laugh, it's twisted and sinister. I allow my pain, exhaustion and grief to become my weapon. Vengeance urges me forward, as static builds around us and I envision tearing Mammon's heart from his chest. Asmodeus blocks my path, holding his hand out.

"He's still dangerous, Larissa. We need to restrain him and take him to face judgment for his crimes." He says. I slam my hands against his chest, adding enough electricity to put him on his ass. Piper calls my name, but I don't look back at her. I have tunnel vision, locked onto Mammon's smug face.

"You took Lilith from me, but we still aren't equally wounded. I'm disappointed your pretty boy is still breathing." He nods towards Blaine. Mammon is on his knees, but he can still look me in the eye. My hair lifts, tickling my scalp as static pours from within me. His eyes widen a fraction, and he leans back as

I struggle to breathe. *Finally, he's afraid.* He knew they wanted him alive. All I want is to watch him take his last breath.

And I'm getting what I want this time.

"Larissa, don't do this!" Blaine shouts. I smile at Mammon, putting every ounce of malice I can into the sneer.

"You'll kill yourself." He spits. My hands raise up on their own accord and I fight to keep control, even as my power sends shocks of pain through my bones. My senses become overwhelmed from the bitter smell of electricity and the brightness consuming everything as it grows.

"Guess I'll see you out there then," I jerk my chin towards the wall, towards all of Hell that reaches beyond this point.

Throwing my head back, a shrill scream of anguish rips through my throat. My ears pop and I can vaguely smell burning hair as I release everything I've been holding back. Mammon flies backwards, his body burning as sparks fly around him.

I can't stop, even as the building crumbles. *Everyone else will get out, but this is where I'll be buried.* The thought doesn't scare me. I nearly find comfort until Elaine's face flashes behind my eyes. Her bright smile, the fake look of annoyance when I take a bite of one of her freshly baked cookies, and the flash of her colorful skirts fluttering behind as she danced around the house. My mother's laughter chimes in my ears, as if she's sharing my memories. But we aren't sharing anything, because they're both gone now.

My eyes roll back as the pain becomes too much for me to bear.

Have I finally found peace?

Chapter 28 - Larissa

Everything hurts and no matter how loud I scream, nobody hears me. I feel the brush of something cool and damp slide across my face, but it's dulled. Every sensation and sound feel like I'm not in my body.

Someone is saying my name, but I slip back under without even putting up a fight.

I'm unsure how much time passes. I keep fading in and out. But there is usually somebody there, yet not here. It's as if I'm just floating in a dark bubble. *If this is the afterlife, then this shit sucks.*

"You are difficult to find, Blessed one." A familiar voice echoes around me, clear and feminine. *Where are you? Where am I?* I can't speak. Panic grips me for the first time as I feel myself being pulled from the shadows. A blinding light glows outside of my closed eyelids and I squint, trying to shield my face.

"You can open your eyes." The same woman says. Her voice is so clear, as if she is standing right beside me. Covering my face with both hands first, my eyes peel open with effort.

"I must warn you I have waited for quite some time and am impatient, darling." She chuckles. I move my hands and blink rapidly up at the bright white ceiling. I try to sit up and a small warm hand presses to my back, helping me. Looking to my right to see who is with me, I nearly fall off the overly plush black couch. There's a woman with long wavy black hair and her eyes, a shimmering gray, are locked onto me. I try to scoot back, staring at the crescent moon twisted into a small bun atop her heart-shaped face.

"There we go. You startle so easily, how odd." she muses, tilting her head. I glance down at her blue dress, marveling at how there are small specks of diamonds that resemble stars across the silky fabric. Looking around us, I realize the entire room is all done in shades of blue and gray. The flooring is black marble tiles, a matching coffee table sits in front of me trimmed with silver.

The beautiful woman picks up a glass pitcher from off the table and pours water into a small glass, holding it out for me. I just stare, wide eyed and confused. Licking my lips, I realize just how thirsty I am. She frowns and then her face lights up as if she has realized something important.

"You are afraid I will hurt you. Let me show you it is safe." She takes a sip from the glass and holds it out proudly to me. Her long, curling black lashes flutter as she smiles fondly. I take the glass and gulp it down quickly.

"Thank you," I say, sitting the empty glass on the table. She scrunches her brows and giggles.

"I just remembered, even if it was poisoned, then it would not affect me. Poison doesn't harm a Goddess." She bursts into laughter and I feel as if I could throw up all over the fuzzy black rug under my bare feet.

"I'm sorry, did you say, Goddess?" My voice comes out a squeak as I grip the black fabric over my legs. It's then I realize I'm wearing a long black dress with a slit up to my thigh and sleeves that fall off my shoulders that are attached to a sweetheart neckline. I cross my arms over my chest and look around wildly.

"Where the hell are my clothes?" Panic sets in. *Who dressed me?* She just sighs and waves her hand dismissively.

"What you were wearing isn't fitting for a woman of your power." She says sweetly before standing and waving for me to follow her. Unsure of any other options, I walk behind her and notice she is also barefoot. She reaches a pair of gray double doors and pushes them open. We step onto a covered patio surrounded by a stunning garden that is alive even in the dark of night. There is a fountain with water spraying from the mouth of a winged horse in the middle of the path and I have to remind myself to close my mouth as I gawk at the sight.

Varying flowers line the garden, but I can't put a name to their bright and colorful petals. We walk along a smooth sand pathway, with lightning bugs dancing around us in the cool night air. She guides me to a bench, and I marvel up at the beauty of the moon. It's nearly three times as big as it should be and shining so brightly that everything is aglow.

"You may call me Selene." She says. I sit down much less elegantly than she does, basically falling into my seat. *The Selene?*

"Do you have questions for me?" she gently prompts, raising her delicate black eyebrows.

"Are you the one who gave me the power to make portals?" I ask quietly, still so confused.

"Yes. Uriel came to me when he had the prophecy. A baby girl born into a world she would one day save. A war that wasn't her own with the help of her soulmate." She sighs sadly, shaking her head. "Mary was such a strong woman, but no mother should have that fear so early on. It broke me when I could not be with her in a time that she needed me most. Knowing what you would inevitably one day face. Yet she still ensured you a normal life, full of good and love. She raised an incredibly strong woman." she says, holding her hand out as a moth lands on her finger tip.

I open and close my mouth, my chest aching at the thought of my mother. But something feels off here, like I should be somewhere else.

"How did I get here? And where are we?" I ask. Images flash through my mind. *Mammon. The rage. The agony I felt as I held somebody in my arms. Who was it?* I grip my head, dizziness making the world tilt.

"Slow down. Your mind is trying to protect you so it may take some time for everything to clarify. Just take slow and deep breaths." She rubs my shoulder and tilts her head while I try to stop my brain from scrambling.

"Your subconscious seems to have created a place in your own mind to protect you. It was like one of those odd human sensory deprivation tanks. Pulling you out was no simple task, mind you. Larissa, you were content to stay there while your body withered away. After watching for nearly two weeks, I had to do something. Even if we aren't supposed to intervene," she throws her hair back over her shoulder "Uriel sure helped you harness Heaven's Fire when Blaine died." she mutters, rolling her eyes.

"Blaine, he's okay? I remember the castle. It was falling apart." My whole world was falling apart because of Mammon. I cover my mouth and wrap an arm around my waist, digging my nails into the fabric as my heart beats faster.

"Blaine is alive and physically healed." She says.

"Elaine is gone," my voice breaks. Selene holds up a handkerchief, waving her hand and producing a small table with a tray of two steaming mugs and assorted teas lying on top. I take the slip of fabric from her stare down at it as droplets hit the fabric, spreading out while more tears pour from my eyes.

"We are in my realm. I brought you to my home as you healed. It appears your mate is not fond of my decision. At least I left him a note," she groans, rolling her eyes as she prepares us each a cup. I take the steaming mug in my hands, watching as the contents shake and tremble. Selene frowns at me and sits her cup back down without taking a drink.

"Elaine is gone from earth, but she gave her life to save you. She wouldn't want you to feel all this pain, darling." She whispers, trying to be comforting. I give a bitter laugh and drink from my cup.

"Then she shouldn't have done it. She shouldn't have jumped in front of me." I snap, slamming the cup back down. I want to scream. None of this is fair.

"My darling girl, I wish I could ease your heartache." she says, reaching out to tuck a strand of hair behind my ear. I jerk away, standing up to turn towards the moon. Fighting to calm my nerves and slow my flood of emotions before I lose control again. *Elaine taking her last breath in my lap. Mammon kneeling in front of me as the earth shatters. A blinding light and explosion that faded to an icy darkness.*

"I remember." My throat stings as I suck in a breath. Selene stands beside me and takes my hand in hers.

"You are still so broken and the path ahead of you will not be an easy one, but I will be there to guide you. I wish I could have been there sooner. Mammon is still alive, darling. There was a traitor within, and you must be ready for what is coming." Selene's voice is steady while she squeezes my hand tightly. She scrunches her brow, staring over my shoulder.

"We are going to have to finish this another day. It's time for me to take you back." She says quickly, gripping my arm and pulling me down the path.

"Wait, I still have questions!" I say, yanking my arm free. She blows out an annoyed breath and puts her hands on her hips, giving me a disappointed parental look.

"I know you do, but I brought you here to heal, and you have. Blaine has caused an uproar and Uriel will be banging at my door soon if I do not return you." She snorts and shakes her head.

"Angels are such obnoxiously obtuse creatures with all their rules. If he wasn't so delicious, he would be a nuisance." She says thoughtfully and my face pinches. She looks around as thunder rumbles and throws her hands up.

"Just try to be patient!" She yells into the sky and stomps her foot. "Give me your hand and try to calm your mind." She says, taking my hand before I can move. I close my eyes and sigh.

"There's so many questions that you can answer," I say, and there's a moment of silence before she pulls her hand from mine. Selene is gone when I open my eyes.

Suddenly, I'm staring at my mother's painting on the wall of the dining room. Above our table, at our home in Nephal. I hear something hit the floor in the kitchen behind me, shattering as the pieces scatter across the floor. Whipping around, I lock eyes with Blaine. Coffee is splattered across the floor and on his plaid pajama bottoms that hang loosely on his hips. His beard is longer and there are dark circles under his eyes. I can't help but admire his bare chest that holds new scars, sculpted from stone and not moving as he holds his breath.

"Larissa," He breathes out my name, a prayer on his lips that I'm real. I nod once, watching him stride over the broken coffee mug as he gets chest to chest with me. I wait for him to touch me, my entire body frozen in place. Breathing deep, I inhale his familiar scent of smoke and spice. He smells like *home*. I slowly look up to him and his nostrils are flared. Blaine's eyes are wide and he presses his lips into a thin line.

"A note. You were in a coma for two weeks, then you up and vanished the moment I left and all I got was a note." His voice is low, full of fear and rage.

"Selene said she left you a note," I say, understanding what he means. Blaine pulls a creased piece of purple parchment from his pocket, the edges worn as if it has been opened and folded dozens of times. He holds it out to me and I take it, noticing he ensures our fingers don't touch before taking a step back. The sting of rejection hurts, but I unfold the note.

"*She will return once her soul has found its way home. You cannot help her this time. Be patient.*" Blaine quips before I can even read the brief letter. *That wasn't very helpful here, Selene.*

"She couldn't have given a better explanation?" I complain, folding the note back up and holding it out to him. He takes it and throws it aside, pressing his chest to mine and backing me into the wall. Feeling his body against mine sends a flush down my neck and I struggle to focus on him.

"Why did you leave?" His voice is just barely more than a growl, and I roll my eyes at him.

"It's not like I had a choice, Blaine. Selene basically kidnapped me," I huff and he curls his lip.

"Glad to see your soul found your body." He snaps. I thought he would be happy to see me. His agitation reverberates through the bond, but there is something else.

"Nice dress," He whispers, dragging his fingers up the bare skin from my knee to my thigh. He shoves his fingers under the fabric and pushes higher up to my hip. I have to fight the excited shiver that crawls up my spine at his touch.

"Selene is a Goddess who apparently doesn't like my choice in clothing," I say, my voice just a breath as he digs his fingers into my bare hip.

"When I left you in our bed, you had my shirt and sweats on. I got out of the shower and the clothes were laying on the floor and you were gone." He hisses.

"I didn't leave you on purpose, Blaine." I whispered, cupping his cheek. The stubble scratches my palm as he leans into my touch.

"You were gone. I begged you to come back to me, but I couldn't save you." His voice breaks and the rage falls away. I throw my arms around his neck, burying my face in his shoulder.

"You are wrong, Blaine. Selene told you I would return when my soul found its way home. You are my home." I whisper, pressing a kiss to his neck. He takes a shaking breath before gripping my thighs and lifting me up to wrap my legs around his hips. I giggle while he peppers my chin and cheeks with his kisses.

"No panties and no bra. You knew I wouldn't be able to hold back for long. That's playing dirty." He groans into my mouth, and I chuckle. Reaching between us, I rub across the bulge in the front of his pants. Blaine sighs, pressing me harder into the wall as he grinds against me.

"I could take you here and now." He stills, groaning in agitation, "Fuck, we need our own place, Angel." Blaine huffs while letting my feet down. I open my mouth to ask him what is wrong when Adrian comes down the stairs.

"Piper wants to try a new tracking spell so I need you to grab something from her room and we can try again." Adrian's voice is full of exhaustion as he walks past us into the kitchen. Blaine cups my cheek and kisses the crease in my bow.

"I hate to see you hurting. It wasn't all your fault, you know?" He smiles, trying to cheer me up.

"What are you talking about, Blaine? Let's get a move on."

153

Adrian stops behind us and meets my eyes over Blaine's shoulder as he steps aside, waving to me "I found her." Adrian stares at me and looks down at my gown, then back to my face. He looks so confused and relieved at the same time. I step to him and he opens his arms, crushing me in a hug as he takes in a shaking breath.

"Larissa, you were gone. Piper couldn't find you. I thought you were gone." He keeps repeating as if he is in shock that I'm here. A familiar ache builds in my chest as I realize how scared they all have been. Blaine calls up the stairs, "You should probably get down here."

Piper thunders down the steps with her tiny feet and I nearly laugh until she slams into me. It catches me off guard and Adrian barely catches us as she sobs into my chest while crushing me with unnatural strength for her size. I awkwardly pat her sides, struggling since she has my arms pinned. Asmodeus stands on the steps, just watching us. He nods to me, then looks down at her with a sad smile.

"Hey, long time no see, I suppose?" I chuckle, fighting my own tears. She snaps her face to mine, glaring at me through angry red-rimmed eyes.

"Where could you have gone that I couldn't find you?" She snaps and I sigh, grabbing her in a hug.

"It's a lot to explain. For me, it only feels as if I have been gone for a few hours." I whisper, and she pulls back, searching my face in confusion.

"I think we should all sit down and hear what she has to say." Levi says, walking up to me. His eyes are bloodshot and his clothes are rumpled as if he has slept in them. I step around Piper and grab him in a tight hug.

"I'm sorry," I whisper. He clings to me and presses his cheek to the top of my head.

"You are home now. That is all that matters." He breathes. I nod as I step back and twist my hands.

"So, the Goddess Selene actually took me while I was still unconscious." I start. Piper's eyes widen and Asmodeus' eyebrows draw together. Levi blows a breath and pulls out a chair, motioning for me to take a seat.

"I'll make a fresh pot of coffee," he says, frowning down at the broken mug and coffee stain.

"I'll grab a broom." Blaine chuckles, walking into the kitchen with him.

Chapter 29 - Blaine

Larissa stares into her mug like she is afraid to hear what we all think about her meeting with Selene. Levi keeps rubbing his face, not making eye contact, as if there is something he wants to say. Adrian has noticed it as well and keeps glancing at him, Larissa and him share a look. Not wanting to push the subject, I just ignore it.

"I didn't get to say goodbye to Elaine." Larissa's voice breaks. I take her hand in mine and rub the pad of my thumb across it for comfort.

"It was beautiful. You would have loved the dress Blaine chose for her. It was a purple one, with flowers stitched along the bottom. We said goodbye for you and asked her to kick your ass back to us if she found you." Piper says, biting her lip as tears well up. A tear rolls down Larissa's cheek even as she smiles at her.

"I gave her two bundles before the fire was lit. One was from you, so I twisted one of your hair ties around it." I shrug. Larissa's lips fall open, and I can feel the gratitude soar through her.

"Thank you so much," She swipes at her eyes and turns to Levi. "What about Mark? How is he?" She asks. Mark told Elaine that when they got out of there, he was going to marry her. Piper leans into Asmodeus, as he pulls her into his lap to wrap his arms around her shaking shoulders.

"He begged us to burn him with her. After all this time, he finally gave her the ring that he was going to propose with." Adrian says, staring down at the table. Larissa covers her mouth, and I can see the guilt reflected in her eyes.

"If Elaine knew you were sitting here and blaming yourself for her death, then she would be crushed, Angel." My

156

voice is low as I lean close to her, rubbing her back. Adrian nods, a serious look on his face.

"Did you try to kill yourself, Larissa?" Adrian asks her, and my entire body tenses. Larissa gives him an incredulous look and he puts his hands up in a surrender.

"All I'm saying is when Mammon told you that you would die, you didn't react. It seemed like you were perfectly fine with that outcome." He raises his brow. I know she can feel my fear as it flows through the bond, and she reaches out to take one of my hands without making eye contact.

"In that moment, I willing to pay the price if it meant killing Mammon." Her words are bitter and honest. I grip her chin and yank her face to look up into mine.

"It wasn't just you that would have to pay the price, Larissa. If you die, then my soul will fade until there is nothing left. I can't lose you." I struggle to speak through my clenched jaw. Larissa's mouth opens, but before she can say a word, there is a knock at the front door. Levi walks away to answer it and I strain to listen.

"What are you doing here?" He asks in an unfriendly manner.

"We heard Larissa was missing, just wanted to see if you needed anything, old friend. That is all." A deep voice says. I don't bother to hide the look of disgust that curls my lip when I recognize who it is before they even walk in behind Levi.

Emery Saint is wearing a white pressed dress shirt tucked into black slacks, the shoulders too tight. My rage wells up inside just from looking at him.

"I thought you were missing?" He asks oddly, tilting his head as he stares at Larissa. His wife Jane is standing beside him and peering between the two of us with curiosity. Larissa stands up and squares her shoulders, facing him.

"Why does a coward like you give a shit if I'm missing? Not like you would help find me. You who hides in your safe little bubble while your son goes off and puts his life on the line." She sneers at him.

"Larissa," Levi snaps at her, but she doesn't back down. Emery's eyes have become slits and his hands are now balled into tight fists at his side.

"You should learn your place, girl. Before somebody puts you in it. From what I have heard, Elaine is dead because of your little suicide mission." he says in a calm voice. Larissa laughs, throwing her head back before snapping back to glare at him. My hands tremble as I stand behind her, reminding him that she is not alone.

"Watch your words, Mr. Saint." Adrian's voice is a low threat. Larissa puts her hand up, stopping him as he advances towards Emery.

"You should be fucking embarrassed to show your face. Don't you dare tell me to learn my place when you don't even deserve your seat amongst the council. And *never* say her name, ever again." Larissa's words are dripping with venom as she speaks. Something dark and twisted crawls through the bond, and I can feel the excitement it brings Larissa.

He steps towards her, and I'm between them in an instant. My shoulders rise and fall as I struggle to take measured deep breaths. My fingers flick and Emery gets nervous, as the shadows dance around him. Jane backs up with concern on her face. She opens her mouth then closes it, shrinking away without saying a word.

"She can run her mouth but needs her half breed to protect her?" Emery scoffs. I grin and shake my head, opening my hands as I stand between them.

"She doesn't *need* anyone to protect her. But I'll be damned if I stand back and let you lay a finger on what is mine. I'll rip your heart from your chest with my hands while it still beats if you ever step to her again, Emery Saint." My voice is a deep rumbling, and the chill in the room is making everyone nervous. He needs to know that I'm not fucking around.

"You are going to let him speak to me this way, Levi? Have you no control over the strays you bring into your home?" Emery turns to him in a fit. But Levi just crosses his arms and cocks an eyebrow up.

"You have a point, old friend. Forgive me, Emery, for not having more control of my home." He says, apologetically. I can feel Larissa's shock as Levi walks up to stand beside him and holds out his hand to shake. Emery takes it with a smug smile before grimacing as Levi grips his hand tightly.

"Get out of my house. We will vote to replace you this evening." Levi nearly spits the words, rage twisting his typically peaceful expression. Jane is already running for the front door, giving me and Larissa an apologetic look over her shoulder. I rub my face in irritation as the door slams behind them.

"You want to explain what that was?" Adrian asks, calm once again with a smirk on his face. Asmodeus has a tight grip on a very pissed off Piper, who is holding a butter knife in her shaking hand. Larissa raises her eyebrows at her, and she drops it with a huff.

"He struck a nerve, okay?" She whines. Asmodeus squints and reaches into his pocket to pull out a folded piece of yellow paper.

"You think it is him?" Levi says to him.

"Can somebody explain?" Larissa waves her hand towards them.

"This letter was stuck in the door a few days ago. Here, take a look." Asmodeus says, handing it to her. She takes the stiff parchment and unfolds it, wrinkling her nose at the sour smell.

"*A traitor remains, within plain sight.*" She reads it out loud.

"When Piper held it, she had a vision. A nephilim betrayed us and told one of Mammon's underlings our rescue plans. She couldn't see his face, just the black mask we all wore." Asmodeus explains as Larissa drops back to her seat.

"Marley had a gut feeling, and she was right," She whispers, shaking her head. "Just like Bertha. What happens if Emery drops the barrier? Selene told me Mammon still wasn't dead." she snarls. Asmodeus takes the note and sighs, flopping down into his chair and staring at the ceiling as if it holds the answers.

"There is something else. When we were in the throne room, I tripped over a body. It was Bertha." She confesses. Levi looks at her in surprise, "Are you sure?" He asks. She nods and he pinches the bridge of his nose.

"Then I should tell you, we found Marcy. They locked her in a cell near Elaine's. Even after her parents' betrayal, we couldn't just leave without her. Adrian saw Dominic get struck down as well. Marcy has lost both of her parents." Levi waits for her to react. It is a struggle to keep her face calm, but jealousy rears its ugly head.

"She was in terrible shape, Angel." I say, rubbing her arm.

"So, could she be the traitor?" Larissa asks, a little hopeful. Levi shakes his head.

"No, she isn't even coherent, and it looks like she was being tortured for quite some time. We won't know anything until she is stable enough to question, but for now, she is innocent." Levi paces. Even her distaste for Marcy has its bounds, and I can see the sympathy she feels for the poor girl.

"It's time I reach out to some of my brothers. We will need their help." Asmodeus says. My anxiety spikes as I rub a hand over my face and bite back a groan at the idea.

"You know I would not summon him if I did not have the need to." Asmodeus says and I give a defeated sigh.

"I just had this hope that Larissa would never have to be in his presence." The admission slips out before I can stop it. Larissa stands up and comes to me, wrapping her arms around my waist and resting her chin on my chest.

"I'll zap him. Just say the word." She mumbles and I finally smile, shaking my head at her as I press a kiss to her forehead.

"You are my heart." I tell her, getting lost in the beauty of her smile, the spark of life in her green eyes and gently tuck a strand of dark hair behind her ear. Adrian blows out a breath, and walks over to Levi.

"We can't stay here." He says and everyone turns to them. Levi nods and begins pulling his boots on.

"Wait, are you saying we have to leave? Why?" Larissa

turns to them in confusion.

"If the traitor opens the ward and allows another attack like last time, we wont survive again." Adrian says. She shakes her head and steps forward to grab her sneakers and shoves her feet inside. "Or we can get rid of the traitors and save everyone the trouble." She tells us, as if it's the obvious choice. Levi puts his hand on her arm to stop her, but she yanks back from him.

"We cannot just declare ourselves as executioners, Larissa. Slow down." He says in a placating tone, but she just gives him a stupefied look.

"He betrayed us and got Elaine killed. You would expect us to sit back while he runs everyone from their homes in fear?" I can feel the darkness rearing its head once again, and an uneasy feeling urges me to keep an eye on her. Adrian leans against the wall with his hands shoved into his pockets.

"We have to be logical. Are you telling me you could murder your friends' parents?" Adrian asks. Larissa finally stops and looks at her brother, shoulders sagging.

"At least let me come to the meeting. I want to talk to Jane." She is struggling and desperately wants to do *something* to ease her pain.

"She kept staring at you. It was like she was trying to send you her thoughts. It was a little creepy." Piper says. Levi grabs his jacket and heads for the door.

"Meet me at the Elder's Hall in half an hour." He says before ducking out and leaving us to all gather ourselves. Larissa turns to me, catching me watching her with a brow raised and arms crossed.

"You might wanna change before we go." Piper giggles as she walks off with Asmodeus to get ready. I'm right on her heels as she heads to our room. Once we step in, I kick the door shut behind us and she looks around the room with wide eyes. The bed is a mess with the sheets and pillows rumpled across it and her clothes are strewn everywhere. Embarrassment makes me nervous as I scratch at the back of my neck when she stares at me, openmouthed.

"Might have gone a little crazy looking for any clues of where you went." I shrug. She muffles her laughter by pulling her dress off over her head as she steps away from me, towards the shower. My eyes drag down every inch of her as I follow, as if I'm pulled by a tether.

"You will take my breath away until the day I die, Angel." Her nickname falls as a prayer from my lips. She giggleswhile turning on the hot water. I have to restrain myself from reaching out to grab the round curve of her ass and grunt as if it physically pains me.

"What is your issue?" She asks, glancing back at me as I close my eyes and tilt my head back.

"I can't believe I'm going to ruin this," I groan before gently pushing her into the shower. She frowns when I cast my clothes aside and step in with her.

"What were you thinking when you said we should go after Emery?" I ask, and she shrugs while lathering shampoo into her scalp.

"I was mad and let it get the best of me." Is all she says. I grab a washcloth and begin scrubbing her shoulders with a gentle massage that has her humming happily.

"I felt it, through the bond. Something that wasn't just anger. It was pure bloodlust and excitement. Larissa, it felt like darkness." I sigh, my hands stilling as she turns to look up at me. I'm genuinely concerned, and she becomes irritated with me.

"You think I wanted to murder for fun?" She rolls her eyes, "Blaine, he is a coward and has put the lives of everyone I love in danger." I study her for a moment before nodding and dropping it. When she raises up onto her toes and presses her slick body against mine, all reason washes down the drain.

Chapter 30 - Larissa

It's early evening when we walk into the conference room and take our seats. I hold my head high, even as everyone stares at us. Emery's face is bright red and I'm curious if he is grinding his teeth down to the gums. Marley gives me a small smile and I frown, noticing the huge burn mark that has started healing on her cheek.

"Now that everyone is here, I'd like to begin the meeting." My father begins, standing at the front of the room. I glance across the table at Mark and my heart throbs painfully at the sight. His eyes are puffy and unfocused as he rubs something between his fingers on the table. *It's one of Elaine's ribbons that she wore in her hair.* I glance back to where Emery sits and my eyes lock onto Jane. She flicks her eyes to the clock nervously, then back at me.

"We should exile them," Mark's quiet voice pulls me back into the conversation. I stare wide eyed up at him as he slowly stands.

"Mark, I'm not sure-" Levi begins and Marley holds her hand up.

"Let him speak. He has the right to explain himself." Marley says and nods for Mark to continue. He clears his throat and looks down at the ribbon between his fingers before looking at me while he speaks.

"He was the one who came up with the majority of our plan to rescue Elaine. When the time came, he was too afraid. Afraid to do the job of a nephilim." He says, his voice becoming angrier. He turns to Emery and shakes his head.

"You were a coward and Elaine paid the price, along with other nephilim and witches. You let all of us down that day. Your own son nearly died saving his friend." He snaps before it looks as if all the energy leaves his body, and he drops into his chair. I close my eyes and swallow hard, trying to keep my emotions in check.

"Elaine essentially killed herself, Mark. You want my family exiled, but I wasn't the one who imprisoned her. I wasn't the one that spilled her blood, nor was I the reason she was taken. Mammon tried to kill Larissa, and Elaine saved her life by sacrificing her own. It's crystal clear to me that the person to blame in this room is not myself." He slams his fists on the table and stares at me. I stand suddenly, kicking my chair over backwards as I do.

"Are you so stupid that you truly believe you're innocent?" I seethe. The lights flicker above us. My power tingles through my fingers, even as I fight to keep it down. A lightbulb in the chandelier above us bursts, sprinkling glass onto the table and Marley lets out a low whistle. Jane is looking at me with uncertainty and I can feel the tension rising in the room.

"There she is. The monster who couldn't control her power in Hell. You killed a little witch during your last fit, but you didn't know that, did you? Everyone here would rather cradle their *princess* instead of hurting her feelings by telling the truth." He says with a smug smile. Confusion locks me in place as I process what he said. Blaine storms past me to grab Emery by the front of his shirt and yank him from his chair.

"You're lying," I say, taking a step back.

"I should save us all the trouble and kill you myself," Blaine says. He's not as tall as Emery, but Blaine isn't the one flinching away. Emery has genuine fear in his eyes. Levi steps in, separating them as he casts a concerned glance back at me. That one look was all the confirmation I needed. *I killed an innocent.* Nausea wracks my body as I stagger back towards the door.

"Go on, Mark. Tell her how she killed two people that day." Emery says. I look over at him, covering my mouth with a hand. Mark's eyes meet mine with sympathy and he shakes his head without saying a word.

"Larissa, Adrian, and Blaine should leave. We obviously will not make any progress, since Emery cannot be a mature adult." Marley snaps and sits back in her chair, crossing her arms. Levi tries to say something to me, but I turn and sprint for the door. Adrian attempts to grab my arm, but I shove away from him and use myself as a portal.

When I drop to the yard behind our house, I sit up and wrap my arms around my legs and hug my body tight. *I'm a monster, Emery is right.* The thought burns into my mind as I stare at Elaine's flowers, even as they blur through the well of tears. This house doesn't feel like home without her, and I decide that I can't stay here anymore. Everyone around me is in danger. I stand on shaking legs and stagger towards the door until Blaine leaps from the shadows and clutches me to his chest.

"You aren't fucking leaving me again," Blaine growls into my ear before pulling back to stare at me. His nostrils flare and his jaw clenches tight.

"What are you talking about?" I hiccup and try to pull myself together. He shakes his head and points to my heart, then to his.

"You were scared and hurting. Then suddenly you had this cold and calm resolve. I'm not an idiot, Larissa." he says, taking my hand in his and pulling me to the house. I jerk on his hold, stopping us both as he glares down at me.

"It's true?" My lip quivers, but my voice is steady. I didn't need to ask, I already know. But I need him to be honest with me more than anything. Blaine sighs and his eyes close. I just wait for a few moments until he opens them and looks at me.

"She was weak and already badly injured. When you lost control, she was caught in the ripple of energy that came from your power. It knocked her into one column, which buckled and crashed down onto her. By the time I pulled her out, she was already gone." He says the last words quietly and looks off into the distance. A pang of guilt and sorrow comes from him and echoes the one I feel.

"Oh no," my voice is barely above a whisper as my knees

give out. Blaine catches me as I fall and kneels to the ground. He holds me tight to his chest as I break down. My sobs shake us both as a scream rips through my throat, leaving me gasping for air. Blaine strokes my hair, rocking me in his lap and keeping a tight grip around my waist.

I hear the back door swing open and somebody runs over beside us.

"What happened?" Piper asks in a worried voice. I can't speak, only shake my head and sob into Blaine's shoulder. His shirt is becoming damp with my open-mouthed crying, but he doesn't seem to care.

"She knows," Adrian says as I hear him run up to us. I dig my nails into Blaine's back as I struggle to breathe. Piper *tsks* before brushing my hair back and trying to look at me, but I bury my face into the crook of Blaine's neck. I can't let them look at me with pity, when I'm the murderer.

"I'm going to go brew some tea. Her throat is going to need it." She says quietly, patting my back before walking away. I hiccup as the tears slow, but the pain in my heart doesn't lessen. Blaine helps me stand, gently pushing me into my brothers' arms. Adrian throws his arm around my shoulder and guides me inside. My head pounds and I'm clutching my elbows so tightly my hands ache.

"I just want to lie down," my voice is a broken whisper. Piper pushes a steaming mug into Blaine's open hands. He takes it and nods towards the living room.

"I can't believe none of you told me. Emery had to tell me." I say bitterly. Piper looks at the ground, hurt by my tone, and I feel even more guilty for lashing out.

"Emery has done what he wished to accomplish. He rattled you and caused pain." Asmodeus says. Just then, an envelope appears out of thin air in a puff of smoke and lands in his open hand. I blink rapidly, thinking I'm seeing things, but he sighs and tears it open.

"Why do they all insist on this form of communication when cell phones exist?" Asmodeus grumbles while reading down the page.

"Blaine," He begins, looking up at him with a frown and nods once. Blaine groans and drops his head backwards.

"What is it?" I ask.

"Asmodeus asked for back up and apparently he got it." He says with an attitude. I scrunch my brow and he looks at me.

"My father," he says. My brow rises as I look between him and Asmodeus. "Is that a good idea?" I ask quietly. Blaine puts his arm around my shoulder and kisses my cheek.

"I'll be on my best behavior. No matter how he pushes my buttons, Angel." He says comfortingly. Shaking my head, I stare down at my black sneakers.

"I meant me, since I tried to kill his brother. I couldn't even kill the right person, but I tried." My voice breaks and Piper walks up to take my hands in her own.

"Sweetheart, nobody blames you. What happened was an accident, that's all." She reassures me. Her voice is sweet, and I so badly want to believe her. *But she is wrong, I blame me.*

"We don't think of each other as brothers typically, Larissa. We all have aligned ourselves differently between Heaven and Hell. When the war began, some ran to hide, others took a chance for power and then some chose to just stay out of the way." Asmodeus says. I stare absentmindedly at the floor, letting my mind spiral down a dark path. Blaine tips my chin up to look at him. He frowns and takes my hand, pulling me through the house and out the back door. He only stops to grab our jackets as we leave and tosses mine to me once we are standing in the yard.

Chapter 31 - Larissa

"What is it?" I ask, shivering as I pull my thick black sweatshirt on. He cracks his neck across from me and takes on a fighting stance. Blaine points to my waistband as I stare at him. I look down at the dagger and back at him.

"Take out your dagger. We are going to work on focusing your energy again. You could use the distraction." He tells me. I drag it out, then shake my head at him.

"No, I can't." My voice wavers as I try to picture the girl's face and fail. Blaine runs at me, pulling his own solid black dagger from his pocket and swiping at my legs. I leap back in surprise and nearly trip over Elaine's small flower bed.

"What are you thinking, Blaine? Knock it off, I said I can't!" I snap at him, annoyed at almost ruining Elaine's beautiful flowers. He gives me a predatory grin and drops into the shadows.

"*Shit*," I blow out a breath and jog through the yard, watching every shadow as I wait for him. The evening sun is giving him plenty of options, putting me at a disadvantage. Feeling his rush of excitement, I realize a moment too late. *I was watching every shadow, except my own.* Blaine leaps from behind me and slams me to the ground. We roll and I see the flash of his dagger as he brings it to my neck. On instinct, I bring mine up just in time to block him. But he is stronger and lands on top of me.

He uses his blade to press into mine, closer to my throat. I am panting and pushing upward with all my force, to no avail. Blaine isn't struggling in the least bit.

"Get off, Blaine!" I huff out, but he just shakes his head and shoves downward. The blade of my dagger brushes my throat when I swallow hard. He leans his face close to mine and whispers.

"What will you do now, Angel? How can you get out of this without hurting me?" He asks. I take a breath and focus my power on my hands. My hand snaps up to grab his arm, letting my dagger slip against my throat. He pulls back, giving me just enough room to get my feet between us and press them to his chest. Channeling my energy into my legs in a split second, I shove him backwards. The momentary contact sends my power sparking through him. The smell of electricity fills the air as he flies backwards and lands on his ass.

"Blaine!" I jump up and run over to him. But he stands up and smiles proudly at me while dusting himself off.

"You put a little more power into that and you can do some serious damage. Controlled damage." He says, cupping my cheek. He tilts my head and frowns down at my neck. I reach up to touch my throat, smudging a drop of blood across my fingertips.

"It's not even a scratch, Blaine." I grumble. He sighs and lays his forehead to mine.

"I may ask you not to hold back, but hurting you makes me sick to my soul." He whispers. I take a deep breath and lean back to look him in the eyes.

"Controlled damage. Instead of going full nuclear."

"You can do it, Angel. I know you can."

"Then why don't we try to practice with no weapons?" I offer, admitting that this is exactly what I needed. Blaine gives a reluctant nod. I drop my dagger into the ground, letting it pierce the dirt, and he does the same. Before Blaine moves, I slam my palms to his chest and throw him off balance with what I intended to be a slight shock. He stares at me in surprise as I dance away from him.

"Why do you look so *shocked*?" I smirk at my pun and he gives me a dry look.

"I'm spanking your ass when I catch you for that horrible joke." He says, and I wag my eyebrows at him, holding my arms out.

"You have to catch me firs-" I don't finish before he snaps his wings out and takes off running towards me. *Okay, that is so not fair.* He leaps into the air and circles above, taunting me. "Poor, wingless, Angel. Maybe I should have nicknamed you Dodo." He shrugs.

Watching him closely, I bite my lip while I weigh the risk of what I'm about to do. He realizes I'm plotting something and stops circling, bobbing in place while watching me like a hawk. Dancing on the balls of my feet, I build my courage before just going for it. I run underneath him while he twists to follow my movement. But I'm not under him by the time he turns, instead I'm dropping on top of him from portaling.

He snatches me in his arms and gives a boisterous laugh as he bobs under my sudden weight. "You actually got me, Angel." He grins at me with pride, and I give him a wink.

"Are you saying I *got the drop on you?*" I laugh as he groans and shakes his head. He tosses me up into the air and I scream, my arms and legs wheeling in the open air. He catches me easily and stays aloft, moving higher into the air.

"Should have let you fall for that," He warns me, wrapping my legs around his waist. I lay my head on his shoulder and grip his neck as the cool air makes my nose burn. A sudden smack on my ass nearly has me jumping from his arms with a cry of surprise. Pulling back, I stare at him in disbelief. My ass stings from the hard slap and he raises his brow. "You had fair warning that you were getting spanked. Don't look at me like that. We are supposed to be training." He grumbles, grabbing my ass in his hands and burying his face in my chest.

"You're distracting me." He mumbles into my boobs, and I watch as my laughter makes his head bounce. Deciding to press my luck, I clear my throat and fidget in his arms. Blaine pulls back and looks at me, expecting me to say something.

Grabbing both of his arms, I shock him. Blaine grunts and loosens his grip enough for me to propel myself away from him.

"Larissa!" He yells in panic, diving to grab me. But I just smile and swing my hands, opening a portal beneath me in the air. Without taking the speed that I'm falling into consideration, which is a big mistake. I drop out about six feet off the ground and land on my side with a hard *thump.* The squeak that escapes me is demeaning as I roll sideways and quickly get to my feet. Blaine dives and skids across the dirt with a look of rage.

"You could've gotten hurt!" He shouts at me. Struggling to put pressure on my throbbing hip, I wave him off.

"Stop worrying, I'm fine. Come and get your ass kicked." I bluff. He crosses his arms and watches me.

"I don't enjoy hurting you, but knocking you on your ass is tempting." He snarls and begins striding towards me, like a predator hunting its prey. I keep my eyes on him until the shadows all pulse towards him. He isn't playing around. A chill cuts through my pants as shadows crawl up my body. He uses them to bind me in place.

I try to swat them away, but my hands brush through them like black fog. They cling to my skin and yank my hands together. He stalks up to me as I blow out a frustrated breath. Blaine's eyes are black and even his skin has taken an ashy tone.

"Well, that's new." I mumble, and he gives me a half smile. *Holy shit, even his fangs are longer.* Fighting against the shadows is pointless until an idea hits me. Pulling my static forward, it sparks across my skin like thin armor. The shadows recede as I push harder.

Sweat breaks out across my brow and I struggle when he fights back. Yanking my hands free, I swing my palm up and throw a ball of electricity at him. It slams into his shoulder, making him flinch. I do it again, but harder this time and he staggers back a step. The third time he throws his hand up, deflecting it with a shield of shadows.

I roll my eyes, but Blaine stills. His shadows melt away as he stares up with brows pinched. Following his line of sight, we watch as the sparking ball swings high into the air and drops, fizzling as it does. He pulls his phone out and rapidly taps the screen with his thumb. When he gets close, he hooks an arm around my waist and launches us into the air. I wrap my arms around him, flinching as my sore hip protests. Blaine presses the phone to his ear as he searches the grounds for *something*.

"Ask Piper to check the barrier." he says, and the color drains from his face as he nods, "We will be there in one minute. It's time to go." Blaine hangs up, shoving the phone back into his pocket.

"What was that about?" I ask, worrying as he dives towards my balcony and carefully lands.

"We need to pack light," is all that he says, swinging the door open and grabbing two duffel bags from under my bed. *Where the Hell did those even come from?* Waving a hand at my dresser, he tosses them onto the bed. I throw my hands in the air and don't move. He steps around me and starts packing the bag with my clothes for me.

"Larissa, I need you to trust me. We don't have time. Somebody broke the wards, and we need to leave." He tells me. A chill covers my skin as I move to help him, my body on autopilot while my mind races.

"Why can't we just put them back up?" I ask and he shakes his head, running from the bathroom with our toiletries.

"It's not that easy, and Mammon already knows where we are. What if they just tear it back down? It's time to get out of here, Asmodeus warned your father."

We stop as sirens blare. Short chirps echo through the city in warning, and we look at each other with a nod. *They're telling everyone to evacuate or find shelter.* I grab my bag and Blaine takes his, running down the stairs. Everyone is gathering in the living room. Adrian throws the door open and Ella sprints in. He grabs her in a tight hug and before the door swings shut, I see people running down the street together.

Blaine takes off towards his room to gather more clothes and I drop my bag on the floor. Going through the kitchen, I pull out all the food that won't expire and begin shoving it into a book bag that was in the laundry room. I stumble across a coffee can stuffed full of Elaine's emergency money and a letter folded neatly inside. Saying a silent prayer to thank Elaine for still looking out for us, I shove it into my bag. An ache builds as I realize this may be the last time I'll be in the home we shared. The bookbag hangs limp in my hands while I stare at her apron. It's hanging beside the sink, exactly where she left it.

Blaine reaches past me and grabs it gently, folding it and putting it inside his bag. "She's coming with us, Angel. Don't worry." He whispers in my ear as he presses a quick kiss to my cheek. I nod and turn to see the worried faces of everyone. Asmodeus looks pissed and Piper is gripping his hand so tightly I fear she may hurt the big guy.

Chapter 32 - Blaine

"So, what happens now?" Larissa asks and everyone looks at each other. I reluctantly step forward and pull out my phone, tapping on the screen. "I'm sending you all the GPS coordinates. We gather here, hide out until we come up with a more permanent solution."

"Stay in groups of at least two if we get separated. It should only take an hour to get there. It's an old safe house, isn't it?" Adrian asks me, and I nod once. Levi and Mark burst in through the front door. Mark is carrying a large pack and Levi goes to his room without a word. He comes back a moment later carrying his own duffel bag and Larissa raises a brow.

"You pack fast." she comments, and he shakes his head with a small smile. "What you are telling me is that you don't keep an emergency bag packed at all times? Looks like I still have some things to teach you, after all." Levi smiles at her.

"Everyone in town is separating. Most are traveling to other Nephilim cities to seek asylum with their Elders, what is your plan here?" Levi asks and Adrian starts to fill him in. Mark steps up and grabs Larissa in a quick and tight embrace as we all discuss options.

"You aren't a murderer, sweetheart. Elaine would not have lived if you, Adrian, or Blaine had died. You kids were her reason for living, so I know she is watching over you." His voice thick as he clears his throat.

"I killed a young girl who only came to help our people. Everything that happened down there is because of," I cut Larissa off by clapping my hand over her mouth and pulling her back against my chest.

"Because of a power-hungry bitch and her psychotic lap

dog." The words come out as a snarl. She closes her eyes and sighs against my palm. "He's spot on," Mark snorts and pats Larissa's arm. Levi walks towards the door and everyone follows.

"Sweet child." A voice whispers behind us. Larissa swings around, but nothing is there. I bump her with my elbow, making sure she stays with us.

"I'll see you again." I hear her whisper while swallowing down the lump in my throat. We step outside and Asmodeus scoops Piper up in his arms and she giggles, kissing his cheek. Adrian helps Ella secure her backpack and grips his own as he wraps arms around her.

"Are we flying the whole way?" Larissa asks with wide eyes. I throw the long strap across my body and adjust the duffel bag.

"We will fly for a while, take breaks as necessary. Piper has offered to cloak us for as long as she can." Asmodeus looks down at her with pride. She smiles back at him, then at Larissa, winking. I pull her against my chest and brush the hair away from her face.

"Everything will be okay." I promise her. Levi looks down at his phone and waves us all on. "I must ensure everyone else gets out safely. I will be right behind you."

Mark drops his bag and slaps him on the back, "You kids get a head start, you are going to need it." Without giving Larissa a chance to argue, I leap into the air with her wrapped around me. She tenses for just a moment until I slowly push us higher. Peering down, she sees her bag dangling from my hand and tries to take it. I jostle her and she throws her arms around my neck again, digging her nails in as she startles.

"Hands off. It's dangerous to interfere with the driver," I tell her in a mocking tone, kissing her neck.

"Can you two at least wait until you're out of sight?" Adrian calls. We look over to see Ella happily wrapped around him, with her head on his shoulder. She looks so blissful, and his tight grip on her tells me he feels the same way. My hand slides up Larissa's thigh to grip her ass as I lick her neck and make her squeal.

"You should be a better flier then, brother." I call out to Adrian and Larissa rolls her eyes. He looks like he is going to be sick, and Ella hides her face as she giggles into his neck. The cold air is much worse up here and Larissa shivers, pressing tight to me for warmth. The motion grinds her against me and I clutch her thighs, putting my mouth against her ear.

"You better stop all that wiggling," I warn. Larissa gives me a heated look and I nearly fall from the sky. "We can't land anytime soon, and *activities* aren't ideal up here with prying eyes."

Larissa bites her lip to unsuccessfully hide her laugh, shifting again as she locks her shimmering moss colored eyes onto me. I bury my face in her neck and huff out a groan. *This was going to be a long flight.*

#

After nearly half an hour of flying, Asmodeus motions for us to land and Larissa looks around in confusion. There are tons of trees here with no vacant place to land and I'm already cursing under my breath. I tuck Larissa against the crook of my neck as I turn and dive towards the ground. Her heart thunders against my chest as we drop, until I snap my wings out and we jerk backwards. The ache of ripping my wings out makes me grunt in pain. I easily weave between trees, protecting my passenger from branches. Her hands slip around my ribs, reaching back to massage where my wings are joined to my back and I suck in a sharp breath. As we hit the ground, she yanks her hand back.

"I didn't mean to hurt you," she says, frowning. "You didn't hurt me, but that spot is extremely sensitive." I explain, holding her hand as she stretches out her stiff legs. I can almost hear her mentally tucking away that little tidbit as she peers at me sideways. Asmodeus drops straight to the ground in front of us and his landing jostles the sleeping Piper in his arms. She yawns and stretches as he sits her down, smiling up at him.

"You were *sleeping*?" Larissa asks incredulously. She giggles and nods. "Yeah, I always get so comfortable that I fall asleep when we are flying. When I can't sleep at night, sometimes Asmodeus flies us around until I doze off." She says, and Larissa makes a fake gagging noise.

"Like a fussy infant during a car ride." I shake my head. Adrian snorts as he and Ella walk up to us. Piper's eyes shoot daggers in my direction before she turns to Larissa with her arms crossed.

"Asmodeus has some attractive friends that aren't mean like this one, if you're interested." She raises her brow, baiting me. I wrap my arms around Larissa, pulling her close to rest my chin on her head and give Piper a crooked grin.

"I'll rip the lungs from anyone who tries to share her air." I say nonchalantly. Adrian widens his eyes at the comment, but just walks away to a fallen tree to sit on. Piper shakes her head and looks at Larissa, mouthing *"Crazy"*. She laughs, reaching up to cup my cheek and I press a kiss to her palm.

Asmodeus takes her hand in his as they sit on the ground, crushing the leaves noisily under them. "I'd just put my spear through anyone's chest who dared come near my mate, much less messy." He whispers to Piper, and she falls against him giggling.

"Why did we land?" Larissa asks. I sit and pull Larissa down between my legs, resting my back against a tree and shuffle to scrape my wings on the rough bark.

"We are all slowing down. We need Mark and Levi to catch up for safety. It's hard enough to fight in the air, harder to do it with our hands full." Asmodeus answers Larissa, and she nods in understanding.

"The leaves have started falling but the trees are still blocking us from anyone flying overhead. How will they find us?" She asks. Adrian holds his phone up. "GPS, or would you prefer smoke signals?" He says with a jesting smile. Larissa holds her middle finger up, falling back against me with a yawn. Asmodeus clears the area of leaves and Piper goes about gathering dry sticks.

"Might as well make a small camp while we wait." She shrugs, and we all pitch in to clear up our little spot.

Chapter 33 - Larissa

The sun has set, but Levi and Mark still haven't shown up. I started getting worried a few hours ago, but keep distracting myself by collecting rocks to surround our small fire. Blaine and Adrian tried hunting. *I'm not sure I'm hungry enough to eat Bambi's mom yet.* Instead, I dig through my food bag and toss a box of granola bars on the ground for everyone. Piper takes one happily and inches closer to the fire with her hands up.

"I'm freezing," she hisses. I nod and rub my arms against the chill, already missing the crowded home we shared. Ella has been weaving branches together with vines and now has a small wall of sticks. She excitedly spears each side into the ground behind us and it covers more than half the camp.

"That thing is gigantic. What the heck is it?" I ask. She beams proudly and I notice there isn't as much wind hitting us now.

"If we had some big leaves, I could make a small roof. But this will do for now. My dad used to be obsessed with survival camping." She smiles sadly at the fire. "I hated it. Coming into the woods with the bare minimum. But he taught me so much." She mumbles. I take her hand in mine and give it a squeeze of understanding.

Blaine and Adrian walk back into sight, both beaming with pride at what they drag in behind them. A deer dangles from a thick branch they have tied its feet to and hoisted onto their shoulders to carry. *I think I just became a vegetarian.*

Asmodeus offers to help skin and prepare the meat. Ella excitedly joins him, and I turn my back. I'm grateful they can do this because my stomach quivers at the mere sounds coming from behind me. Blaine sits beside me, pulling me against him.

"They will be here. We just need to wait." He says softly. I nod and stare up at the sky, still so unsure. Losing Elaine has reminded me that I could lose anyone at any moment. Anyone I love can disappear between one moment and the next.

"Knock it off," Blaine bumps me with his knee and distracts me from my train of thoughts. His eyes are threatening slits when I glare at him. Feigning innocence, I shrug.

"Just not a fan of the deer chopping going on over there." I lie and he snorts.

"You are so full of shit." He sighs and grabs me, dragging me into his lap. I yelp at the suddenness and my cheeks heat with embarrassment as everyone looks at us. He rubs my cheek with his thumb, softly stroking my neck with his fingertips.

"I'll do everything in my power to make sure you don't lose anyone else," He whispers, kissing me softly. I sigh against his mouth, letting his tongue brush over mine. His fingers dig into my hip and side, only heightening the sensations between us. A tap on my shoulder makes me jump, but Blaine's iron tight grip prevents me from getting away. Piper hands me a stick, wrinkling her nose. A bright red chunk of meat is speared on the end.

"You looked hungry over here, devouring each other's faces. I figured you could use some meat. Before you jump his meat in front of us." She snickers. My mouth drops open in mortification. Blaine takes the stick and holds it over the flame. [7]

"She's my *soulmate.* It's a little hard to keep our hands to ourselves," He grumbles, burying his face in my neck for emphasis. Blaine makes smacking noises as he licks and bites my neck noisily. I squeal and try to wrestle away from his tickling. "Blaine, stop it!"

He lets out a boisterous laugh as Piper covers her face with a chuckle. "You two are going to have so many babies." She sneers. I violently shake my head no, and Blaine stiffens beneath me. His brows are pinched in confusion when I turn to look at him.

"Why not?" He asks innocently. I stare up at the sky and shrug, waving my hand.

"This isn't a place for a child. This world sucks and our children's lives would be in constant danger." I breathe. He shrugs and looks off into the trees.

"And they would have us to protect them." He says. That's when I realized we have never discussed our future. *Because you didn't think there would be a future.* After everything I've lost, I never expected to live that long. The thought catches me off guard and I clutch my arms to chase off the chill. He leans forward to lay his head on my shoulder and settles me between his legs. Blaine pulls the meat off the stick and holds it out for me, but when I reach for it, he pulls away.

"Open your mouth, Angel." he says with a threatening tone. I swallow hard and do as he demands after I realize he isn't caving. Blaine softly pushes the meat between my lips and gives me a wicked grin. He licks his fingers clean, and I hear Piper awkwardly cough and whisper, "That was *hot.*"

"Our children would have something we never did." His voice is low. I wait for a tense moment for him to finish. "They would grow up with both parents by their side." He whispers and kisses my neck. Warmth floods my heart and I feel the prick of tears threatening to spill. He rubs my arms and I lean into him. Those words made images of a small baby with big brown eyes and dark curling hair spin through my head. I quickly shake them off.

Love isn't enough sometimes. All of Hell will follow us wherever we go, and hurting our child would be the fastest way for both of us. My thoughts stall out as a stick breaking in the distance makes the hair on the back of my neck stand up. Blaine reaches back and pulls his sword from somewhere behind us. When I give him a confused look, he shrugs and puts his lips to my ear.

"You never know when you'll need to defend yourself. Always have a weapon within reach, Angel." He kisses my temple and stands slowly, motioning for me to stay down. *Like Hell I will.* I sneak over to my pack and unstrap my blade, turning to see his annoyed squint.

Another rustle sounds, coming even closer. Ella is holding a bloody hunting knife out as she crouches, peering through the trees. Adrian wastes no time in taking to the sky and landing on a tree above us to look around. Asmodeus steps in front of Piper, who rolls her eyes at the back of his head.

Adrian drops from the tree and waves us off, "It's Mark and Dad." He says, relief obvious in his voice. I blow out a slow breath, strapping my sword back onto my bag. Blaine startles me, giving my ass a hard slap.

"You turn your back and drop your weapon without checking if they are being followed?" He *tsks* me and shakes his head. "I thought I taught you better than that." Blaine says. I roll my eyes and wave around us.

"I am a weapon, remember?" To prove my point, sparks jump around my fingertips, making him grin.

"That you are, Angel." His voice is low as his eyes drag over me. My dad walks into the light of the fire and I realize how rough he and Mark look. They both drop beside the fire, their wings slowly drawing flush to their back. I watch as Asmodeus and Adrian prop the deer over the fire, cutting pieces off so everyone can skewer and cook their own.

Nobody speaks. We all wait patiently for them to gulp down water and catch their breath. They look unharmed, just exhausted and worn ragged.

"We got everyone out that we could. Some adamantly refused to leave, so a few warriors stayed to stand guard. By the time we left, there were still no signs of any demons." Levi says, rubbing his shoulder. Mark groans as one of his wings struggles to tuck against his body.

"I'm getting too old for this. Should have stayed behind." He grumbles. I kneel beside him and put my hand on his shoulder. Mark looks up to me and I can see how desperately he wanted to stay where Elaine was put to rest.

"You should take over Elaine's bookshop." I say softly and

for a moment I think he will laugh it off. But he smiles and nods at me. "Not a bad idea, kid." He says.

"She'd love that." Blaine says, holding more meat out to me. This time he allows me to take it with my fingers, giving me a wink. The rest of us eat quietly while Adrian and Mark fill both groups in on everything and make plans to leave tonight.

We each gather our belongings and stomp the coals out. I'm watching Mark nervously, he is still sitting and staring off into the sky. He is so broken without her. I wouldn't want to go on without Blaine.

"He needs time, Angel." Blaine whispers, taking my hand in his. Levi says something to Mark. He slowly gets up, grabbing his bag and stretching his shoulders.

Chapter 34 – Larissa

Soon enough, we are back in the freezing sky. It's so dark that I'm afraid we will smack into a flock of birds. I expressed this to Blaine, and he let out a boisterous laugh.

"You should have more faith in me than that. I am part demon." He says and I watch as he tilts his head up. To prove his point, the stars seem to reflect more brightly in his eyes than they should.

"Why do you think I don't argue when you ask for the lights to be off during hanky panky?" His mouth tilts up in a smirk as he kisses me softly.

"Drop!" Asmodeus bellows. Without hesitation, Blaine tucks his wings in. We fall at least ten feet before he snaps them back out. My grip on Blaine is iron tight as my head whips around. There's finally a break in the clouds and the moon illuminates around us. A cambion with black wings and hair the same shade is just above us. She has a hideous snarl on her lips as she dives at us.

Blaine twists and takes off, using his body to protect mine as she throws a knife. Holding tight to him, I yank us backwards to portal above her. Throwing him off balance causes Blaine to drop low. Pulling one leg away from his waist, I kick at her. My clumsy motion still lands a blow to the side of her head. She screeches and swipes at me, tearing my pants and flesh with her claws. Blaine roars as he pulls me away, stomping his foot onto her arm. The sick *crack* that fills the air makes me flinch more than my wound.

"We need to get you out of here." Blaine says, adjusting his grip on me as he looks around us. More cambions have been diving in and out, aiming for Asmodeus and Adrian as easy targets. But Mark and Levi have done a good job of protecting them. Ella has her legs wrapped around Adrian's waist as she bends over backwards. He is clutching the front of her jacket while she swings her sword at the cambion below her when he tries to swipe at Asmodeus' wings.

There are six cambion, and eight of us. The issue is, three of us are nearly useless up here and are making things more complicated. Blaine takes my face in his hands and presses a quick kiss to me.

"I'm going to get you as close to the ground as I can, Angel. The second your feet hit dirt, you need to run. I'll be right behind you as soon as we take care of this." He tells me. I shake my head, terrified of leaving him behind.

"Piper, there's no time to argue." Asmodeus snaps behind us. She nods, her lip quivering as he peppers her face with kisses.

"My heart will always find yours." He promises as they drop towards the ground. Adrian doesn't seem keen on letting Ella go, but she looks at me in desperation. I nod and she whispers in his ear.

Just as Blaine drops lower, the same cambion woman appears behind him. She throws a dagger, and it makes a *thunk* as it sinks into Blaine's shoulder. He hisses a breath, and we tumble sideways while he reaches over his shoulder to rip the blade free with a snarl. She is closing in on him again and I look up to Ella. "Now!" I scream.

She shoves away from Adrian. He dives for her, desperately trying to catch her hand. She tucks away as she falls and I launch off Blaine, slamming into her as she drops past us. I quickly portal us, clenching my eyes shut as I hope we don't splatter the forest floor or get skewered on a branch.

We slam to the cold, hard ground. The impact knocks the air from my lungs, and I gasp like a fish out of water. I tried to take the brunt of the impact, but Ella still landed hard enough on her shoulder that she grips it as we stand. Helping her stand, I try to watch the fight above us. One of the cambion men isn't near anyone else. I watch as he turns quickly, searching the trees with green eyes. *Glowing* green eyes.

His eyes lock on mine and I back away, searching for the packs that we dropped. My sword was still strapped to the bag. I'm mentally kicking myself for not carrying it. The loud crack of a branch breaking above me echoes, and I don't move fast enough. It slams down onto my back, knocking me forward with a cry of pain.

"Get up, Larissa!" Ella screams. I twist and throw the thick branch off me, looking up into those glowing green eyes. He reaches down to grab me, and I let him. His skin has a soft gray tint to it and his long black hair falls around his face as he pulls me up. I slam my hands on his chest, and he doesn't budge. His lip curls into a sneer and I smile back.

With some concentration, I focus on creating an energy field between my palms and his chest. It explodes against him, and he grunts, staggering backwards. His grip falters and I yank free, nearly tripping over the broken branch behind me. Ella is slashing over and over at a short girl, managing to corner her. The cambion backs into the tree and Ella tries to stab her, but the girl slams her foot outwards, sending her sprawling.

I can't run to her side, because green eyes grabs me by my throat and throws me against a tree. My head bounces off the hard bark, making me groan, and he presses against me. His hand grips my throat, but he isn't cutting off my airway and only pulls me up to stand. I bare my teeth and try to kick him. He sighs and crushes his body to mine, pinning my hips with his own.

"Watch where you put that thing," I hiss. He chuckles and grips my wrists. I'm getting ready to build up a small burst when he whispers something that catches me off guard.

"Just hold still, princess. I won't let them hurt you." His deep voice makes me falter. There's honesty in his voice, but he still attacked me first.

"You just tried to kill me." I point out, still wriggling to get loose. My movements slow when I feel the prick of an icy blade graze my chin. I shouldn't have hesitated, now if I shock him it could force his arm to jerk upwards.

"The cambion girl that your friend just decapitated tried to kill you. I got here a second too late." he says, dipping his face to brush his nose along my throat. The intimate contact makes my body lock up. He takes a deep breath and sighs.

"What the fuck are you doing?" I rasp. His grip tightens as he tenses.

"Loverboy is going to rescue you now." He says, his lips brushing my skin as I try to cringe away from him.

"Get off of her!" Blaine roars, as familiar shadows dance around us. I feel them brush my skin tentatively as if they are checking for injuries. The man lets me go and steps back, turning to smile at Blaine. I pull my power into my hands, ready to defend Blaine. Asmodeus suddenly grabs the guy by the front of his shirt and tosses him away from me.

"Why are you here, boy?" He shouts.

Piper runs over and grabs Asmodeus' arm, stopping him as he storms after green eyes. Blaine gathers me in his arms, looking over my face. I breathe a sigh of relief when I realized he is mostly unhurt and his shoulder has already stopped bleeding. He grips my back and I flinch enough for him to notice.

Blaine spins me around and yanks my shirt up before I can stop him.

"Who did this?" His voice is low and full of rage. I try to answer him, but he is already storming over to the man who is now sitting on the ground. He tilts his head while watching Blaine and I realize his eyes are no longer glowing. *Maybe I was just imagining it?* But then they scour over my face and glow again as he winks.

"Blaine, it wasn't him. He didn't hurt me." I call out. This stops him in his tracks, and he looks at me, doubt clear on his face.

"He had you pinned to a tree by your throat." He deadpans.

"She didn't ask me to stop." The man says, dusting himself off and crossing his arms. "Learn to protect her better. It'd be a shame if she fell into the wrong hands." He baits Blaine.

"What are you doing here, Hayden?" Asmodeus snarls. I look at him in confusion.

"Uncle Lucifer sent me for you," Hayden says. Blaine's jaw clenches and I walk to him. I hate the reaction that the mere mention of his father causes. Hayden watches closely as I take his hand in mine. Blaine kisses my knuckles and nuzzles his face against my neck. Levi has been watching in silence and he tilts his head as realization dawns.

"You were working with the informant that set up our trackers." He says.

"My father, Beelzebub. He's also the one that ratted out your rescue, with the help of a little cambion. But I'm not against you." He waves his hand. Hayden's tone is bored, but I can see his eyes constantly flicking around.

"Why did you attack us if you aren't an enemy?" I ask. He shakes his head and points to the trees. "Because I didn't attack you, I've been following from below. I was going to wait for you to land, but when you were ambushed, I had to step in." He says, as if it should be obvious.

"Lucifer is thrilled to meet you and made it clear I was to protect you." He tells me. Blaine growls behind me, wrapping his arms protectively around me.

"I don't give a fuck what he says. You can stay away from Larissa." His tone is hostile. Hayden puts his hands up in mock surrender, "Then next time make sure she doesn't free fall through the sky and break her ribs again." He motions to my sore side where I'm resting my hand. Blaine lifts my shirt again, making me hiss a breath through my teeth. As the adrenaline wears off, I'm realizing how injured I really am. My leg is killing me and the wound is still bleeding down into my shoe.

"I'm curious. If you are Beelzebubs kid, then why should we trust you?" Ella asks. I feel Blaine stiffen and I shoot her an annoyed look.

"Our parentage doesn't decide who we are, that's why." She looks embarrassed when I snap.

"I didn't mean it like that." she breathes. My skin is hot

and has become itchy. It's putting me on edge, and I don't like it. Blaine gives me a weird look and I turn back to Hayden and he's regarding me with a look of humor.

"I turned away from my father the moment I heard he was siding with Mammon. That idiot made Hell *worse*." Hayden says with a chuckle. I blow out a breath and turn to Asmodeus.

"Do you trust him?" I ask.

"No." Blaine says behind me, but I pinch the bridge of my nose and ignore him. Piper nods to him and Asmodeus sighs.

"Yes, for now. We asked Lucifer for help." His voice is quiet and annoyed. Blaine blows out a breath of frustration and Adrian stares down at Hayden with obvious distrust.

"We can't just stay out in the open. How far are we from the safe house?" Mark asks. I pull my phone out and huff when I see the shattered screen. Blaine checks his phone while I jam mine back into my pocket. He and Adrian lead the way, both glancing back at Hayden.

Chapter 35 – Larissa

"*Shit.*" I hiss between my teeth as I stumble, twisting my ankle and straining the gash on my leg. A powerful pair of arms caught me, and the smell of pine mixed with mint hits me. I look up in surprise to see Hayden holding me as genuine concern flashes in his eyes.

"If you want my attention, all you have to do is ask." He grins at me, and I shove him away. Cringing when I put weight on my bad leg, he slowly wraps an arm around me. His touch is so gentle that I nearly sink into his warmth. He's careful to avoid my ribs but still takes my weight off the sore leg. Ready to fight him off, I grind my teeth.

"I'll behave. Just let me help." He says in a calm voice. It relieves the pain, so I stop fighting against him. Until he jerks me backwards and I watch Blaine's fist sail past Hayden's smug smile. Hayden shakes his head and nods towards me.

"Don't be stupid, she's in terrible shape and needs help." He snaps at Blaine. I shake my head and try to step away.

"Stop trying to pick a fight," I grumble. Hayden sighs but doesn't let go of me. Blaine slides his hand under my knees and snatches me from Hayden's hands. White spots flash behind my eyes from the pain that burns through my ribs and leg.

"Put me down!" I shout and he sits me on the ground beside him as I lay back to clutch my head. Everything is spinning and I'm exhausted. Their fighting is pissing me off and I don't want to deal with it.

Piper takes my ankle softly between her hands and turns my leg to examine it. The moonlight doesn't show much with blood covering the wound.

"Give me your dagger," she says and holds out her hand. I

pull it from my waistband and drop it in her palm. She carefully cuts away pieces of my pant leg and groans.

"You need stitches! Why didn't you say anything?" She admonishes me.

"It's just a scratch." I bluff, getting dizzy just sitting here. Blaine lifts my head and lays it in his lap, and Hayden hands him a bottle.

"Levi said to make her drink this." He tells him. I glance over to see Levi and Asmodeus arguing over the phone that Mark is holding up. Somebody is on speaker, but I can't hear what they are saying. Blaine holds the cold bottle to my lips as Adrian helps Piper dress my leg. Ella holds out something and Adrian grips my leg tighter. Piper sits on my lap and Ella holds my hand.

"Blaine, this will not be easy." Adrian says. Then a sharp stabbing burns in my leg and I try to yank away. A brush of cold races along my body and Adrian sighs.

"I can't see. Get your shadows out of my way." He grumbles. Blaine brushes the tears from my face as I squirm under the stabbing pain. He kisses my forehead over and over, doing everything he can to comfort me.

"He needs to do this, sweetie. I'm sorry." Piper tries to tell me, her voice cracking.

"Stop it!" I wail, shaking as I fight against their restraints.

"Look at me." Hayden commands. Through the blur of tears, I lock eyes with his glowing eyes. Everything stills, and darkness surrounds me. It's as if I've dropped into a dream. I'm just a thought floating in the dark. I gasp and his voice is in my ear, yet far away.

"It's okay. I'm just taking away your senses, temporarily." He explains, and I try to rub my eyes. *I can't even talk. What the hell is happening?*

"You can speak, and I can hear you perfectly fine. Stop panicking, Larissa. They're almost done. I figured this was preferable to the agony you were in." His voice is soft, trying to comfort me.

So, this is your fancy cambion power?

"I suppose you could say that. My mother is a witch." His voice is dismissive. I raise my brows in surprise, or at least I try to.

"I'm not playing twenty questions with you, so don't be nosy." He grumbles.

My mother was a witch, too. There's a long pause before he clears his throat.

"You need to brace yourself. I'm going to wake you now." He whispers and I blink, my eyes feeling like sandpaper. The agony returns and I try to clutch my leg. Blaine's large hands hold me back and he keeps whispering in my ear, telling me I'm okay.

"What did you do to me?" I groan out through my teeth. Asmodeus glares at Hayden as Adrian finishes wrapping a thin bandage around my leg.

"That cambion had venom in her claws. It slows down healing and prevents clotting. But this should help until we can get you to a healer." Adrian says, standing up and helping Blaine get me off the ground.

"Hayden," I say in a stern voice.

"If I can lock eyes with someone, I can take their senses." Hayden says dismissively. Blaine helps loop my arm around his shoulder while I gape at Hayden. I gingerly put weight on my foot and cringe as the stitches strain. *This blows. I miss my bed.* When we walk, Mark is sticking close and keeps looking at me from the corner of his eye.

"Well, spit it out, old man." I say jokingly, smiling at him. He chuckles and rubs the back of his neck.

"I promised Elaine that if anything ever happened, I would protect you kids. I'm not doing a great job of it." He sighs sadly, massaging his shoulder.

"We are still alive and together. You're doing fine, Mark." Adrian says behind us. I smile and nod in agreement.

"I personally could go for a five-star resort with room service, but Adrian has a point. You aren't doing too bad." Blaine grins beside me and I smack his chest playfully. Mark lets out a short laugh and nods. "I'd kill for a good steak." He says.

Piper giggles, "A hot tub would be mind-blowing." She says dreamily, and I have to agree with her. My sore muscles could use a good soak. After walking for a while, the sounds of the forest suddenly fall silent. The comforting sound of owls around us has stopped to just a few heard in the distance. A stick breaking makes me jump and Blaine whispers in my ear.

"I'm the scariest monster out here." His breath tickles the hair on my cheek, and I smile at his words. There was a time when the things that go bump in the night were my biggest fear. I had no idea what was really lurking this entire time and how scary this world was beyond what we could see.

We finally make it to the safe-house, and my skin is prickling. Something just felt wrong, and I'm not the only one. Levi waves everyone to stay back and creeps up to the door. Before he can open it, it swings open.

One look at the man in the doorway makes my blood chill. He's handsome, with curling brown hair that is styled on top of his head with the sides shaved short. There is a dusting of stubble on his sharp jaw and a nose that I've seen every day this past year. *Blaine looks so much like him.*

"Lucifer." Asmodeus grumbles, storming up to us. I notice he stands in front of Blaine, protectively. No matter what he says, he cares about his nephew. Blaine's hand has started shaking and his fingers dig painfully into my aching ribs. But I don't move, not daring to let go of him. His jaw ticks as he clenches it tighter. I could claw Lucifer's heart from his chest with my bare fingers for what he's done to my Blaine.

"Oh, dear brother. Your pathetic lot needs me, if I recall correctly." Lucifer waves his hand, grinning.

"I asked you to meet me and work with *me.* Nobody else here wants you around." Asmodeus snaps. Lucifer shrugs, his muscular arms stretching against his crisp white button-up shirt.

"My son is here, and his lovely mate. I figured two birds, one demon." He cackles as if his joke is hilarious. I shift uncomfortably, my energy draining with every breath. I raise my hand without thinking, and rage burns through me. More than just a tingle, an all-out vibration fills my chest and shoots down my arm. It's as if I'm not in control of my actions. A ball of sparking electricity flies from my palm and slams into Lucifer. It knocks him into the wall of the cabin, and he wheezes out a groan as he staggers forward. He braces his hands on his knees and coughs violently.

Asmodeus whips around to stare at me in disbelief. Blaine grabs my hand and shoves it down before I can do it again.

"What is wrong with you? That was suicide!" Blaine hisses between his teeth. Levi is glaring at me in rage and slowly shakes his head. Lucifer's dark laugh draws our attention as he brushes away the burnt fabric and gives me a thumbs up.

"That was a magnificent little firework, darling. I can see why Blaine has kept you around for so much longer than all the others." He tilts his head, gauging my reaction. My fingers twitch as I fight Blaine's grip, ready to fire another one at his father's face. Just as suddenly as it came, my agitation melts away and I shiver at the sensation.

"Enough, Lucifer." Blaine snarls. Asmodeus runs his fingers through his hair in frustration.

"Can we just stop for a moment?" Asmodeus asks. Levi waves towards the cabin and gives Lucifer a once over.

"If you step out of line, I'll kill you myself." Levi warns him and Lucifer puts his hand over his heart, acting hurt.

"We are going to be family. Truly, I am wounded." He says. His tone is nearly genuine enough for me to believe it. Blaine keeps looking at me out of the corner of his eye before flicking his gaze back to Lucifer.

"This place is dilapidated." Mark groans, drawing our attention upwards. The roof is collapsing inwards, the wood looking decayed from years of neglect. Well, shit.

"We also have company." Hayden says, glancing behind us.

"More cambions?" I ask. Blaine nods and looks around at our surroundings as he tries to come up with a plan.

"They have more fliers." Asmodeus sighs. Lucifer holds his hand out to his brother.

"I have a lovely place that would accommodate you all. Come now, I don't feel like fighting tonight." Lucifer says, his tone serious as he waves his hand to open a portal. As he does, I hear the shrieks and laughter as it echoes through the trees.

"Mammon's army found us." Adrian says. He takes Ella's hand in his.

Chapter 36 – Larissa

I don't trust Lucifer, even if he healed my demon poisoning. If he keeps pushing Blaine, a burn on his shirt will be the least of his worries. We didn't have a choice but to go with him, even though death at the hands of Mammon's army might have been preferable to this torture.

"I don't think you understand how serious this is. Orange satin button ups are tragic with purple pants." Piper says for the tenth time. Lucifer doesn't look any less offended as he continues to defend his choice of style. *Why is this happening?* Piper seems to like Lucifer.

"You will also lack appreciation for your rooms, no doubt." Lucifer sighs and waves to Asmodeus. He just glares at him harder. I didn't realize he could look grumpier than before.

"This is my nightmare," Blaine groans as he flops down onto the couch next to me. I pat his knee affectionately. Levi, Mark, and Adrian are currently scouting our proposed rooms to check for any signs of a trap. After everything that we have been through, trust is scarce. Hayden sits in a chair to my right and rests his elbows on his knees. He props his chin on folded hands and watches me. It makes me fidget uncomfortably under the intensity of his stare. This room is huge, yet I can't seem to get away from him.

"So, you're prophesied to save the entire human and nephilim race? That must be a colossal weight to bear. I cannot say that I envy you." Hayden says.

"She is doing just fine." Blaine quips, wrapping his arm around my shoulders. *I wouldn't be surprised if he peed on my leg, too.* Blaine gives me a curious look when I snort at the mental image.

"I didn't exactly ask for it, but not much you can do against fate, is there?" My tone is bitter. Talking about the prophecy when I keep failing is like salt in my wound. Mammon is still alive, and we seem to be the only ones suffering any genuine loss.

Lucifer points at Blaine and waves him over. He shakes his head at him once, then pointedly turns away. *He sure has the defiant bad boy routine down.* I nudge him and he looks over to where his dad has opened his hand. Light seems to bounce around his palm, bending and twisting a flurry of colors.

"He will pull you over by force if you don't go willingly. Lucifer isn't above using something important to you as leverage." Hayden says, tipping his head towards me. Blaine presses his lips into a thin, hard line as he stares at his father.

"Should I come with you?" I offer and he shakes his head once, standing and dragging himself towards Lucifer. It hurts to see him so distraught over this one person. Lucifer has ruined his life repeatedly.

"Uncle Luce still hasn't learned how to express his feelings. He simply expects his son to fall in line and respect him as his father." Hayden says, as if it excuses him.

"He hasn't earned Blaine's respect. Blaine became the man he is despite Lucifer." I stare into Lucifer's eyes, ensuring he can hear every word. "Elaine and his mother Kate are the only ones who deserve any credit. *Lucy* can go fuck himself." I sneer. Hayden chuckles and shakes his head.

"You are playing with fire, little one." He whispers. Breaking my stare down with Lucifer, I shrug and look at him.

"I've taken on bigger and scarier things." My voice is steady, even if I doubt myself. Hayden shakes his head at me, amusement on his face as he leans back. His arm rests on the chair and it almost looks comically small under his enormous frame. His arms are twined in muscle, with speckles of scars along them. I didn't notice before, but it looks as if he has burn scars peeking from the collar of his shirt and up to his throat. Hayden flashes me a sharp toothed grin, catching me staring.

"Can't say I mind the ogling, but you should buy me dinner first." He says. I roll my eyes and absently run my fingers across my collar bone. "What's the story there?" I ask. He watches my motion with vague curiosity until my question registers. It's as if an icy wall slams down behind his eyes and he becomes visibly agitated.

"Are you just trying to get me to take my shirt off? I thought you were spoken for. Is there trouble in paradise?" He asks. But his words lack his teasing humor. They hold more bite than before.

"Because you are *so* charming," I snort and Blaine walks up to hold his hand out to me.

"Let's go to our room. We need to talk." His voice is weary. I stand, taking his hand firmly in mine. Hayden chuckles and tilts his head at our entwined hands.

"Did daddy tell you that the prophecy is false? That it was *tainted*?" He sneers. Blaine turns to him with rage in his eyes and I push against his chest, trying to keep Hayden alive. *Even if he doesn't deserve it.*

"What are you talking about?" I ask. Hayden shrugs, waving his hand at Blaine, and I wait for him to explain. His eyes lock on mine and I can see it. Blaine looks so hurt, so broken. I shake my head and pull him towards the grand staircase that leads upwards. "What is our room number, Blaine?" I ask softly, taking the ornate key from his hand. *Has Lucifer ever heard of key cards? Sheesh.*

Blaine guides me up the stairs, his mind a million miles away as we navigate the massive mansion. The bond strums in my chest, like a bird trapped in a cage.

"Blaine. Can we even trust Lucifer?" I ask softly. He gives me a sad smile and looks down at his shoes.

"The angels chose our parents. They chose them and altered our bloodlines without telling them. Uriel may have had the prophecy, but another archangel planted it. Only a few King's of Hell knew of their little indiscretion. Apparently, if Hell knew they were creating weapons to use against them, then they could have attacked Heaven on their own turf. Of course, the cowardly angels couldn't have that." He rolls his eyes and stares up at the ceiling. "Lucifer isn't easy to deceive, so he knew right away. But he decided that having a powerful bloodline was worth it. Asmodeus had his suspicions, but he was out of touch with both worlds when we were created, so he never knew for sure." We continue down a hallway, and I have no idea where we are as I struggle to understand everything he is saying.

"What does-" I ask, but Blaine cuts me off with a look, pressing his fingers to his lips as he looks around. We don't know who is staying in any of these other rooms. Anybody could be listening in. Blaine nods to a door as we come closer. *Room 158.* He waves me in before locking the door behind us. I scrape my hand along the wall, looking for a switch. When I finally find it, I'm caught off guard by the room.

A large gray couch sits across from a flat screen television that is mounted on the wall. It is mounted above an electric fireplace, and the room is decorated like a rustic cabin would be. The door to our left leads into a bathroom with a wall-to-wall shower. I look up at the waterfall shower head and nearly forget everything Blaine has said. *Nearly.* The bedroom is just as luxurious, with a king-sized bed across from another oversized television. They covered all the windows with light blocking curtains. I know I'm going to sleep so well in the middle of all those pillows.

Blaine drops onto the couch and pats the seat beside him. When I sit down next to him, I nervously rub my palms on my thighs.

"They did not fate us to be soulmates. Larissa, an archangel decided for us that our blood lines would make strong offspring. That a child born from a Goddess and nephilim would become one with a child from a demon and nephilim. One day, they would create an entirely new race together. They altered our future by tying us together." He says the words as if they make him sick. I scrunch my brow and shake my head.

"That can't be right. My mother was a witch." I say. Could

they have tied him to a different woman? My pulse races and it feels as if my veins are filling with ice water.

"Your mother carried you, but they created you from another woman's DNA. Those sick bastards apparently got permission from a certain Goddess to create you with her assistance." He drops his head into his palms. My hands grip the cushion on each side of me so tightly that my nails dig into the fabric.

"No. He is lying to you, Blaine. My mother was a witch. She carried me. She gave birth to me." I whimper. He takes my face in his hands and forces me to look into his red-rimmed eyes. He's telling the truth, and it's breaking his heart to do so. Yanking my head away, I jog to the bathroom. The door slams off the wall as I drop to my knees and empty every bite of venison that I had in me. Blaine holds my hair up and rubs my back softly.

I drop my head into my arms and shake my head. This can't be happening. The faucet squeaks and a cabinet door clicks shut before a wet cloth is pressed into my hand and a cup of water hovers beside me.

"Blaine, please tell me it's not true." My voice is hoarse, my throat still stinging from the stomach acid that burned its way up. But he won't look into my eyes.

"Screw them. They may have decided who our parents were, but they didn't decide who I fell in love with." I spit the words with venom, standing to point into the sky.

"You don't get to mess with our lives like this anymore!" I scream and Blaine grabs my arm, whipping me to face him.

"I'm so sorry, Angel." He crushes me to his chest, a shuddering breath leaving his lips. My grip on Blaine tightens and all I need is for him to know my love for him is real. Our mothers both died because of the selfishness from Heaven. They wanted to win a war so badly, they were willing to pay the price of anyone else's life.

"That's it. They can fight their own war. I'm done." My voice is callous. He pulls back, shaking his head.

"They may have orchestrated this, but Lilith and

Mammon killed those who raised us. No matter what, she was still your mother. Mary gave birth to a beautiful baby girl that she raised to be an incredible woman. Selene and the angels cannot take that from you, or from her." He says. *Selene.* I stop his hand as it strokes my cheek.

"She was right there. Selene was right in front of me and never told me the truth." My voice cracks as rage pushes aside the pain. My heart aches as it makes room for so many overwhelming emotions.

"I'll rip their wings from their body and lay them at your feet when I find the angel responsible for this. I swear it." He says fiercely.

Chapter 37 – Larissa

My decision was made, and nothing could change it. Mammon would die for what he took from all of us. But after that, I was coming for Heaven's army. They will regret the weapon they created when it blows up in their faces. My fate was my own to decide from this moment on. A soft knock comes from the door and Blaine leaves to check the peephole. I finish brushing my teeth and step from the bathroom. Blaine gives me an apologetic look over his shoulder before unlocking and swings the door open.

Levi stands there, his hands fisted tightly at his side. His eyes are glassy, and he looks me over as if he is seeing me for the first time again. Seeing that I'm not the child of the woman he loved.

"Larissa," he says, stepping inside slowly. I shake my head, clasping a hand over my mouth. He stops in front of me and I'm afraid to move. I went so long without a father and now that I have him, he's going to reject me. Levi grabs me tightly in his arms and lifts my feet off the ground. I feel like a little girl who has fallen and scraped her knee, with my father scooping me up to promise that everything will be okay.

"You are our daughter. We brought you into this world from love, the same as your brother." He grits out, choking back his own tears as I nod into his shoulder. I hear the front door open and he puts me back on my feet, brushing my hair back and kissing my forehead. Adrian looks at me over Levi's shoulder, his face pinched in pain. Did Lucifer tell the entire world?

"I told him to keep his mouth shut until Larissa could talk to you." Blaine grumbles, slamming the door behind Adrian. We stand there for a few tense moments before Adrian breaks the silence.

"So, you are part nephilim, part Goddess and you were grown inside a dormant witch? That's a lot to take in. You don't exactly have any mind-blowing gifts, other than when you brought him back to life." He points his thumb over his shoulder at Blaine who is staying silent. "I still think that was some kind of fluke." Adrian says dismissively.

"Lucifer said Selene is my biological mother." Even saying the words out loud hurts, and I can see the pain as it flashes in Adrian's eyes. He shakes his head as he walks around me to flop down on the couch.

"Mary was your mother. Selene doesn't get any credit for who you are today, Larissa." Adrian tells me. He sounds so tired, and I hate to see everyone around me suffering. Blaine comes up and wraps his arms around me.

"Stop blaming yourself. That's what Lucifer does. When he showed up, you hurt his pride, so he dropped this bomb the first chance he got." His tone is angry. Another knock at the door makes my shoulders sag because I don't know how much more of this I can take.

"Son of a-" Blaine snaps as he opens the door, takes one look at his father, and slams it so hard the wall rattles. I bite my lip to hide a smile as he flips off the closed door and walks back over to me.

"He has a key," I whisper to remind him. Blaine gives me a devilish grin and pulls two spare keys from his pocket and dangles them in front of my face.

"I may have grabbed all the spares I could find on his key ring." A deep sigh has us all spinning to look at Lucifer as he leans against the wall.

"I can teleport, son. Don't doubt your father so quickly." Lucifer says with a chuckle.

"You knew about everything from the very beginning?" I ask him, and he nods. He sits in the recliner and motions for the rest of us to take a seat. Blaine pulls me into his lap on the couch and my dad gives him a glare, still uncomfortable with the show of affection. I grip Blaine's hands as they hold me around my waist, knowing this is more to keep me from blowing a fuse.

"I knew. One of those overgrown pigeons came to me one day to ask me to create a weapon. A child with a nephilim woman. I figured it couldn't hurt to throw my name into the hat on the winning side. When I began following Kate, it wasn't even a question. I had to have her." Lucifer says, dreamily staring off as her memory hits him. Blaine growls and I pat his hand, trying to calm him down. His arms have started shaking and I know he's getting worked up.

"Blaine will say otherwise, but I cared for her. She was lovely. Even when she was being stubborn. I tried to get her to leave the nephilim life behind when she became pregnant. I had changed my mind and would not let the angels have him. But when I told her the truth, she wasn't forgiving. Kate sent me packing and told me never to come back." He shrugs.

"But you came back and tried to take him?" I ask, remembering what Blaine had told me. Lucifer nods and winks at me.

"Smart girl. Yes, I did. I planned to take him with me so they wouldn't find him and set their plans in motion. She refused to come with me and wouldn't let me take him alone. That pushed her closer to Elaine, which was the one that connected all your little dots." He waves his hand in the air and gives a dramatic yawn.

"Such a boring story. Until Lilith decided to send an incompetent cambion to follow you home, Levi. She apparently thought you'd lead him right to Mary. The silly prick didn't even hesitate to kill Kate and flee. He was a coward, truly." He snarls. I feel the temperature drop and I dig my nails into Blaine's arm, trying to keep him from losing his calm.

"Why didn't you protect her?" I ask softly. He gives me a sad look and crosses his legs. His eyes take on a murderous red shade as he looks away.

"I tried. But I was too late. I chased him down and tortured him for days. The poor bastard was so weak that he succumbed to his injuries before we got to anything exciting." Lucifer tries to sound nonchalant, but his entire demeanor has lost its joking appearance. In his own twisted way, he cared for Blaine's mother. Blaine has gone still under me, and I look over my shoulder to see the vacant look in his eyes.

"The council failed you, and I failed Kate. Simple." Lucifer smiles at Blaine. "If you have any more questions, then find me in the morning." Lucifer stands to walk away, but I jump up to block his exit. He gives me a bored look as I cross my arms defiantly.

"Why should I believe you that Selene is my mother?" I ask. He rolls his eyes and brushes past me.

"Don't be dull, girl. I said to find me *tomorrow* with any further questions. I couldn't care less about playing 'Who's your mommy?'. Poor not-so-orphan girl. I wonder how you turned out so uninteresting, coming from a Goddess." He waves over his shoulder as he leaves. I'm fuming and Adrian just groans.

"Right now, there isn't a way to tell if what he says is the truth or a lie, but your DNA doesn't define who you are." Levi says, looking mostly at Blaine. He pats his shoulder. "I'll always see you as one of my own, even if you still have not forgiven me for stopping you all those years ago." He says to Blaine before leaving and I rub my hands over my face with a long whine.

"My dad is a total jackass, but your dad is sappy as shit." Blaine says to Adrian, who lets out a snort.

"Apparently I'm the only one in here with normal genetics though, so screw both of you freaks." He jokes and my jaw drops open at him. "Larissa, you are my sister. Not *half-sister*, either. I know this may change things for you, but it has changed nothing for anyone else. We are all in this together." He says with a nod before walking out as well. Leaving Blaine and I to stare at each other.

"Why are they taking it so well? Why am I the *only* person losing their shit?" I ask. He blows out a breath and holds his hand out for me to sit with him. I tuck myself under his arm as he plays with my hair. This man can make me melt like putty between his fingers.

"Because they don't see you differently. You seem to think that everyone is looking for an excuse to cast you aside, but you're wrong, Angel." He says softly, kissing the top of my head. Blaine grabs the soft blanket from the back of the couch and pulls it over us. He lays down and drags me with him. Nothing is different, yet I still feel like something has changed. I close my eyes and just cling to Blaine, breathing in the comforting smell of smoke and spice.

I feel as if I am drowning in my guilt, and he is the only thing keeping my head above it all.

"How do you feel, knowing the man who murdered your mother has been dead this entire time?" I ask him. He nods, his chin bumping my head as he holds me tighter.

"I'm still not sure if I feel relieved or if it pisses me off that he felt he had some right to avenge her. It doesn't change the fact that Lilith was the one who sent the cambion after Levi. You are the one who took her down and I will forever be in your debt, Angel." He whispers, kissing me slowly.

"Well, I'm going to need a lot more of these kisses. I'm talking *years* of this." I giggle against his mouth as I feel the corner tilt up.

"In that case, I pledge to please my lady until the day I take my last breath." He promises. Chills crawl up my spine as he hooks my knee over his hip and presses me into the back of the couch. For tonight, we are in our own little bubble, and I can push everything else aside to just enjoy this.

Chapter 38 – Larissa

"Wake up, Larissa. We must speak." A sweet voice reaches me, and I groan. My body feels as if I've barely slept at all. I blink and look around, confused about where I am. I'm still wearing Blaine's shirt, wrapped in the blanket we snuggled under. But Blaine is gone and I'm somewhere I don't want to be right now.

"Selene," I say, glaring at her. When we fell asleep, I wasn't wearing pants. Even if I were, seeing her face so soon feels like a nightmare.

"Reaching you in your dream is even harder than I expected, with that delicious man that was wrapped around you. Even while asleep, he is protecting you." She says affectionately. Did she just call Blaine delicious?

"Why am I here? How the hell do I get back?" I snap, wrapping the blanket around me as I stand and begin walking towards the garden she showed me when I was here before.

"It appears that you could use a brush up on manners." She whispers, while following me out. I give a bitter laugh and spin to face her.

"Good, I look nothing like you." I hiss before turning my back to her again. It was a low comment to make, but she should just send me back.

"That is not true. Our hair is nearly identical. You have my overflowing breasts as well." She giggles. I give her a shocked look. This woman has no boundaries.

"Just give me a moment, please. I wanted to be a mother-" Waving my hand near her face, I cut her off. "You are not a mother. Not mine at least." I say bitterly. She gives me a sad look and walks toward the bench among the white blooming flowers. The bright moon overhead makes the entire world look as if it glows. Even with *this anger, I can still appreciate the beauty.*

"Say what you will, but you came from my ovary." She says dismissively, "It's quite easy to enchant even a nephilim doctor. Planting it was no trouble, and just a small nudge of hormones ensured a full night for Mary and Levi. I was only doing what was in the best interest of the witches. Taking power back to our side was the obvious choice." She tries to condone her actions, but I still can't wrap my head around it.

"Did I ask for the dirty details?" My lip curls in disgust.

"You're sick and I am done playing these games. I will not be a tool for the cowards in Heaven. I'm declaring war on them. They are power hungry and willing to screw with everyone else's lives. Those assholes are no better than Mammon! You included!" I shout at her. She covers her mouth, surprised by my outburst.

"You will do no such thing. You have a prophecy to fulfill-" She tries to talk but I stand and lean over her. "Fuck your prophecy. Here's mine. Heaven will fall to be rebuilt again. Balance will be restored as the rightful King returns to Hell, and I'll kill anyone who gets in my way." I warn her. She stands up to challenge me, but it's too late. Moments ago, I felt the familiar tug from Blaine on my soul as soon as I got too worked up. He was pulling me back home.

Just to be petty, I stick my middle fingers up to her as I'm swallowed by black shadows that have wrapped around every inch of me.

"You found me," I whisper, smiling with my eyes still closed. I'm wrapped tightly in his large, warm arms and my heart has started beating faster.

"I will always find you, Angel." he says, peppering my face with kisses. "You were so angry and scared. I wish I could have gotten to you faster." His voice is soft, but I can feel how worried he was.

"Selene has serious issues with boundaries. I may have also said I'm declaring war on Heaven." I whisper the last sentence. Blaine yanks back, nearly tumbling us to the floor. His face is shocked as he waits for me to tell him I'm joking. I bite the inside of my lip nervously, and he throws his head back with a boisterous laugh before burying his nose in my hair.

"You are incredible. Not sure how smart it is to challenge a Goddess within her domain and to declare war on all of Heaven. But you never back down." he says, beaming with pride. I laugh at his reaction, crushing my lips to his. His kiss sears my flesh, drawing goosebumps across my bare legs. Blaine's fingers brush under my shirt, shoving the fabric up as his hands slide across my skin. He cups my breasts, pinching my hard nipples between his fingers as he bites down on my lips.

My back arches and a gasp escapes my lips as he moves his teeth to the sensitive skin of my neck, biting harder as he goes. I dig my nails into his back, grinding against his lap. It draws a low moan from him that vibrates against my throat. Just to be interrupted by the phone on the end table that begins a sharp ring. I groan and he pulls the shirt off that I was wearing, throwing it aside. The cool air hits my skin and makes me suck in a sharp breath.

"Ignore it," He growls as he bites my nipple. I laugh, tangling my fingers in his messy hair. *His hair is getting long, I love it.* The phone stops ringing, and Blaine grabs the shirt at the back of his neck, pulling it off and dropping it in one fluid movement. *Things that aren't inherently sexual but turn me on, number five hundred and seventy two.* Blaine's fingers grip my hips punishingly as he grinds me across his erection.

The phone rings again. Blaine snarls as he lays me back on the couch, pressing himself between my thighs. He blindly reaches over the arm of the couch to rip the phone from its chord and tosses it aside. I cover my mouth, partially in shock and partly to cover my giggle. He grins, the dull light from a lamp across the room reflecting off the short fangs I've become so fond of.

"Maybe you are part vampire." I whisper, teasing him. His smile drops as he gives me his grumpy glare. My smile falters as he reaches between us and *tears* my panties off. One of my favorite pairs.

"Blaine, I didn't bring enough for you to do that." I gasp. He grins as he teasingly drags his fingers across the ache he is building between my legs.

Until somebody is pounding on the door. *"Sonofabitch"* Blaine hisses. I huff and sit up, but he gently pushes me back down with his palm, a wicked gleam in his eyes. He presses a finger to his lips and shakes his head. Before I can ask what he's doing, he reaches between us and presses two fingers inside of me. My mouth flies open, but he smothers the moan with his hand. Whoever is at the door is pounding on it again, grating on my nerves.

"I'm coming in, so I suggest you put your clothes on." Lucifer calls outside the door. Blaine reluctantly pulls from me and grabs the shirt from the floor to drag it over my head. I stomp to my duffle bag that sits near the bed, pouting at being interrupted. Blaine delivers a solid slap to my ass, making me yelp as I bend over to find pants.

"I'm not done with you yet, Angel. Better hope these walls are soundproof." He says casually, pulling his shirt on and taking my leggings from me. "Because your sweet little cries are for my ears only." He says, holding the pants up to help me dress. Blush heats my cheeks as I hold my foot up.

"I can dress myself." I say and he gives me a panty dropping smile.

"If I can undress you, then I can also help you get dressed." He drags my pants up and over my ass at a snail's pace before burying his face in my crotch. Gripping his hair, I squeal and try to pull him away. *And he bites down.*

"You bit me," I whisper shout, trying to escape the death grip he has on my thighs. He pulls back to grin at me and stands as we hear a gag behind us. Lucifer is standing in the doorway. *With my dad right behind him, who looks mortified.* I would almost prefer standing in front of Selene as opposed to this. Blaine gives Lucifer a matched look of disgust, preventing him from coming in any further.

"Morning Levi. Luce." He says his name with a drop in

tone. Lucifer is wearing a red satin button up that is tucked into gray skinny jeans. I nearly laugh at the contrast between him and my father's gray t-shirt and black slacks.

"It smells like Asmodeus in here," Lucifer chuckles at his lust joke. "But would anyone care to explain why there is a moon Goddess in my lobby? Accompanied by a pissed off *Archangel?*" He snaps. Blaine doesn't even look at me, just shifts his weight so I'm almost completely obscured from their sight.

"No clue. Who did you make a deal with this time, Lucifer?" Blaine asks casually. Levi steps forward and holds his hands up in a placating motion.

"I just need to know the entire truth, son. So I can stand by your side when we get down there. No surprises." Levi says softly. Blaine glances back at me and I step towards my dad.

"Selene decided to pop into my dreams last night and carry my soul off *against my will*. I said some things and may have declared war on Heaven." I say in a rush. Levi rubs his eyes and lets out a long breath. Lucifer has a glint of excitement in his eyes.

"Oh, darling girl, you continue to *shock* me." Lucifer grins.

Chapter 39 – Larissa

I drag my feet while getting ready, but we end up in the foyer in the blink of an eye. When I blew up on Selene, I didn't consider the consequences. I still don't regret what I said, now I have to deal with it. Blaine is gripping my hand in his as we walk towards the two ethereal beings glaring at me in the foyer.

"We called for you quite some time ago." Selene huffs in a sharp tone.

"We were occupied." Blaine lies, covering for my nervousness. The man beside Selene holds his hand out for me and I take it. I give his white button up and crisp white pants a weird look. His skin is overwhelmingly hot, and it's hard to resist the urge to yank my hand from his. The Angel's blonde hair is short and slicked back, giving him a fully manicured look. *He's radiating purity. It's a little startling.*

"You are a tiny little thing, aren't you?" His gravelly voice says. "Uriel." he says, bowing his head slightly. I nod and pull my hand back, completely unsure of what to say.

"Can't imagine what would be more important than being summoned by us." Selene scoffs, and I bite my tongue to hold a snarky response.

"I can promise you that burying myself inside of her is more important than whatever you want to say. Have either of you heard of cell phones? You could just text us. I don't get your obsession with the dramatics." Blaine says. He makes a scene of rolling his eyes and my mouth falls open. Lucifer cackles beside us and Levi clears his throat. Selene's face turns pink as she tries to contain her anger, and Uriel just looks flustered.

He's taking the attention off me. Blaine is egging them on purposefully, so they'll turn their anger to him. I shake my head, not willing to sit back while he takes them both on.

"What do you want?" I address Selene. Uriel holds his hand up.

"You should speak to your mother with respect." He admonishes me. Before I can react, Levi steps up to him, every bit as tall and powerful as the angel.

"She never disrespected her *real mother*. Mary earned the respect that was given to her. Your Goddess has no honor and has earned nothing from my daughter." Levi crosses his arms, his stance casual. But there is a storm brewing in his eyes.

"Watch your tone. Details aside, we deserve to be spoken to with respect. You excusing her behavior is the reason she is acting like a petulant child, Levi." Uriel says.

"You bring so much entertainment to my domain, darling." Lucifer purrs behind me and Selene looks disgusted. I'm just so sick of all of this.

"Who did this? Who decided to violate my mother by shoving some random woman's egg inside of her?" I ask, just wanting to get this over.

"I wish you could see the bigger picture, Daughter of Prophecy." Uriel bows slightly. I drop unceremoniously onto the large armchairs near the fireplace, not wanting to stand through this. Blaine perches on the arm of it and rests his hand on my shoulder. Hayden walks in with two cardboard trays of coffee cups, giving me a sly smile.

"Dealing with ethereal beings requires you to consume caffeine. It's basically law," he says in a conspiratorial whisper. I laugh as I gratefully take the warm foam cup from him. He drops a bottle of creamer on the small sitting table, and I scrunch my brow.

"A little birdy told me you drink more cream than you do coffee." He says with a shrug, and I gratefully grab it to pour into my coffee. I take my time with it, using this as a delay, and Selene sighs in annoyance. How dare I inconvenience the woman who literally screwed with my whole life?

"You declared war on Heaven. That is a serious claim

and I'm sure it was spoken with more emotion than sincerity. I came with Selene to help smooth this over and to answer any questions I can." Uriel sits across from me, man spreading, and all. Asmodeus jogs into the lobby, doing a double take at Selene and Uriel.

"Is everything alright?" Levi asks.

"We need to talk." Asmodeus says, giving a pointed glare at Uriel before looking back at Levi and Lucifer.

"Let's go to my office. It's safe from nosy busybodies." Lucifer grins maliciously at Selene before turning on his heel and leading them away. Levi stops and frowns down at me, hesitant to leave me.

"Don't worry about me, Dad. I can hold my own." I smile up at him and Blaine waves him on.

"Levi, I won't leave her side." He promises. This must be enough for him because he gives a sharp nod before following behind the two Kings of Hell. Selene adjusts her silver skirts of the dress she is wearing as she gracefully sits on the edge of a chair to my left.

"You still haven't answered my question." I say pointedly. Uriel rubs his jaw, nodding with a beaming smile.

"Fair point, Larissa. I do not know the name of the Angel who triggered the prophecy that I saw. I will do my best to find the answer for you and return once I have found it. Now, why would you decide to fight against us?" He asks. I have a feeling he is being genuine, but I won't be holding my breath.

"Because you preach how the nephilim are fighting for humans to have free will, but here you are, taking that from us. You were all willing to alter our lives how you saw fit, to *create us* how you wanted. But the loss we suffered, the guilt that we carried, it was all set-in motion because of the selfish actions within Heaven. The blood on our hands is on yours as well. You chose to make *weapons* and then chain them to their future, fating them to fall in love. Just so we would make little super weapon babies!" I throw my hand up in frustration, seething at their obvious lack of understanding. Hayden coughs, choking on his drink from my freak out.

"We did not fate you to fall in love, per se." Uriel comments, snagging a cup of coffee from the table and giving Hayden a once over. Blaine stops rubbing my shoulder and his fingers dig in when he tenses.

"You were fated to be together, yes. But even fated mates have been together simply out of their obligation to the pull of their souls. The two of you seem to be rather cozy. We may be able to alter some things, but we cannot force two people to love each other." Uriel says as if it excuses everything else. I roll my eyes and tip my coffee back.

"We won't fight your war. You wanted to wipe Hell out, but there are good people down there. Nephilim took an oath to stop the slaughter of innocents. Craving full power, control over all realms, is greed. What Larissa's saying is that she isn't just your pawn to control." Blaine says, tilting his head as if waiting for them to argue.

"Larissa," Selene says in a pinched tone. "You surely see the need for Heaven to take control. We don't want Hell wiped from existence, our will is for there to be peace across the realms. No child would have to wake up motherless because of evil deeds from uncontrollable demons." She says. No matter how hard I fight, her words find their target. My heart constricts as I glance up at Blaine's face. If looks could kill, Selene would drop dead this very moment from the way he is staring her down.

"Yes, since you would have Larissa murder dozens of others when they won't bow at your feet. She isn't stupid, give her some credit. Emotional manipulation, why am I not surprised?" Hayden *tsks* as he winks at me.

"We do not need you within this conversation, *cambion*." Uriel spits the word as if it disgusts him. I laugh, standing to wave my hand at the large double doors across the foyer.

"Get out. We are done here." I say, dismissing them. Uriel makes no move, but Selene rubs her temple as if I'm giving her a headache.

"Withdraw your declaration of war and we will be gone

for this day." Uriel states.

"Fine, we have a *temporary* truce. I won't rain Hell down on your mighty asses today. Now, just go." I say, my voice bordering on bloodthirsty at how exhausted this entire conversation has made me. Selene and Uriel share a look, both hesitating. I stand and turn to leave, but a low rumbling catches me off guard. The ground seems to shake with a sudden strike of thunder just outside. Adrian runs into the room, looking around wildly. Piper is hot on his heels, and Asmodeus is with her along with Lucifer.

"We must go now. I fear that soon you may make my life a living Hell, for lack of better words." Lucifer says, visibly shaken. Blaine puts his hand on my lower back, steering me towards them.

"Beelzebub and Mammon are nearly here. I could sense *something* in the distance, but their rage was overwhelming. They sent a messenger ahead of them." Asmodeus says. His face is grim as he holds out a blood-stained piece of parchment. I take it gingerly between my fingers, feeling sick as I peel it open. *The blood is still wet.*

"*Lilith has died at your hand, so you will die at mine as I finish what was started. You will fall to the Forgotten Army.* I didn't think she was actually dead, though?" I mumble in confusion.

"If they are warning us of their arrival, then they must be fairly confident that we can't run." Hayden says, thinking as he stares at the rapidly darkening skies. Asmodeus looks nervously down at the two reflective papers he is holding. I reach towards them, and he reluctantly allows me to take them both. My hand flies up to cover my mouth. Another rumble of thunder vibrates through the ground. *Not thunder, an army of forgotten soldiers.*

"*You will lose what has been lost when you face the Forgotten,*" Selene whispers. I swing around to look at her, the words she first spoke to me.

"The blood of a Goddess. You were telling me all along." My voice falters and she nods.

"The Forgotten are exactly what their name suggests.

They were once cambions that fell to carnal desires. Feeding on even each other as they were trapped within the pits of Hell. They are husks of the ones they once were. They can only be commanded by the ruler of Hell." Selene glances at Asmodeus. Blaine takes the pictures from my hand and grunts in disgust.

In the first picture, Jake is dangling upside down from a rope twisted around his body, as he hangs from Mammon's monstrous hand. The monster grins maniacally into the camera as the photo was taken. Jake looks badly beaten, blood marring his gigantic frame. His eyes are closed with one of his arms dangling loosely below him and I think I'm going to be sick.

The second photo is of Eric and Micah. Eric is trying to shield Micah's blue head from something above, but it's plain to see. Micah's throat is slit, his head bent at an unnatural angle. He's dead. Eric's face is contorted in rage, but the massive gaping wound across his side is on full display. As he kneels over Micah, gripping a piece of shattered glass in his bloody hand as a weapon. Are they all dead? The world swims for a moment and Blaine's arms circle around me, holding me upright.

"The back of the photo says that if we run, they will all die." Adrian says in a broken voice. Uriel steps towards the doors, watching lightning strike the sky as rain pours.

"What will you do, Larissa?" He asks. His tone is light, as if he knows what I'm going to say.

"I'm going to fight," My jaw clenches as I look around at my friends and family, "But all of you need to leave. I can't risk hurting anyone else if I lose control." My tone is final. Blaine shakes his head, planting his feet to prove his point.

"I'm not going anywhere." He tells me. Asmodeus and Piper nod at me. Everyone else shares a similar air of confidence and I sigh, knowing I don't have time to fight them.

"When I say to run, you all get the fuck out of here." I grit between my teeth. Lucifer throws his hands up and groans, "So, you are planning to destroy my mansion?" He asks. I raise a brow at him.

"Do you even like this place, Lucy?" I ask. He laughs and

shrugs, "I was actually planning to demo and make a nice little bed and breakfast. But death is bad for business, so try to not get killed, hm?" He grins. I roll my eyes at his eccentric behavior, but I see him step protectively closer to Blaine.

"*Larissaaaa,*" a voice hisses between the cracks of thunder. Hayden steps in front of me, his fist clenching into a tight white-knuckle grip. Mark runs through the room, panting and soaking wet with Levi in the same condition.

"There are thousands with them out there." Mark coughs, his tone grave.

"Where is Ella?" Adrian asks, in a slight panic. Piper raises her hand while bouncing excitedly on the balls of her feet. "I sent her to Aunt Willow. She's bringing reinforcements. We already sent out an SOS to the nearest nephilim town." She explains. Their numbers are massive, and the Forgotten are feral creatures. Can we truly survive this, or are we just bringing more to their death?

Chapter 40 – Larissa

The glass shatters, blowing inward as a roar bellows through the building. We all drop to cover our heads, protecting ourselves from the debris sailing in. I stand and step out into the rain as I square my shoulders, glass crunching under my sneakers. Blaine tries to call to me over the storm that rages outside, but I'm standing before the towering Mammon in the blink of an eye.

"Accepting your fate so easily, pathetic girl?" He snarls down at me. I shake my head, opening my arms wide. The empty driveway is sinister, as the pole lights flicker around us.

"I'm *choosing* my fate." My voice barely carries past the storm. Pulling my power from deep within, I push it around me as a beacon. Lightning sparks overhead, urging me on as I push harder and a bolt of lightning hits me before I can blink.

"Stay back!" I scream to Blaine, hoping he listens for once even as I feel his panic ripple through our bond. The pain is bearable, even as I feel the lightning arcing across my skin. A deep ache has permeated my body, all the way to my scalp as my hair floats around me and an orb of light surrounds my body. The glow comes from *within* me.

"You will pay for what you've done, Mammon." I say, leaping towards him. Mammon tries to swat me away. When his arm strikes my chest, I grab onto him. He lets out a yell that is cut short as his body trembles. Another lightning strike hits me, knocking both of us to the ground from the explosion it produces. I couldn't hold it all in and I pray nobody around me is injured as electricity ripples over the ground.. A dark, hulking figure rears up as I crash to the earth, trying to protect my head as I roll.

"Larissa!" Blaine bellows, slamming into the creature as I

drag myself up from the mud. I swipe the rain from my eyes and watch as the Forgotten twitches on the ground. Blaine helps me stand as I take in the sickly mottled purple toned skin. It looks melted in most places, the creature's face sunken and hollow. The eyes are pitted sockets, even as it turns its head to look at us. I can feel its gaze, even without eyes, tracking my movement.

"Look out!" Adrian calls and we both drop to our knees as a chunk of metal sails overhead.

"Father!" Hayden shouts, taking to the sky to face the man advancing on us. *So that's Beelzebub?* He has short black hair that curls against his temples, and skin the color of dark concrete. He is huge, easily eight feet tall and more than a little intimidating.

"Stay out of this, boy. Unless you wish to join your sister." He snarls at him. Hayden roars and dives at his father. Forgotten begin swarming us, their numbers overwhelming ours. Adrian is swooping in and out, driving his sword into any he can reach. Mark and Levi are trying to use their firepower, but the torrential rain is making it difficult and I realize we won't be able to keep up like this for much longer. I watch as Piper sits atop Asmodeus' shoulders. She creates a massive portal under a group of Forgotten, plummeting them through it. Piper waves her hand, opening the other half of her portal hundreds of feet above us. They sail through, splattering onto the ground and crushing those that were beneath them.

"You bitch," Mammon coughs up a spray of black blood onto the ground behind me, standing once again.

"Can't you just fucking die, and maybe stay dead?" I grumble. Blaine pulls his sword from the shadows, charging at Mammon and I curse myself for leaving my sword in our room. I take off behind him, my shoes slipping in the wet grass until they slap down onto the pavement as Mammon backs across the expansive driveway.

He suddenly stops and his form swells and morphs, doubling in size and looking less humanlike. I was now staring up at a sixteen-foot-tall Mammon beast. His right side has new burn marks, showing where I had clung to him. I melted half of his shirt to his flesh, and he's favoring that arm. Blaine drops into shadows just to leap back up behind him. He drives his sword forward, directly into the back of Mammon's right leg.

"You little half breed," Mammon snarls, swiping a clawed hand down at him. Mammon's talons scrape the front of his chest. Suddenly Blaine's form blows outward into a puff of smoke. He vanishes before Mammon can react. I slam my hands together, using the sting to create a sparking orb from my hands. This one is stronger from the one I had thrown at Lucifer. The blast I create is unstable, sparking sporadically before I send it sailing towards his face.

Taking advantage of his distracted state works perfectly and it explodes on impact. Mammon howls, clawing at his face. But I don't have time to celebrate as I clutch my head, dizziness rushes through me and I stagger sideways. The world tilts and I look up into the eyes of Lucifer as he catches me.

"Easy there, my girl. You're pushing yourself too quickly." He admonishes me, and I can feel his healing energy flitter over my body. I try to push away from him as I stand, but Lucifer materializes a short sword with a curved blade. He presses it into my hands as I blink in confusion.

"A Scimitar. Don't stab with this, sweetheart. Slash at him, then back away before your enemy has even seen you. Go on, now." He says, turning to throw a thin black wire around the throat of the closest Forgotten. A swift yank causes the head to bounce and roll as it's torn from the body. Lucifer winks over his shoulder at me as he hacks his way through the growing crowd.

Just then, Mammon thunders towards me. I grip the handle and allow Mammon to close the space between us. Using a wide arc, I slash towards his face with one hand on the hilt. My other hand flicks a portal across my body, landing me on the wet ground just behind Mammon and he gives a snarl before swinging around to stare at me. Blood has gurgled from the wound on his chest, and I smile to myself as I adjust my grip on my new blade.

Something grabs my hair and yanks me backwards with

otherworldly strength. I cry out against the burn in my scalp as I jerk to face my attacker. A Forgotten clutches my hair, diving to grip my throat in his leather skinned hand.

"You need some lotion." I croak against his iron tight grip. But this creature just clutches my back to his chest as he forces me to walk forward. Mammon grabs the Forgotten by his head and crushes it in his palm. I nearly vomit from the warm, sticky splatter that covers me. Mammon tries to grab me but I duck away. I'm not fast enough and he slams his hand downwards, striking the center of my back. I sprawl onto the ground with a cry of pain, knocking the air from my lungs. Mammon slams his hand down onto the back of my head, shoving my face into the mud as I struggle to fight him off. My sword is gone, I must have dropped it when I fell.

"Let her go." Levi demands. The rain is slowing and Mammon snorts, yanking me from the ground. Coughing desperately to clear my lungs, I spit mud down the front of my shirt. I reach back to grab his hand, but he squeezes me to his chest.

"Get sparky on me and I'll crush you." He rumbles in my ear, and I clench my eyes shut. I struggle to think clearly while my dad tries desperately to get him to release me, he switches from threatening to offering to take my place. That pulls me from my thoughts.

"Absolutely not." I tell him, whimpering as Mammon tightens his hold. My ribs are aching, straining against his hold. The witches aren't here yet, reinforcements still haven't showed up, and we are losing. I lock my eyes with Blaine, mouthing for him to run. His eyes widen in horror as he shakes his head, sending water flying from his drenched hair.

I push the pain away as I commit him to memory. Even with the clouded sky darkening the world, I know the soft golden tint to his deep brown eyes. His thin scar that is hidden just along his jawline that I love to rub my fingertips across. The small freckles I trace with kisses on his cheek. *I love you so much, Blaine.* I flood our bond with overwhelming feelings of love and his fear strengthens.

Piper calls my name as I look around the field.

"Run!" I shout as loud as I can with my walking prison crushing me tighter with every breath. Adrian has tried to get close to us, but I see the realization dawn as he nods in understanding. Hayden is trying to hold himself against his father, but Beelzebub appears to be even stronger than Mammon. Hayden's father has him dangling in the air by his throat. Panic washes over me as I struggle to lift my hand just enough to send a small blast. It bursts against Beelzebub's cheek. He drops Hayden in surprise, snapping to look at me. Mammon snorts and slams a hand over my throat, choking the air from my lungs.

"Give me the girl." Beelzebub's voice croaks as he steps towards us.

"Settle brother," Mammon snarls, "I'll kill her now." He tells him. Panic claws at me as my vision darkens. My lungs are screaming for air that I know won't come. If he's going to kill me anyway, I'm going down with a fight. I jerk and buck against him, hearing Blaine give a cry as he charges towards us. Mammon's grip slips, just enough for me to gasp in a quick breath of air and open a portal beneath us with the last of my strength.

"Stop!" Blaine cries. But he's too late. Mammon and I are dropping through the sky. We tumble dizzyingly as we fall, while Mammon thrashes me in his hands.

"Put us on the ground. You stupid bitch, we'll both die!" He shouts in terror. I look down, my eyes growing heavy as they struggle against the cold air. Everyone is so small beneath us, like tiny little spots.

"That's the point." I say with a voice so broken I doubt he can hear me. Mammon rakes his claws across my chest, and I scream. No matter how hard I had tried to hold it in, the pain is blinding. Blood flows into the air behind me as we free fall towards the earth. He was going to make this as agonizing as he could for me.

Digging deep within myself, I jam my feet to his chest and kick off. I flip backwards, separating from him. That was all the energy my body had left, it was drained. My soul was becoming cold, the sparkling tingle long gone. As if my power had known what was waiting for us and it didn't want to be there. I was so exhausted and the earth was alarmingly close. I should be afraid, but I just can't force myself to feel anything right now. My body had flung around in the air, like a doll unable to control its movements. Blaine's desperation was all I felt as my eyes closed. My heart had slowed as my body jerked. I smiled, knowing I had finally done it.

"Hang in there, Larissa!" Blaine's voice cradles my body and I no longer feel myself falling. *I can die like this. Imagining he is here with me.* "Please don't let go, just hang on a little longer." My body is frozen. *Numb.* Through it all, I can almost feel the warm droplets of tears as they hit my face. *I wish I could tell him everything. I hope he knows how much I love him.* "Then tell me, open your eyes and look at me, Angel. I need you." His voice is right in my ear, nuzzling my cheek.

I'll love him until the very end and beyond.

Epilogue

Blaine is fluffing my pillow again, hovering like he has every day for the last week. I bite my lip and let him continue as he pours me a glass of ice water from a pitcher on the nightstand. He keeps looking at me from the corner of his eye, expecting me to fight off his mother hen act.

"Thank you." I take the glass gratefully and gulp it down.

"Today we are going to try for a walk outside." He smiles. I sit up quickly, spilling some of the water on my oversized shirt.

"Are you serious?" I ask excitedly. He rolls his eyes and grabs a towel from the bathroom, wiping my shirt off when he comes back in.

"Settle down before I change my mind." He grumbles. Two days after I woke up in the mansion's makeshift infirmary, I went for a walk after going insane staring at the same walls. Blaine found me collapsed in the hallway just outside the doors on my way back. I had been dealing with overwhelming dizzy spells and he hasn't left my side since. That was five days ago, and I was feeling like a bird trapped in a cage two sizes too small.

"Selene still isn't sure why your power is dormant. Uriel has been trying to find cases of this in the past. But so far, we don't have any answers." He says in a soft voice. I grip the glass in my hand so tightly my knuckles turn white. I still can't feel even a whisper of my power, and nobody has any idea why.

"Now I'm not the daughter of prophecy, so there's that." I say in a flat tone. Blaine frowns at me but says nothing as he pulls the blankets back to help me stand and dress. This part I didn't mind. I enjoyed his feather light kisses on my chest, arms and even legs as he pulled my clothing on. Piper taught him how to braid my hair and he was getting pretty good at it, even if it always came out a little lopsided. He felt powerless when I sacrificed myself to kill Mammon, again, so he enjoys having something to do. Something he can control.

"Piper and Ella are going to drive this entire place crazy if we don't join them. Let's get you some fresh air, Angel." he says, wrapping an arm around me to steer us towards the hotel room door.

"Pretty sure your dad is ready to kick all of us out," I snort, and he laughs.

"The man is a nuisance, knocking on our door more often than room service. I didn't expect him to be so hospitable." He grumbles.

"He enjoys having you close." I say and Blaine stops walking, just for a moment before pulling me along a little quicker.

"We should hurry. The sun makes it look warm out there, but snow is sticking." He changes the subject. *Oh no,* there are some feelings, better avoid them until they blow up in my face as opposed to acknowledging them. I roll my eyes but keep quiet for now. Blaine tries to zip my puffy jacket up as we reach the front doors and I swat his hands away.

"I'm not a child. I can do that myself." I mumble as I yank the zipper up. Only to get it stuck on my scarf.

"Could have fooled me," Adrian laughs as he holds the door open for me.

"Piper told us if we didn't find you in ten minutes, she was going to stab us, and I am inclined to believe her." He shrugs. Asmodeus nods behind him, glancing back over his shoulder to where Piper and Ella are talking on the sidewalk. I huff past everyone, nearly running in my excitement at being outside. The wind is bearable, even with the large flakes of snow that have begun falling.

"Larissa!" Piper squeals, running to jump on me in a hug.

"Easy," Asmodeus grumbles.

"What he said." Blaine says in a huff. Piper steps back and sticks her tongue out at them over my shoulder. I laugh and turn my face up to the sky.

"So, what did you drag us all out here into this frigid bullshit for?" Ella asks. Piper fidgets nervously, looking at Asmodeus. He walks over and affectionately wraps his arm around her. He has to lean down to rest his chin on her head.

"We're having a baby." Asmodeus declares. *They're so cute-*

"You're what now?" I ask, grabbing her from Asmodeus. She nods excitedly, tears in her eyes. Ella and I scream, crushing Piper between us in a flurry of hugs. She laughs while awkwardly trying to pat our arms and I can hear Blaine congratulating Asmodeus. The entire time his eyes are burning into the side of my head. I'll kill him if he ruins this later with his baby fever.

"That is incredible, Piper. I am so happy for you." Ella says, as we finally separate.

"It really is. You're going to be such an amazing mommy." I say, my voice thick. She pats the front of her puffy pink coat with a small smile.

"Well, he is going to have the best aunties." She grins.

"You already know?" I ask in shock. Asmodeus shakes his head. "She had a vision. Cheating, if you ask me." He sighs. But the excitement is visible in the way he smiles down at her.

"We are totally celebrating." Ella says, clapping her hands.

"Somebody should ask Lucy if we can order pizza." Piper says, nearly drooling at the thought.

"I'll go let him know that's what we are having for dinner." I wink at her. We excitedly chatter over the prospects of having a tiny witch-demon-halfling running around until the cold chases us all inside. I immediately try to search out Lucifer, but Blaine intercepts me.

"Let me talk to him. You should rest before dinner. If you overdo it and miss out, then Piper will be crushed. Like, hormonal burn the mansion down type of crushed." He smiles at me. I can't argue with that, especially since my limbs are shaking and my teeth still haven't stopped chattering.

"Do you think they'll stick around until the baby is born, or if they will take the throne in Hell?" I ask absentmindedly.

"It would be safer for her if they went back to the Kingdom, but she would miss you." He says. I nod in agreement. When we get back to the room, Blaine pushes the door open for me to go in first.

"After everything we have gone through, I feel like this blessing is a sign of better things to come." He admits and I smile, nodding as I drop onto the couch. I yank my jacket over my head, frowning at the caught zipper.

"Asmodeus said that the castle is nearly rebuilt, and they found where Lilith was being held. When the castle collapsed, she was crushed. The entire place was full of bodies, but they weren't buried in the rubble. These were fresh. It looks like Mammon used the Forgotten to kill off his own people. Cambions and demons alike. The sick bastard left Jake and Eric to die slowly in the basement," he tells me and I shake my head in disgust. I'm grateful they both lived, but my heart still aches for my friend Micah.

"This might be wrong to say, but I'm glad he's dead." I say and Blaine laughs.

"If that son of a bitch had a grave, I would dance on it." Blaine remarks.

"Where do we go from here? Beelzebub could come back at any time." I ask him. He stares out the window, looking for answers to questions we can't put into words.

"Levi is bringing some of our people from Nephal here tomorrow. Third time's the charm for building a safe town, I suppose. Don't get mad, but Marcy will be here." He watches me, waiting for my reaction. I throw my head back with a loud whine.

"The healers are doing everything they can, but Jake and Eric are still hanging on by a thread. Micah would have wanted everyone to stick together, to be here for each other." He reminds me. Micah's bright smile and blue hair flashes in my mind. When they found them in Hell, Eric was unconscious and cradling Micah's body. Jake was delirious and barely able to hold his head up.

"The Saint's are still missing, and Hayden said they were working between the angel's and Beelzebub. Whatever storm is brewing is a lot bigger than just this. Bigger than us." I say solemnly. Blaine nods his head and walks towards the door.

"Maybe it's time Heaven answered our questions. Let's make the Archangels come to us." He grins and I smile back at him.

It's about time we fight our own war.

The end.

Thank you for reading *Against The Forgotten*!
I would appreciate it if you would leave a review on amazon or goodreads if you would like to! As always, happy reading, Darling's!

Follow my socials for updates on upcoming books through Insta, TikTok and Facebook!

@NatoshiaBaer_Author

The third and final book in the Fallen series, Against The Fearless, will be released Fall of '24!

About The Author

Natoshia Baer

Natoshia has had a fondness for writing since she was a young girl, sitting with her mother at the computer as they created fantasy worlds full of adventure in short stories. Flash forward to today, and she is still sitting far too close to the computer screen as she types away. But now her stories are a little darker, with a pinch of  excitement and a touch of spice. She has written a little of everything, from brooding mafia men to the paranormal, and now the monstrous side of books. When she's not reading or writing, Natoshia is spending time with her husband and their two children, or her beloved cat Chunky. Her favorite colors are Morally Gray and Red Flags, which is reflected in every new character she writes. She hopes you find a beautiful escape within the pages of her books.

Books In This Series

The Fallen

Against The Fallen

Larissa has finally found some normalcy in her life after the tragic death of her mother. Each day she drags herself out of bed and puts aside the recurring nightmares and longing for something more.

Until one evening, her nightmare appears in the real world.

Larissa is pulled into a life where Hell is waging war against Heaven, and she's stuck in the middle.

Lilith has put a bounty on her head, but luckily for Larissa, someone in Heaven wants her alive. While struggling to find her place in a world she was destined to lead, everything changes when Blaine comes along. He seems to have the answers she's been looking for, until sparks fly between them. Can she survive Hell's army long enough to find the life she yearns for, or will she meet the same fate as her mother before her?

Against The Forgotten

Books By This Author

Our Darling Isabelle

She spent her entire life fixing her mother's mistakes, but this one was different. What can Isabelle do when she is offered up as payment for her mother's debt? The Barone brothers aren't used to being told no and they don't have any hesitation taking what they want. And they want her. Isabelle's problems only grow when she develops feelings for these brothers, and their enemies become her own.

"Two years. Give us two years and if at the end you still want out, you leave with your debt erased." I offer. Her eyebrows raise as she thinks it over. A few tense moments pass before she gives a curt nod.
"Fine. But at the end of the two years, I'm leaving." She says firmly. The thought nearly tears my chest open, but I smile and nod, kissing her lips.
"Deal." I whispered against her mouth.
I'm a lying son of a bitch. She's never getting away from us.

Jared's Redemption

He ran from his misery the day he became an adult, but that freedom came at a cost. Trusting a crooked man shattered the person Jared had strived to become, and he vowed to spend the rest of his life paying for his mistakes. He knew that a man like him wasn't worthy of a happy ending. Until she came along.

Luna lived a life where people constantly treated her as a possession to be polished and presented. She finally saw her chance to show her family she could be more than a pawn. All she had to do was take on the bounty to kill Steffen before anyone else. Until she saw him, tall, dark, and his face caught in a scowl. Except he was ready to take the shot that would ruin all her plans. Luna only had one choice. Tackle him to the ground, crush her lips to his, and vanish into the woods with his gun. Until her obsession became too much to bear as she fell in love with the man that she spent her days watching.

What happens when the brute of a man becomes the prey, hunted and followed his every step?

His Paradise

Coming Fall of 2024
Aden has spent his entire life following in his father's footsteps, and he was content to continue on this path. He knew his life would be one danger after another, but Aden was never afraid when he stared down the barrel of a loaded gun. The one thing that scared him was witnessing his best friend Isabelle, and his sister Luna, finding love in the very world he wanted to shield them from. The idea of dragging another person into this life wasn't something he planned for. But when he sees her being married off to a murderer, his heart calls the shots.

Being the daughter of a family that has deep ties with the local mafia isn't a problem for Nina. She knows how to sit up straight, has perfected her shy smile and never speaks out of turn. She is the ideal wife, and David Killinger has chosen her. Unluckily for her, David is a cruel and violent man who likes to break pretty things. When Aden steps in to save her, Nina is finally given a chance at genuine happiness with her new husband and son. They create their own path, one that leads to a life neither could have imagined.

Until her past comes back to haunt them.

Can Aden save his little paradise, or will it all fall apart when Nina disappears?